ONE BEATS
THE BUSH

A gripping action thriller

The Max Donovan Adventures #1

RIALL NOLAN

THE BOOK FOLKS

Published by The Book Folks

London, 2023

© Riall Nolan

ISBN 978-1-80462-091-5

www.thebookfolks.com

For Chris, who held up half the sky

PROLOGUE

I flipped sideways in the water as the second shot hit inches away from my ear. Then I jackknifed and dived under the boat. Looking up, I saw three other bullets drill into the water at the spot where I'd been a second ago. I moved down under the keel, where I knew he couldn't hit me, and hung motionless in the water, trying to figure things out.

Just then the first of the sharks arrived, attracted by the smell of blood in the water. It bore straight in, twisting its head sideways just the merest bit to gulp down a chunk of fish bait. It gave me a flat-eyed stare as it went by. Farther out on the reef I could see two other sharks headed this way, nosing in from the deeps beyond the reef. Another load of fish bait hit the water above me, sending a pink cloud of blood out. The blood would attract more sharks and drive them into a feeding frenzy, where they would snap and rip at anything, even each other.

CHAPTER ONE

1981

Old-timers will tell you it's practically impossible to crash-land a C-47, but I knew better. I'd done it twice before, and now I was about to do it again.

A routine early morning medevac from one of the forward firebases had just been turned into a bloody nightmare by a stray ground-to-air that had come twisting up at us out of the jungle. We were lost, out of fuel, and on fire, airspeed dropping fast as I fought the pedals, trying to bring the nose up.

The port engine coughed and died, dropping us another hundred feet closer to the trees below. I scanned the horizon frantically for a landing site as acrid smoke billowed into the cockpit. Behind me the surviving members of my crew cursed as they heaved equipment out of the cargo door, desperately trying to lighten the crippled airplane.

I glanced across at my copilot, trying to remember his name. He'd been brand-new that morning, brash and full of confidence; now he grinned at me with Death's embarrassed smile, long gray loops of gut erupting from the hole in his belly where the shell fragments had gone in. He'd died instantly, and if I couldn't get us down safely in the next sixty seconds, he would have gotten the best deal by far.

We staggered down through the morning sky, streaming smoke and fuel. Then the trees opened up, revealing a pretty little village in the middle distance, its fairylike pagoda spire poking up out of the rice paddies at the edge of the jungle.

We thundered in over the first of the paddies, rolling crazily, barely fifty feet in the air. I caught a glimpse of Charlies scrambling along the dikes below us, sharks around a crippled whale. One of them opened up with a Kalashnikov, and a second later my windshield starred and shattered, blowing glass into my open mouth.

The little bastards are trying to kill us, I thought. Can't they see the red cross on the fuselage? Another burst ripped through the plane, and behind me someone screamed. Well, fuck that, I decided. I bent down, fumbling for the .45 I kept under my seat. Just then the stall warning buzzer sounded.

I sat bolt upright in bed. Through the open window, the rosy-fingered dawn was coming up over Bangkok, filtered through the remains of a bottle of Mekhong whisky I had left perched on the sill.

I wasn't in the burning plane anymore. I was in the Ambassador Hotel, there was someone else in the bed with me, and I'd just traded my favorite recurrent nightmare for a hangover, courtesy of Bangyikhan Distilleries.

Across the room the telephone rang again.

"Bloody hell." Beside me Joyce Lindsay-Watson, the protocol officer at the British Embassy, turned over, stuck her bare rump in the air, and pulled a pillow over her head.

I swung off the bed and staggered toward the phone.

I was almost to it when I got my feet tangled in something pink and silky that Joyce had been wearing last night. I crashed heavily to the floor, as if poleaxed.

"Jesus," muttered Joyce from under her pillow.

The telephone kept ringing.

Stretched full-length on the floor, I snaked my arm toward the receiver and brought it to my mouth. Someone had snuck in during the night and poured asphalt on my tongue, but after a moment I got it to work.

"Do you have any goddamn idea what the hell time it is?" I croaked.

There was a long-distance hum. "It's four o'clock in the afternoon in San Francisco, friend, which is where I happen to be." Whoever was talking to me had a voice like a bullfrog. "Is this Max Donovan?"

I considered his question carefully as I gazed around at the wreckage of my hotel room. The Chinese Army had obviously used it for war games after Joyce and I had gone to bed. The smell of smoke was probably the Golden Duck cheroots I'd bought in Rangoon last month. Or maybe one of us had set some furniture on fire. "Who wants to know?" I said finally.

"This is Lieutenant Luther Crake," the voice boomed. "Homicide Division, San Francisco Police. Where in blazes am I calling to, anyway? All I've got in front of me here is a bunch of damn numbers."

With a voice like yours, you don't need a telephone, I thought. "This is Bangkok," I said.

There was a stunned silence at the other end of the line. Got you that time, I thought.

"You say Bangkok?"

"Bangkok," I repeated. "Bangkok's in Thailand," I added helpfully. "Thailand's west of San Francisco, between–"

"I know where Thailand is, for God's sake," Crake growled. "Let's stop farting around, okay? Are you Max Donovan or not?"

I pulled myself to a sitting position. Then I leaned forward and opened the fridge beside the dresser. Inside lay two cold bottles of Singha beer, their labels gleaming wetly. I stared at them with quiet loathing. Joyce turned over in bed and began to snore softly.

I pushed the fridge door shut. "I'm Donovan," I said. "What are you calling me for? And who gave you my number?"

"Fredrick Fields gave it to me," Crake said. "He says he knows you, Mr. Donovan. Is that true?"

I suddenly came alert. "Fat Freddie? Of course he knows me. Is something wrong?"

Crake's voice turned careful. "You a lawyer, Mr. Donovan?"

"A friend of his. What's going on?"

Crake grunted. "Too bad; he could use a lawyer right now. He's been arrested, Mr. Donovan. We're charging him with homicide." He paused. "Does Fields have any relatives?"

"Freddie's an orphan," I said as I clambered to my feet. "Hey, you're kidding about this, right?"

"No joke, Mr. Donovan. Your friend's in a lot of trouble. The arraignment's tomorrow."

A hard, icy lump was forming in my stomach. "Let me talk to him."

"Sorry, Donovan." He didn't sound particularly sorry, though. "Fields assaulted an officer after we arrested him and we had to give him a little Thorazine. He's sleeping it off right now. Before he went under, he gave us a phone number and all the money in his pockets. 'Tell Max Donovan,' he said. Then he went to sleep."

Crake paused and cleared his throat. It made my head ring. "He had fourteen dollars and twenty cents in his pockets, Mr. Donovan. I reckon you've got about another thirty seconds left. He told me to tell you he'd been arrested, and I've done that. Anything else you want to know?"

There were a lot of things I wanted to know, but I had the feeling that Crake wouldn't have the answers. I stood up and stared out the window at Bangkok's tin-roofed anarchy trying to think about what to do next. Sighing, I opened the fridge and fished out one of the Singhas, twisting its pointy little head off on the opener attached to the door.

"You still there, Donovan?" Crake's voice thundered across the international line.

I swallowed the beer and came to a decision. "Tell him I'm coming," I said.

"What?"

"I'm coming back to San Francisco. Tell Freddie I'm on my way."

Crake grunted. "Save your money for a good lawyer, Donovan. There's nothing you can do here, if you ask me."

I took another swallow of beer. "Nobody asked you, Crake," I said. "Just tell me where I can find you."

"Your nickel, Mr. Donovan. You know the Hall of Justice on Bryant Street?"

"I do."

"Homicide's in Room 750. Speak to the case officer, Sam Young."

"Sam Young," I repeated. "I'll be there just as soon as I can. You tell Freddie that. As soon as I can get a flight."

"Don't bust a gut, Mr. Donovan," said Crake. "Fields isn't going anywhere." There was a click and a buzz as he hung up.

I jiggled the phone, and Kenat, the Thai desk clerk, came on. "When's the next flight out to San Francisco?" I said.

While he checked his schedules I glanced over at Joyce. She was sound asleep.

Kenat's voice came back on the line. "Missa Donovan? Pan Am 002 next flight. Leaving Don Muang later this morning. I don't think you gonna make it. They say you should be there plenty time before."

I stood up, groping for my trousers. "Book me," I said. "I'll pay cash at the airport. Some of that cash is for you if there's a taxi waiting downstairs in five minutes."

He chuckled happily. "Can do." It was the kind of challenge he liked.

I pulled on my clothes and packed my single bag. Joyce slept through it all. I found a pen and wrote 'Sorry' in big letters on a piece of hotel stationery and propped it on the bedside stand. Then I picked up my suitcase and walked out the door.

CHAPTER TWO

Behind the door to Room 750 a beefy man with a mustache like a painter's brush and a nose like a fire hydrant sat behind a nameplate that read 'Lieutenant Luther Crake.' It was just before eleven in the morning, and I'd come straight from the airport. I looked and felt like a dog's breakfast.

Crake looked up, his blue eyes calm and steady. "What'll it be, friend?" The sounds he made came from a voice box that must have been drop-forged in Pittsburgh. Or maybe Crake was just fond of turpentine on the rocks before dinner.

"I'm Max Donovan," I said. "Bangkok, remember? I want to see Freddie Fields."

Crake flashed me a hard smile. "I remember, Mr. Donovan. You didn't waste any time." He looked me over professionally. "Have an accident on the way over?"

I remembered the bruises on my face. "I've been working," I said.

Crake's eyebrows went up. "Yeah, no shit? What do you do for a living, wrestle alligators?"

The phone next to him rang once and he picked it up. "Crake."

While he was busy I inspected myself in the wall mirror. His crack about alligator wrestling hadn't been too far off the mark. I'd looked like hell getting on the plane at

Bangkok, and what seemed like days of transpacific flying hadn't improved things. My hair was filthy and uncombed, and my mustache drooped raggedly. I still had cuts and bruises on my face from an unfortunate encounter in Bangkok, plus a fading shiner. My bloodshot eyes had bags under them that looked like coal sacks. Oh, yeah, I thought, you're a real beauty.

"On my way," Crake said into the receiver. He hung up. "I've gotta go up to Forensics." He jabbed a blunt thumb at the door behind him. "You want to find out about Fields, talk to Sam Young, the case officer. Through there."

"I want to talk to Fields," I said. "Not another cop."

Crake grimaced. "Fields isn't talking to anyone right now. You'll excuse me for putting it this way, but he made a real pain in the ass of himself around here yesterday. He got a little excited again at the arraignment this morning, and so we had the doc give him another jab. He's still sleeping it off." He stood up. "I'm expected upstairs. Sergeant Young will tell you everything you need to know." He hoisted his beer belly and sailed out the door.

I went behind Crake's desk and through the door he had indicated. Inside, a tall Asian woman was stuffing papers into a bulging file cabinet. I coughed discreetly.

The woman turned around. "Can I help you?" She had the widest pair of almond eyes I'd ever seen.

"I'm looking for Sam Young," I said. "Are you his secretary?"

She looked at me for a moment. "That's very funny," she said. "I'm Sergeant Young."

I blinked. "You? You're Sam Young?"

"Samantha, actually. Samantha Wai Ling Young." She gave a small, tight smile. "Luther's a sweetie, but his sense of humor really sucks sometimes. What can I do for you?"

She was tall and slim, with the pale, delicate skin that you see among northern Chinese. A touch of lipstick drew attention to her wide mouth. Her straight black hair was shoulder-length, falling in wings around her face, setting off her high cheekbones.

It took an effort to pull myself back to business. "I'm Max Donovan," I said finally. "I'm here about Fat– I mean, about Freddie Fields."

She nodded. "Oh, right. Luther said you might show up. You're the person he called in – where was it – Thailand?" She indicated a chair. "Sit down, please."

I watched her as she walked behind the desk. She moved like a show horse in the ring, placing her long legs firmly and precisely. She sat, located a file, and pulled a pen from the pocket of her blouse. "What's your connection with Fields, Mr. Donovan?"

"He's my best friend. We're sort of in business together. Or were." I ran a hand over the stubble on my face. "Look, I don't understand this. How can Freddie be charged with homicide? He's supposed to be down in Mexico."

"Surprise, Mr. Donovan. Fields is down the hall, about to be taken up to the psychiatric ward at San Francisco General. You can see him in a moment, but first I need some information." She bent to the form. "How long have you known him?"

"We met in 1968."

"And where was that?"

"In Vietnam. Long Dinh prison camp."

She stopped writing. "You were a prisoner of war?"

"We both were."

"And, ah, when were you released from the camp?"

"We weren't released," I said. "We escaped. Together." I leaned across the table and took the pen out of her hand. "I've answered five of your questions, Sergeant – suppose you answer one of mine. Just what the hell happened to Freddie?"

She looked at me for a moment. Then she put the forms away. She took a pack of cigarettes from her handbag and offered me one. I shook my head. She lit one, blew out smoke, and pushed a stray lock of hair back behind her ear.

"Okay," she said. "From the top. There's an X-rated motel called the Party Time up near Broadway and Columbus, a real sleaze farm. Know it?"

I shook my head.

"Two days ago, at around noon, the clerk heard someone yelling in the hallway. A minute later he saw a pickup truck tear out of the parking lot." She paused.

"A lot of yelling goes on at the Party Time," she continued, "but not at noon. So he took a walk down the hall. He found the door to number five open and a dead man on the floor."

She dragged deeply on her cigarette. "A squad car caught the pickup truck five minutes later on the ramp of the Bay Bridge. Your friend Fields was driving. He resisted arrest and was forcibly subdued. Later – in this office – he attacked an officer and had to be sedated. Before he went under, he asked that you be called… He was arraigned this morning. He again became hysterical, so they gave him another shot. He's still recovering."

She stubbed out her half-smoked cigarette and glared at it. "I'm supposed to be giving these damned things up. What else do you want to know?"

"Who's the dead man?"

"An Australian diplomat named Brian MacKenzie," she said. "He was clubbed to death with a heavy blunt object, which we haven't located yet. The motive doesn't appear to be robbery. MacKenzie had plenty of money on him, but Fields had less than twenty dollars when they picked him up."

I found it hard to believe I was hearing this. "This is incredible. You really think that Fat Freddie killed this guy?"

She returned my gaze steadily. "Brian MacKenzie is eight floors down, in the morgue. He didn't die of old age, Mr. Donovan. Somebody killed him… Your friend Fields is the district attorney's prime suspect right now." She stood up. "Let's go see him."

I followed her down the hall and into a smaller room. There was a cop outside the door standing guard. He sniffed at me like an old dog, grunted, and stepped aside.

Freddie was inside, lying flat on his back on a stretcher, eyes closed. Sam Young hung back in the doorway as I walked over and looked at him. He seemed to be asleep. His face was puffy, his breathing heavy and laborious. He had a dull purple bruise over one cheek and scabs on his knuckles. His uncombed hair frizzed out like an electric halo, giving him the look of a stoned owl. Then I noticed the restraint straps on the bed. They'd tied him down.

One red eye opened, and his huge bulk stirred. "Max." It came out as a low-register croak. "Max, you came." He tried to sit up, but the straps held him back.

I put my hand on his shoulder. "Easy, buddy. Just relax. How're they treating you?"

Both eyes opened and rolled slowly around the room. "They put me in jail, Max." His voice was thick and slow. His big lion's head came up an inch off the bed. "The fuckers put me in jail. All of 'em had guns. They turned the lights out, too, so the rats could run around free."

His voice started to climb, the words spilling out of him in big chunks. "I heard 'em, Max, I really did. The goddamn rats. When I woke up, I hollered to the guards and they came and took me into another room, and then it all got crazy again and they hadda give me another shot. I told 'em to call you, Max. You'd know what to do."

I smoothed his hair, trying to calm him down. "It's okay, buddy. I'm here. You're not going back to jail. Everything's fine."

He looked at me with moist eyes. "They told you yet what they said I did? About killin' that guy? You gotta tell 'em, Max. Tell 'em I didn't do it."

A white-coated intern, all teeth and tan, put his hand gently on my shoulder. "Don't get him too excited," he said quietly. "It's not good for him. We've gotta take him up to General in a minute."

I turned to him. "What have you got him on?" I said. "He's as stuffed as a Christmas goose."

"Thorazine," the intern said. "He was a little psychotic when they brought him in." He grimaced. "A lot psychotic, in fact. We've got him on a maintenance dose now, just to keep things shipshape."

"Where you're taking him," I said, "is it a jail?"

"Naw, just a secure ward. He'll probably have to stay in restraints, though." He smiled to show there were no hard feelings.

I turned to Freddie. "Can you hang on until tomorrow?"

He nodded weakly. "I guess so. But jeez, Max, we gotta talk. I didn't kill anybody, but we gotta talk about a couple of things. I got us into a little trouble, I guess. What happened was–"

I put a finger on his lips. "Freddie, don't say anything. Wait until tomorrow, okay? There's cops outside."

It was the wrong thing to say. "Cops? Where?" Freddie's voice had gone high and quavery. Just then the flatfoot guarding the room appeared in the door, his hand on his service revolver.

Freddie's eyes locked on the cop and widened. "He's got a gun, Max," Freddie whimpered. "A fuckin' gun!" Then he started to scream and buck against his restraining straps.

The intern moved right in, needle held high. "Shit," he muttered as he plunged it into Freddie's arm. "I told them no goddamn visitors."

In sixty seconds Freddie was sleeping peacefully. "Show's over for today, ace," the intern said to me. "Now why don't you be a prince and get the hell out of here?"

Back in the office, I turned to Sam Young. "This is all bullshit, Sergeant," I said quietly. "You've got no motive, no weapon, and no witnesses. Everything you've told me is circumstantial. You've got no case – no reason to suppose that Freddie had anything to do with this at all."

"Are you a lawyer, Mr. Donovan? No? Then let me respectfully suggest that you don't know what the hell you're talking about." Her dark eyes held mine. "The district attorney can treat this case in any one of three ways – as manslaughter, homicide, or murder. Manslaughter means it was an accident. Homicide means it happened because of some other illegal act in progress – robbery, for example. Murder requires premeditation."

She paused. "Fields was arraigned this morning on a homicide charge. To prove it the state's not required to produce either the weapon or any witnesses. In fact, they don't even need the body. All that's needed is proof that death was caused by a criminal act."

I stared at her. "You're serious, aren't you?"

She nodded. "Absolutely. The trial's in three weeks, and the DA's office is charging hard on this one. They're going to try to get the charge raised to first-degree murder. And they might just manage it. Your friend's record doesn't help."

"Drunk and disorderly once in a while isn't much of a record," I said.

She tapped the file in front of her. "Once in a while? Over a dozen times, according to this. Plus indecent exposure, vagrancy, and using insulting language to a police officer."

"Indecent exposure? When was that?"

"Last May in Berkeley."

"Oh, yeah." I shrugged. "Okay, so Freddie took a whiz once on the hood of a cop car. Big deal."

"Twice."

"Huh?"

"He did it twice. He, ah, whizzed on the car on two separate occasions. The second time he used insulting language. He's got what law-enforcement people call a bad attitude."

I spread my hands and sighed. "When they say nobody's perfect, Sergeant, they've got people like Freddie in mind. Have you seen his hospital file?"

"No. Should I?"

"He was in a counseling program up at the veterans' hospital," I said. "For his bad attitude. PTSD – post-traumatic stress disorder. Check it out."

She made a note. "Is he still in the program?"

"There's no more program. The shrink in charge blew his brains out. He was a vet, too, and he had about thirty patients like Freddie. It must have been a lot of stuff to carry. After he stepped out of the picture, things kind of fizzled out."

She looked at me for a moment. "I'll follow it up," she said finally. "Let's get back to you, Mr. Donovan. What do you do for a living?"

I stood up and let my breath out. "Sergeant, I'm not really interested in answering any more questions. I came in here to see Freddie, and now I want to get him out. If you put him in jail, he'll die. Has bail been set?"

Behind me a voice I hadn't heard in years said, "One hundred thousand dollars. And if you ask me, it ought to be ten times that."

CHAPTER THREE

Delbert Ackroyd stood in the doorway, grinning like a shark on its birthday.

Sam Young stood up. "Good afternoon, sir."

"Stand easy, honey," Ackroyd said as he swaggered into the room. He came over and looked me up and down. "Hello, Donovan. Crake told me you were up here. It's been a long time, hasn't it?"

At least ten years, I thought as I stared back at him. But not nearly long enough. District Attorney Delbert Ackroyd was sleek and well fed, an expensive Italian suit draped over his bulging paunch. He still had his acne scars and yellow teeth. He'd acquired a toupee since I'd seen him last, and he looked ridiculous.

But then he always had.

"Freddie's innocent, Ackroyd," I said.

Ackroyd flicked cigar ash on the floor. "He's scum, Donovan. And I'm going to nail his ass to the wall. Stick around, you can watch me do it."

He moved around the desk and pointed his cigar at me. "You know who he killed? A fucking Australian diplomat, that's who. Shit like that gives the city a bad name. The voters have had enough of trash and scum in this town. It's getting so bad that honest citizens can't walk down the street."

He was puffing himself up like a tree toad now, his voice going tight and high, as if it were being pulled out of a bottle by a corkscrew. "The way to make the streets safe again is to make an example of some of the germs that are underfoot." He grinned at me. "Beginning with your buddy Fields."

He turned to Sam Young. "Donovan told you yet about how he was an ace pilot and a war hero in Vietnam?" He snorted. "Some hero. He and that fat freak spent most of the war sitting on their asses in the jungle, eating rice with the gooks, while everybody else was getting shot at. Or maybe he told you about the goddamned book he wrote when he got back here, the one attacking the administration for their conduct of the war?"

He turned to me. "What the hell was the name of it, Donovan – something about a horse, what was it? Oh, yeah, *The Horse You Rode In On*. That's the title. I thought it was a shitty book."

"Always gratifying for an author to know he's been read," I said. "I hope you bought a copy instead of stealing it from the rack."

"Cheap shot, Donovan. You got brought back to the US at taxpayers' expense, and then you turned around and bit the hand that fed you. What makes guys like you so goddamn ungrateful, anyway?"

I shrugged. "'When the water's high, the fish eat the ants. When the water's low, the ants eat the fish.'"

Ackroyd looked blank.

"That's a Lao proverb," I explained.

His lips curled. "I suppose you've been there too."

"As a matter of fact, yes."

"On whose side?"

"Excuse me, Mr. Ackroyd." A laboratory technician stood in the doorway.

Ackroyd turned. "What the hell do you want?"

The lab technician held up a clear plastic evidence bag. "No luck on the analysis, sir," he said. "They're bird feathers, all right, but nobody knows what kind. The report'll be down in an hour." He set the bag on Sam Young's desk and escaped.

Ackroyd picked up the evidence bag and peered at it. "Goddamnit, any fool can see they're bird feathers! I want to know what they were doing scattered all around MacKenzie's body." He flipped the bag at Sam Young, who caught it awkwardly. "You find out about that, sweetie. And get a move on."

Distaste glittered briefly in her eyes. "Sir, I don't know if—"

He leveled the wet end of his cigar at her. "I don't give a purple rat's ass what you don't know, honey," he said. "Pull your goddamned finger out and come up with some results. Didn't you hear me the first time?"

"Delbert? Delbert, are you in there? Answer me!" A woman's voice swept in from the corridor outside.

Ackroyd started violently. "Ah, shit," he muttered. Raising his voice, he called, "I'm right here, love. What is it?"

A large, red-faced woman appeared in the doorway. Queen Victoria dressed as Mary Poppins, and so wide that she shut out most of the light and air. I guessed she was Ackroyd's wife.

I hoped so, at any rate.

"Delbert, where on earth have you been? I've been searching for you everywhere." She had a voice like a wood rasp, and a little pursed mouth out of which her words flew like poison-tipped darts. "We're supposed to be at the Choral Society meeting in ten minutes, and here you are wasting time with these people. Come on." She gave us commoners a look that could have driven a tenpenny nail and stepped back out into the corridor to avoid contamination.

Ackroyd stuck his pitted face close to mine. "Let me tell you something, Donovan," he said. "You want to go bail for Fields, be my guest. But we're gonna charge him with murder one, and when we do, bail is canceled and he goes back inside." He blew smoke at me. "Which is right where he should have been put years ago. Along with creeps like you."

"Delbert, come on. I'm waiting!" His wife's voice was a chain saw through hard timber.

Ackroyd turned and walked out the door, leaving behind the smell of dead cigars and doom.

Sam Young looked down at the evidence bag in her hand and shook her head in disgust. "Mystery feathers, Christ. And I was due to go on vacation in two days."

I stepped closer and peered at the bag. Inside were half a dozen fragments of feathers. They were long and slim, banded with alternating blue and white lobes. The blue was the most brilliant and perfect hue I had ever seen. Something in the back of my mind stirred and then subsided.

She'd caught it. "Know what they are?" she asked.

I looked at the feathers for a moment longer. "I guess not," I said finally. "Sorry."

She put the feathers away in the desk. "You, ah, certainly seem to have made a big hit with our district attorney, Mr. Donovan," she said. Her voice was carefully neutral, but I caught a hint of something savage in her eyes.

"Years ago," I said, "in another life, I spent some time at college with Delbert Ackroyd."

"College? God, what was he like back then?"

"Del?" I thought for a moment. "Let's put it this way," I said, "he gives new meaning to the word 'asshole.' If I'd said to a girl, 'I can fix your roommate up with Adolf Hitler, Idi Amin, or Delbert Ackroyd,' she'd say, 'Oh, no, not Ackroyd.'"

She was smiling now, looking at me thoughtfully. "I remember now," she said.

"Huh? Remember what?"

"You. Or rather the book you wrote. About the war and what it had done to the soldiers. I read it." Her eyes grew soft. "My older brother was killed over there. In the Tet Offensive."

I didn't say anything.

"He was killed by our own troops," she continued. "One of them mistook him for the enemy." She looked at me. "For a gook, as Mr. Ackroyd might say."

She took a deep breath. "For years I was bitter. I hated the ones who'd made it back. They seemed like the winners, and it didn't seem fair." Her eyes were glistening now. "What you wrote helped me see things differently."

"There weren't any winners in that war," I said quietly. "Only losers. I'm going to try to get one of them out of jail now."

"You'll need ten thousand for the bail bondsman," she said. "Most people don't have that sort of cash lying around."

"I'll manage somehow," I said. "I don't have a choice. Being locked up will destroy Freddie. If you knew him, you'd understand that. He couldn't have killed that guy."

"Somebody did, Mr. Donovan. Got any ideas?"

"No," I said finally. "No, I don't."

"Then let's just let justice take its course, shall we?"

I turned and stared at her. "Are you kidding?" Then I walked down the hall and out of the building, into the cleaner air.

I was almost to the parking lot when a woman stepped in front of me, blocking my path. "Excuse me," she said in a clear, high voice. "Are you Max Donovan?"

I was feeling as irritable as a snake with blisters. "What the hell do you want?" I snapped.

She drew back, stung. She was slim and attractive, and her cornflower-blue eyes were brimming with tears.

"I'm sorry," I said. "Let's start again. Yes, I'm Donovan. Who are you?"

"My name is Kathy Armlin. I'm… well, I'm sort of responsible for what's happened to Freddie. And I need to talk to you about it."

CHAPTER FOUR

She drove a late-model Nissan sport coupe with a sunroof. Whoever Kathy Armlin was, she wasn't starving. "Freddie and I met in Mexico," she began as we pulled out of the parking lot. "About six weeks ago." She looked across at me. "I guess you could say we're kind of involved right now."

I nodded. That explained why I'd never seen her before. I'd been on the Thailand job for the past two months. Before that, the Ivory Coast. I'd had three days in

San Francisco in between – just enough time to have dinner with Freddie, check on the status of our Mexico project, and give him the phone number of the place I usually stayed in Bangkok, just in case. I hadn't really expected to hear from him.

I glanced across at her as we turned onto Market Street. She was attractive in a wholesome, Midwest cheerleader sort of way – slim and petite, with a peaches-and-cream complexion and white, even teeth. Her wide blue eyes made her look like a startled doe. Freddie's track record with women wasn't too impressive, but even a blind squirrel finds some nuts, I thought, and if he and Kathy Armlin were 'kind of involved' right now, there was no harm I could see in that.

Before Freddie's therapist had shot himself he had told me that a stable, loving relationship with someone supportive would do wonders for Freddie. 'The healing power of love,' he'd called it. I believed him. I could use a little of it myself, I thought, remembering Joyce Lindsay-Watson in Bangkok and calculating the rough odds on getting her to ever speak to me again.

"Things were just great until about two weeks ago," Kathy Armlin was saying. "That's when my baby brother got into some trouble in Reno." She looked at me, an appeal in her eyes. "This is… well, difficult to explain to someone I don't really know. But Freddie said I could trust you – that you were his only real friend. He told me that if anything bad ever happened, I was to find you. That you'd know what to do."

She took a deep breath. "Billy's only seventeen, but he looks a lot older. He's a little wild. Last month he went to Reno on a weekend deal. He didn't tell Daddy, or even me. He said later he just wanted to see what it was like to gamble in a casino."

"He's not old enough to gamble," I observed.

"Billy looks twenty-five, Mr. Donovan. He's fooled people that way for years."

"Call me Max," I said. "And keep talking." I had the feeling I wasn't going to like this story.

"He got into some poker games," she continued. "Just for fun, he said. And then he met these three guys."

I nodded. "And they told him about a private game where it was a lot more fun."

She looked at me. "Did somebody already tell you about this?"

I sighed. "I'm a good guesser," I said. "Go on."

"Well, they took him to this hotel room and they started playing poker. They played all night, and when they were through Billy owed them ten thousand dollars." She paused. "He had less than three hundred dollars in his wallet."

"What happened then?" I had the feeling I could guess this part of the story too.

"They argued about the money. Billy said he'd send them a check, but they didn't want that. He started to get scared then. They took him out in the desert, ten or fifteen miles out of town. One of the men pulled a gun out. They threatened him with it, and then they beat him up and left him out there. He had to walk back to town."

"He was lucky," I said. "It can get a lot worse."

"It did get worse. They were waiting for him at the motel. They slapped him around some more and told him they'd kill him unless they got the money. That's when he called me in Mexico and asked me to help him." She hesitated. "And I did."

"You paid the ten thousand dollars?"

She bit her lip. "I stole it."

I swung around to look at her. "Stole it? From whom?"

"From my father, Max. Randolph Armlin."

I whistled softly. "Randolph Armlin's your father?"

She nodded. Everybody knew Randolph Armlin, and they either liked him or they didn't. I liked him. He was a liberal philanthropist who spread his money around among the poor and needy – the kind of guy who was fast becoming an endangered species in these days of bottom-line thinking.

"Well, well," I said. "And what's Randolph Armlin doing these days?"

She looked at me. "He's running for state senator, of course. Against Delbert Ackroyd. Didn't you know that?"

In the back of my head several large pieces suddenly fell into place with a dull thump. "Jesus Christ," I muttered.

"You must be the only person in California who doesn't know that," Kathy Armlin said. "Where have you been for the last six months?"

"That's a whole other story," I said. "But it's not important right now. Ackroyd for senator? He couldn't get elected dogcatcher."

"You'd be surprised. Ackroyd's got the law-and-order vote and a lot of the big corporate money. They took a poll last week, and Daddy and Mr. Ackroyd were dead even. The election's in three months, and the papers say that everything depends on what happens between now and then."

"So how did you steal the money, Ms. Armlin?"

"I got it from Daddy's campaign chest. It wasn't hard to do – I'm a registered CPA. When Daddy decided to run for senator I stopped my practice and went to work for him as his manager."

My head had started to throb. "Let's get back to your brother for a minute," I said. "Do the guys who wrung him out know who he is?"

She shook her head. "Billy used a fake ID in Reno; they had no idea. I gave him the money in cash, and he paid them. That part's finished, thank God. Now I've got another problem."

"Which is?"

"The law says that Daddy has to file a financial disclosure statement and his campaign finances have to be audited. He didn't tell me that he'd arranged for the audit to be carried out in three weeks. They'll spot the missing money right away."

I thought about that for a moment. My headache had picked up the tempo, hammering like an outhouse door in the wind. "And if they do, he'll lose the election," I murmured. "How does Freddie fit into all this?"

"I made a mistake, Max. I called Freddie and told him what had happened." She bit her lower lip. "I never should have mentioned it to him. He flew up from Baja last Friday night and called me from somewhere in town. He said he'd thought of a plan that would fix everything. He told me to stay home for a couple of days and he'd be in touch once he got the money. Then he hung up."

She was crying now, tears spilling down her cheeks as she shook with sobs. "I didn't hear from him again, and I started to worry. Then I saw his picture in the paper this morning. I called your number, but there was no answer. So I went down to the Justice Department. I was trying to get up enough nerve to go in when I saw you coming down the steps. I recognized you from the picture Freddie has – the one of both of you in the camp."

We were still on Market, heading slowly northeast toward the Bay. "Pull over," I said. When we had stopped I reached over, turned off the ignition, and put my arms around her. She smelled of soap and sunlight.

Her head slumped forward. "I haven't seen him in four days," she whispered. "I don't know where he went or what he did. I'm scared, Max. Freddie's the kindest person I've ever known. He could never kill anyone." She surrendered to another fit of crying.

I held her until her sobs began to subside. After a few minutes she dried her eyes with a tissue and sat up straight. "Should I just tell the police, Max? About Billy, about the ten thousand dollars? Mr. Ackroyd's going to make an example of Freddie, for the election. Why don't I just tell them the truth?"

I shook my head. "Telling Ackroyd will just make matters worse. He'll see to that. Your father will lose the election, your brother will get arrested for gambling, and you'll be charged with embezzlement. And Freddie will still go to jail."

"But what can we do? I mean, we've got to do something, don't we?" Her eyes were desperate.

"The first thing we do," I said, "is keep Fat Freddie out of jail. He'll go crazy if they lock him up again."

She nodded. "I know. He told me all about what happened in the camp, Max. He says you saved his life."

"He's got it backward," I said. "But it doesn't matter; the principle's the same, right?" I gave her a cheer-up smile and handed her back the keys. "If you're up to driving again, why don't we go and see if we can find some bail money?"

CHAPTER FIVE

We went across the Bay and down San Pablo Avenue into deepest Oakland, where the liquor stores look like Fort Knox and every third house is a gospel church. The brown-bag crowd was out in the warm weather; small clumps of men sat quietly in doorways, taking quick sips from their bottles and talking in low voices about the General Situation. In the street, paper and plastic trash lay in depressed little piles, waiting for the next wind.

Kathy Armlin glanced through the safety of the windshield at the ruined storefronts, their neon signs smashed and dark. "What exactly are we looking for down here?" she said.

"Money. There's a guy I know named Lorenzo Marx. He's worth a try."

"Lorenzo Marx? That's an odd name, isn't it?"

I smiled thinly. "He's an odd man. Not a very nice one, either. He's a pusher and a loan shark, and he's got the morals of a wolverine in heat." I pointed to a rusting late-fifties Cadillac squatting by the curb. "That must be his new car. Pull up behind it."

Kathy Armlin made a face. "His new car? That awful thing?"

I grinned. "You should have seen the other one," I said. "He had one of those old Imperials with the taillights up on cocktail toothpicks. Something unfortunate happened to it a while ago."

She parked behind the Caddy and both of us looked at it without speaking. Definitely Lorenzo's car, I thought – a gross, dirty guzzler, just like its owner. It sat there covered with dust and freeway slime, baroque tail fins nearly rusted through, the fabric top showing signs of terminal leprosy. There were dents in the bodywork and two of the rear taillights were smashed. The nearly bald whitewalls were nicely set off with ornate silver spinners and mud flaps decorated with colored-glass jewels. The kind we'd called 'Tennessee Go-Fasters' in high school. The license plate said 'REPTILE.'

Some people make a statement with their cars. Lorenzo issued an ultimatum.

The street was quiet. A stray dog moved along the sidewalk, sniffing suspiciously at the empty beer cans spaced like trail markers every few feet. A kid with orange hair and zits cranked by on foot, wearing a T-shirt with a picture of a submachine gun and the legend 'Peace Through Superior Firepower.'

I opened the car door and slid out. "If you hear shooting," I told her, "drive to a pay phone and call the cops. Don't get out of the car."

A couple of dudes in digger hats cruised by in a low-slung Camaro, the clash of heavy rap blaring from the windows. They glanced at Kathy, saw me, and kept moving.

She was looking at me as if I'd just turned into a frog.

"Got that?" I said.

"I… I guess so."

"Good. Now roll up the windows, lock your doors, and don't talk to anyone."

I paused at the entrance to the alley to scan the newspapers in the machine. 'Mom Sells Ugly Twins to Circus' was the headline on the scandal rag, but it was the city paper I was interested in. Down at the bottom of the front page was a story about weapons thefts from military installations in the Bay Area. Next to it was the story of MacKenzie's murder, together with a picture of Fat Freddie.

I scanned the story, but didn't learn anything new. I straightened up, took a deep breath, and went down into the alley.

Lorenzo's office was upstairs in the back, above the Sayonara Massage Parlor and Social Club. It didn't have a sign on it. In Lorenzo's way of thinking, you either knew where it was or you didn't. And if you didn't know where it was, you had no damn business looking for it.

I walked up the rickety wooden stairs at the end of the alley and pushed open the rusted screen door. There was a long hallway with two doors going off to the left and a door at the end. The end door was ajar, and the sounds of the Grateful Dead playing *Scarlet Begonias* drifted out from inside. The pusher is in, I thought, and started down.

I was on my way past the first door when it opened and a hand shot out and grabbed my arm. "Hold it; motherfuck."

I turned and saw a skinny black kid in his early twenties dressed in Levi's, a white T-shirt, and pointed patent-leather cockroach-snappers. The kid wasn't big, but he looked strong and capable. His eyes were flat and slightly slanted, the whites tinged with yellow. They were giving me the sort of look you see in the python cage around feeding time. Definitely not a junkie, I thought. More like a New York subway bopper – alert and mean. I reached up carefully and pried his hand off my arm, backing up slightly so that I was against the corridor wall.

"What the fuck you want?" His eyes never left my face.

"You the receptionist? I'm looking for Lorenzo."

"Ain't in."

"His car's parked outside." I sniffed. "Besides," I said, "I can smell him."

He didn't crack a smile. "He ain't seein' nobody. Now get the fuck out of here."

"That's three 'fucks' in four sentences," I said. "You really ought to watch your mouth."

The knife appeared very quickly. One moment we were staring at each other, and then suddenly I was looking at a long, narrow stiletto pointed directly at my throat. His eyes changed slightly, and then he lunged.

I reacted by instinct. As the knife came toward me it seemed to slow down, as everything started to unfold in slow motion. I stepped sideways, taking his arm with both hands. Moving with him, I turned his body and ran the point of his knife into the drywall beside me. It went all the way in and stuck there.

I let go of him with one hand while I pushed with the other, still in the direction of his forward movement, slamming him hard against the wall. I chopped down once on his wrist and he let go of the knife.

Then I slapped him hard against the side of the head. His skull bounced off the wall with a loud smack, and he started to go down. I rose up on the balls of my feet and brought my right knee up hard into his solar plexus. I caught a whiff of Dentyne as the breath whistled out of him and he crumpled like a punctured balloon. I got in two more slaps as he hit the floor.

I moved back out of range and watched him for a moment. He lay quietly, curled up on the linoleum in the fetal position. I thought about kicking him in the head for good measure, but decided not to. After all, we hadn't really been introduced yet. Instead, I patted him down. Finding no other weapons, I pulled out the knife and walked down the hall to Lorenzo's office. My head had started throbbing again.

Lorenzo sat hunched up behind his desk, looking like the King of the Toads, eating a large cheese Danish. He froze in mid-gobble as I came through the door, his tiny eyes gleaming like wet rabbit turds.

Then I saw the dog. A huge St. Bernard, hunkered down about four feet away from my boots. It noticed me at the same time and brought its wide muzzle up with a low growl. I showed the dog my knife, and the dog showed me its teeth. I'd never killed a dog before, but the way the day had gone so far, anything seemed possible.

The dog and I looked each other over. Finally the dog seemed to nod, giving me a look that said clearly, 'I won't bother you if you don't bother me.' Fair enough, I thought, and nodded back. As a gesture of good faith, I tossed the knife on Lorenzo's desk. In response the dog's massive head dropped down and settled on the floor between its huge paws.

I turned my attention back to Lorenzo. It had been more than a year since I'd seen him, but neither of us was likely to dwell on old times. He hasn't changed much, I thought. Bad complexion, rotten teeth, and the same rat-bright eyes peering out of a fleshy face that reflected a lifetime of dedicated and varied forms of abuse. He wore his usual two-day Yasser Arafat beard and his ponytail was greasy and matted. He had a stained sweatshirt on with the words 'State of Hawaii – Do It in the Road' plastered across it.

Fat Freddie had once speculated that Lorenzo's mother had at some stage got hold of a large ugly stick and beaten her boy severely with it. Personally, I doubted that Lorenzo had ever had a mother.

He reached over and turned off the music, keeping his eyes on me as he pushed the rest of the Danish into his mouth with a wide dirty thumb. It was like stuffing a down sleeping bag into a sack. As I watched, his other hand appeared from under the desk with a sawed-off shotgun.

He leveled it at my buckle and thumbed the hammers back. "Just so nobody gets excited," he said.

I looked at the weapon. It had once been a 12-gauge side-by-side, but somebody had chopped it down to about eighteen inches. The barrels were wide and dark, practically big enough to stick my fists down.

I stood very still. "Bird shot?"

He shook his head. "Deer slugs. Don't even think about it." He belched loudly and leaned back in his seat. "Okay, Donovan. You got ten seconds to tell me what you want."

Here goes nothing, I thought. "Heard about Fat Freddie?"

He smiled, his face lighting up like a boil. "Yeah, I heard about it. Ain't it a bitch?" He shook his head. "Homicide. Maybe murder one. Man, that's heavy." There was a trace of admiration in his voice.

There was a noise from the doorway and I turned. The black kid stood there holding an Ingram MAC-11 fitted with a sound suppressor. I looked at the Ingram with curiosity. It wasn't the sort of weapon you usually see on the street.

"He sucker-punched me, Lorenzo. Want me to waste him?" The kid's eyes radiated hate.

"Meet Festus," Lorenzo said to me. "Festus is my new troubleshooter." He chuckled, showing blackened teeth. "Any sumbitch gives me trouble, Festus shoots 'em." He paused, and his pupils shrank to pencil points. "He'll shoot you right now, I tell him to."

And Kathy Armlin wouldn't hear a thing, I thought. Oh, my, this is really wonderful.

Just then the St. Bernard farted. A full, wet, ripe sound like a garbage bag bursting. The dog beamed ecstatically at us, tail thumping on the floor, as a foul stench spread through the room like poison gas.

"Jesus." Lorenzo heaved himself out of his chair, setting down the shotgun. "Keep this scumsucker covered, Festus." He waddled across to a heavy safe set back against the wall. The dog watched him adoringly, eyes bright in anticipation.

Lorenzo kept his back to me as he worked the dial. "Got the dog last month," he muttered over his shoulder. "On account of a coupla break-ins over the summer. Fuckin' neighborhood's going bad, Donovan."

He heaved the door to the safe open. I caught a glimpse of papers and something much more interesting. Money, stacks of it. A lot of money, I thought, for Lorenzo to have in the office. I wondered if he'd gone back to dealing crack and made a mental note to ask around.

Lorenzo slammed the safe door shut, spun the dial, and thumped back to the desk. He threw a twenty at Festus.

"Get a dozen burgers for the dog," he growled. "The place down the street. Take the car if she'll start."

Festus looked at the money, then at the dog, and then at me. "Aw shit, Lorenzo—"

"Just shut up and go do it. I can take care of Donovan here. Go on, git. An' leave that goddamn gun in the bedroom where it belongs."

Festus scraped up the money and started for the door, giving me a look that could melt marbles. "Ain't finished with you, friend," he whispered.

I nodded pleasantly. "See you in church."

"And tell 'em not to put any of that fuckin' sauce on," Lorenzo yelled as Festus went out. "That's what makes the dog fart so bad." His chair groaned as Lorenzo sat down. "You got lucky just then, Donovan. Festus is a mean little shit, and he's gonna remember you. You won't be so lucky next time." He raised the shotgun. "Let's get back to business. You was telling me what you wanted."

I thought for a second about how best to appeal to Lorenzo's better instincts and concluded that it would be like panning for gold in a cesspit. I decided to take the direct approach. "I need bail money for Freddie," I said. "Ten thousand dollars. Today."

Lorenzo stared at me. His shoulders seemed to twitch and heave slightly. Then his mouth opened and a deep wheezing noise came from it. It took me a moment to realize that he was laughing.

"Short-term, full points," I continued. "Just for a couple of weeks. I've got to get him out of jail; otherwise, he'll go crazy."

The wheezing subsided. "He's already crazy, you shithead. And so are you for coming in here. The answer's no."

"No?"

Lorenzo raised the shotgun. "Suck pond water, Donovan. No money. Not now, not ever. You got a lotta nerve comin' in here, actually, but I'm glad you did. I've been waiting to stick it up your ass ever since you blew up my car."

"The Imperial? I had nothing to do with that," I lied.

He glared at me. Lorenzo might be playing down in the shallow end of the gene pool, I thought, but he isn't completely stupid. "You're a lying sack of shit, Donovan," he growled. "Somebody blew the Imperial up with a coffee can full of C-4, right out there on the curb. Word on the street is that you supplied whoever did it." His eyes narrowed. "You're lucky I'm gonna let you walk out of here in one piece. That car was practically cherry, man."

I shrugged. Sometimes results, sometimes consequences. It had been a long shot. I started backing slowly toward the door.

"One thing, Donovan." Lorenzo always liked to have the last word. "Tell Fat Freddie to keep his mouth shut. Tell him that."

I stopped. "Keep his mouth shut about what?"

The shotgun came up. "Nothing you need to know about. Freddie'll understand; just tell him. Now git. And don't come back."

* * *

Kathy Armlin looked very happy to see me. "The meanest-looking man just came out and drove away in that old car," she said as I slid into the seat beside her. "Is he the one you went to see? Lorenzo?"

"One of his helpers." I told her about my encounter upstairs.

She bit her lip. "No money?"

"No money. I'll have to try something else." I rubbed the whiskers on my face. "But first I need some sleep. My place is up in Berkeley; you can drop me there."

As we pulled out I saw Festus coming back down the street in the Cadillac. I rolled down the window and gave him the finger, but got no reaction. Maybe he didn't see me. Maybe he had something else on his mind.

I certainly did. Figuring out how to steal ten grand from Lorenzo Marx before tomorrow morning.

CHAPTER SIX

"Say what?" The kid's acne-scarred face looked at me suspiciously across the greasy counter.

"A dozen burgers to go," I repeated. "With extra sauce. Lots of it."

He regarded me warily for a second. "Havin' a party?"

I gave him an extra-wide smile. "They're for me and my brothers. We always like a little late snack."

"Uh-huh." He turned back to the grill and started slapping down hunks of meat. "Dozen burgers with lots of sauce," he murmured to himself. "Oh, boy. Man's mama musta raised some serious fools."

I was the only customer in the all-night restaurant. Odors of sweat, cooking fat, and leaking drains fogged the air around me. From back in the kitchen the sound of Dion and the Belmonts drifted out of someone's transistor radio. Outside in the dark, cars moved slowly up and down San Pablo Avenue, cruising the near-deserted neighborhood for any leftover pieces of the action.

There wasn't much to be had. The solid citizens were home in bed, the streetwalkers had gone home, and the bars wouldn't be letting out for at least another hour. I checked my watch; just past midnight. Time to get moving. Although there was no real reason to start at midnight, I'm a traditionalist at heart. Besides, jet lag was catching up with me. Do what you have to do, I told myself. And then go home and get some sleep. So I yawned and waited for my burgers and tried to calm the pounding of my heart.

* * *

Earlier that afternoon Kathy Armlin had dropped me off at my apartment after my escape from Lorenzo's office. "Meet me at the hospital at ten tomorrow morning," I'd told her. "I should have Freddie bailed out by then."

"With what? You already said that man refused to lend you any money."

"I'll think of something," I said.

She nodded doubtfully and drove off, leaving me alone on my front porch.

I had already thought of something, of course, but I wasn't going to tell her that. The less she knew about my plans for the evening, the better. It wasn't a very smart plan, either, but it was the path of least resistance, and I didn't have time to dream up anything more creative.

I opened the door to my apartment and went into the kitchen. The bugs and I have an arrangement whereby I get to use the kitchen in the daytime and they get to use it at night, but discipline had gone to hell while I'd been in Thailand. Four huge cockroaches looked up at me in astonishment, their feelers quivering indignantly. Then they shot under the sink to tell the others.

The fridge didn't smell too good, but the half-empty bourbon bottle was on top, right where I'd left it, and booze doesn't spoil. I poured an inch into a nearly clean glass and went out and settled down on the couch to think things over.

Problem: How to locate ten thousand dollars before tomorrow morning. I'd already decided on a plan of action, but just for form's sake, I ran through my options while the bourbon warmed the cockles of my heart, whatever they were. Kathy Armlin was out – she had no more money and no hope of dipping into Daddy's campaign chest again. Freddie was broke as usual. The bank was out. The first payment on the business loan that Freddie and I had co-signed was coming up in three weeks. We had confirmed reservations for a full boatload for our first charter next month, but with the captain in jail on a murder charge, it didn't look as if we were going to weigh anchor after all. I sipped my drink and sighed. No, the bank was definitely out.

I took off my money belt and counted what was inside. Just under three thousand dollars. The Thai job would net me twenty thousand, but that wouldn't arrive for at least a month. I cursed softly and looked around at the apartment. Nothing in the place was worth much, and even if it were, I didn't have time for a garage sale. So scratch one more possibility.

I went to the kitchen and sloshed a little more bourbon into my glass. There was a nice view from the sink out across the bay to San Francisco, and the late afternoon sun was glinting on the city's spires, making the place look like fairyland. For a lot of people it was.

I stared for a few minutes and then wandered back into the living room. So now, I thought, we're down to the bedrock. As Sherlock Holmes used to say, when you've eliminated everything else, whatever remains – however unlikely – is the solution. I took a sip of bourbon, lay back on the couch, and began to think about how exactly I was going to rob Lorenzo Marx of ten thousand dollars.

It was practically a victimless crime, I told myself. Lorenzo's money had originally belonged to lawyers and investment brokers from Marin County who'd exchanged it for small plastic vials of white powder, which they promptly snuffed up their greedy noses. I felt no remorse at the thought of stealing the money of those worthy professionals; after all, they had obtained it from their own clients in virtually the same fashion.

I'd feel worse, I thought, if it were high school kids' lunch money gone for crack or joints laced with angel dust. But Bone Brown and I had put a stop to that when we'd blown up Lorenzo's Imperial six months ago. I'd been out of town at the time, on a job in northern Pakistan, but I'd given Bone the C-4 before leaving. He'd wired it and set it off with a remote radio signal, right in front of Lorenzo's beady little eyes. He said the expression on Lorenzo's face quite took his breath away, it was so wonderful.

It had apparently worked too. Since then Lorenzo'd been staying away from the jump-rope set and dealing only with consenting adults with more money than sense. But judging from what I'd glimpsed in his safe this afternoon, Lorenzo seemed to be making even more money than before.

So imagine you're Robin Hood, I told myself – rob the undeserving rich and give to the poor. Namely, yourself. It's Lorenzo's fault, really. He never should have opened the safe and showed me all the money inside.

I could get the safe open again – of that I was certain. I was almost equally certain there'd be at least ten thousand dollars inside it. People like Lorenzo distrusted banks, preferring to leave no chicken tracks that might be followed by eager IRS men.

So I sat and sipped my bourbon and thought about various ways I might do it. When I had it figured out, I lay down on the couch and slept.

My wrist alarm woke me at eleven thirty. I got up and put on my heavy climbing boots with the thick Vibram soles and laced them tight. Then I made some coffee, drank it, and started assembling the equipment I needed. I put a flashlight, some tools, and a length of nylon cord into a small rucksack. I searched my closet until I found the old pair of air force coveralls I'd inherited years ago and put them in the rucksack too. I got a pair of thin gloves from the dresser, along with a set of handcuffs and a weighted sap. From under the dresser I drew out the last of my C-4 explosive. From a box in the closet I took out a detonator and a small length of fuse.

All I needed now was a disguise. I thought for a moment, and then burrowed into a sack of old clothes I'd been meaning to throw away for several years. There it was, crushed down at the bottom. I drew out the rubber Nixon mask and looked at it with pleasure. It had been a gift from a former girlfriend, years ago, on the occasion of a costume party. It fit over the entire head. The eyeholes were large and gave a clear view to either side.

Perfect for what I was about to do.

* * *

"Here you go, man." The kid pushed a large bag, prominently printed with the name of the restaurant, across the counter at me. "Lots of extra sauce, just like you said." I gave him a twenty and took the change. The kid grinned at me. "Sure hope you got some Alka-Seltzer at home."

I parked my car two blocks down the street from Lorenzo's office. I waited a few minutes, watching the street carefully. As I watched I bit into one of the burgers. A moment later I tossed it out the window. Eat enough of those, I thought, and your palate would look and feel like a steel-belted radial.

A cop car flashed by me, hooting like some great demented night bird. I watched its red taillights disappear into the urban murk. My palms were sweating, my breathing a little ragged. Perfectly normal, I told myself. After all, it had been nearly a month since I'd done this sort of thing, and unlike most complex skills, it never seemed to get any easier. And sooner or later the law of averages would catch up with me.

But not tonight, I told myself.

I got out of the car, picked up the rucksack, and melted into the darkness of the alley leading to Lorenzo's office. The main problem, I thought, would be to figure out where Festus and the dog would be. Festus didn't like the dog, and the dog likely felt the same way about Festus. I certainly would have. So they would probably be in separate rooms.

Get Festus first, I decided. Then get the dog. Of the two, Festus was faster, smarter, and a whole hell of a lot more dangerous, and not just because of that Ingram he'd been waving around this afternoon. I'd been lucky earlier when I'd laid him out, and he and I both knew it. I could probably beat him anytime in a fair fight – which was basically what we'd had. But given the slightest advantage, he'd win the next time, and the reason was simple. Because Festus would kill me if he could, and I didn't want to kill him.

And that made things about as difficult as they ever get.

I put on my coveralls and gloves and pulled the Nixon mask down over my face. I took out the sap and put it in an outside pocket where I could reach it easily. Then I started slowly up the stairs, pausing at every tread, probing the darkness with my senses. A stair riser creaked and I stopped for a long moment, feeling the sweat dripping down under the mask.

The door was locked, but I had expected that. I reached into the rucksack and brought out a small ball peen hammer and a roll of tape. In a few seconds I had taped one of the windows and broken it with the hammer. I reached inside with a gloved hand to unlock the door.

I paused in the doorway, letting my eyes adjust to the darkness in the hall. I wasn't worried about burglar alarms. The very last thing on earth Lorenzo wanted was for the police to take an interest in his premises. I was thinking about the St. Bernard. Sooner or later the dog would sense me. I had to find Festus and deal with him before that happened.

I started down the hall. Five steps, then ten. I passed the door to the bathroom and stopped momentarily, listening hard. No sound. Festus had to be in the next room. Either there or in the office.

I could see the dim outline of the door, three feet in front of me. Right now he might be waiting in there with the Ingram, ready to blow my head off. I let out a slow breath. Only one way to find out.

I eased the door open, ready to throw myself to the floor if anything moved. No sound from inside. I snapped on my penlight and advanced the thin beam into the room. Festus was asleep on his back, snoring lightly, an empty six-pack and an open paperback on the floor beside the bed.

I crossed the floor quickly, just as he opened his eyes. He sat halfway up in bed, staring bug-eyed at the face of Tricky Dick, and I hit him just behind the ear with the sap. I handcuffed him to a convenient water pipe and taped his mouth shut.

The Ingram was under his bed, fully loaded, with the safety off. I picked it up and headed for the door, pausing to take the bag of hamburgers out of my rucksack. It was time to say hello to the dog.

I opened the office door and snapped on the light. The dog was there, all right. He opened one surprised eye and heaved himself upright, a growl building in his throat. I held out the bag of burgers with one hand, the Ingram with the other. "Nice doggie," I croaked.

Brand identification did it. The dog's eyes lit up as he spotted the brightly colored logo on the bag of hamburgers and the smell reached his nostrils. "Yurp," went the dog, pounding his tail on the floor.

A whore after my own heart, I thought. "Suppertime, doggie," I said.

The dog shook himself delightedly and trotted forward. Holding the burgers up high, I led him down the hall and into the toilet. I spread out the burgers in a big circle. "Enjoy," I said as I shut the door.

I had to work fast now. I went back into Lorenzo's office and headed for the safe. As I crossed the floor, I slipped on something soft and slick, nearly losing my balance. I looked down to see one of my climbing boots thickly covered in dogshit. I swore under my breath. It would take me forever to scrape it out of the Vibram cleats, but I couldn't afford to stop now. Breathing through my mouth, I kept on.

I stuck a lump of C-4 against the safe door near the lock and looked around for something to tamp the explosion with. I settled for a couple of cushions, strapping them tightly in place with lengths of nylon cord. Then I attached the detonator, lit the fuse, and backed into the hallway.

There was a noise like a large book falling flat on a coffee table. I walked back into the office and brushed away the smoke to find the safe's door hanging open, and a small snowstorm of cushion stuffing settling to the floor.

Whistling between my teeth, I reached inside for the money. I counted out ten thousand dollars in hundreds and fifties and stuffed them into my rucksack. There was lots more money in there, but I decided not to be excessive. As Tricky Dick himself might have said, that would be wrong.

A lot of other junk that had been in the safe was scattered around on the floor. Address books, bills, invoices. One sheaf of papers caught my eye. It was a bill of lading for the motor vessel *Sea Witch*, of Panamanian registry, bound out of Oakland for the Port of Suva in the Fiji Islands with a cargo of automobile spare parts. Lorenzo's name was entered as the shipper.

Auto parts? Somehow it didn't sound like Lorenzo. I shrugged and threw the papers back in the safe. None of my business, I told myself, and anyway, it was time to get moving. Festus was going to start making noise pretty soon. The dog might cause trouble, too, once he'd finished his dinner.

I snapped the lights off and headed down the hall. I took out the Ingram's magazine, put it in my rucksack, and threw the empty gun into the bedroom. Festus was awake, his eyes glowing with hatred as he strained against the water pipe I'd chained him to. I gave him the double V sign on the way out.

In the bathroom the dog sounded like he was throwing up, but I didn't stop to check. I went straight out the door and down the stairs.

The alley was quiet. I pulled off my coveralls and stuffed them into my rucksack. I ripped off the Nixon mask and mopped my face, willing my breathing to return to normal. Then I started walking with what I hoped was a law-abiding spring in my step down the street to where I'd parked the car.

I shut the door and started the engine. I suddenly felt exhausted. I had been going full bore ever since Crake's phone call in Bangkok and I was ready to drop. I needed sleep, immediately.

But no. As I sat there, I became aware of a sharp, distinctive odor rising up to tickle my nostrils. I sighed and put the car in gear. I had one more thing to do before I could sleep. I had to clean the dogshit off my boots.

CHAPTER SEVEN

I pushed the plate with the last sandwich across the table. It was a corned beef and lettuce, one of my favorites. "Go on," I said. "Have it." Fat Freddie's face brightened. He picked it up and began to chew. It was his third sandwich in fifteen minutes.

We were in the Tivoli on upper Grant Avenue in North Beach, and Kathy Armlin and I were in the process of restoring Fat Freddie to somewhere near normal operating condition. Right now he looked like Jerry Garcia on the Scarsdale diet, and he probably felt that way too. His scabs and bruises were beginning to clear up, but his eyes were still puffy from the Thorazine. He needed a shave and his clothes needed washing.

I sipped Anchor Steam from the bottle and watched him devour his sandwich. At least he's still got his appetite, I thought. Even if he hasn't got a hell of a lot else.

It had taken me less than an hour to spring Freddie, with the help of an enterprising bondsman named Reuben Archuleta. Everybody had turned out for the farewell. Luther Crake's expression was calm, serious, and unreadable. Ackroyd looked like a blister about to pop. Sam Young nodded as we went out the door. "Good luck," she murmured. Ackroyd shot her a warning glance. Nobody, I noticed, had asked me where I'd found the bail money.

Now Kathy Armlin watched Freddie eat, her eyes soft and full of concern. He finished his sandwich and brushed crumbs from his mustache. Then he shyly put his arm around Kathy and gave her a hug.

"She's a good woman, Max," he said. "She tell you what happened?"

"Some of it," I said. "I need to hear the rest. You told Kathy you had a plan to come up with the money she needed. What'd you do – rob a bank?"

Freddie laughed nervously. "Hey, Max, you know me and guns, right? No, I thought of something better. Something straight." He caught my look. "Well, okay, a little illegal. But honest, it was practically foolproof."

"Except that you got charged with murder."

Freddie looked down at his hands. "So things got a little fucked up, Max. I admit that. But–"

I leaned across the table. "Freddie, tell me something. Straight, no bullshit. Did you kill anybody?"

He looked at me like a kicked spaniel. "Nobody got hurt, Max. I swear. Max, you know me. You think I could do anything like that?"

I reached across the table and took his hand. "I just wanted to hear it, buddy," I said softly. I sighed. "Now tell me about your plan."

He cleared his throat. "You remember that place we found a couple years ago when we were hiking up in Sonoma County, up outside Napa?"

"The sinsemilla farm?" I was quiet for a moment. Shit. "Freddie, how much did you take?"

He shrugged. "Only about a hundred pounds. I took an old duffel bag and a machete and snuck in one night and trimmed a few plants. They'll never miss it. The hard part was getting through the tripwires and the dogs. They got Dobermans up there, Max."

"Who had you planned on selling it to?"

He hesitated. "You're not gonna like this, Max."

"I haven't liked it so far," I agreed. "So what's one more piece of bad news? Come on, Freddie – who was the buyer?"

"Lorenzo Marx."

I choked, spraying most of a mouthful of beer on the tablecloth. A passing waiter with a sullen face gave me a disapproving look.

"You okay, Max?"

I nodded. "Keep talking," I said.

"Well, once I had the weed, I called Lorenzo. We set up an afternoon meet in one of the knock shops off Columbus. I checked in a little before three and waited for him. He showed up half an hour later with some real nasty-looking dude he called Festus. He took a look at the stuff in the duffel bag and we were all set to deal when all of a sudden there's this shouting from the next room, somebody screaming his guts out, and then doors started slamming."

"What happened then?"

"Lorenzo panicked. I think he figured I'd set him up. The other guy pulled a shotgun out from under his coat, but Lorenzo wasn't waiting around. He started crawling through the bathroom window. Festus had to push him through. They both took off through the alley at the back."

Freddie made a small sad face. "The shotgun spooked me – I picked up the duffel bag and took off down the hall like a big-assed bird. The door to the next room was open and I could see a guy lying on the floor with blood all around. Just then the manager came running out of the office."

"What'd you do then?"

"Got into the pickup and got the hell out of there. They picked me up on the Bay Bridge ramp." He turned tortured eyes to mine. "They had guns, clubs, everything. I hit one of them, I guess, tryin' to keep them away from

43

me." He stared at me, his eyes red and tearful. "They put me in a cell, Max. In a fucking cell."

His eyes were squeezed shut and his voice had passed into a high wavery register. We were starting to attract attention from nearby tables. Kathy Armlin took Freddie's hands in hers and held them, making soft soothing noises, the way you would to a frightened animal.

"I tried to explain to 'em, Max. They locked me up." He was sobbing now. "All those goddamn... guns." He raised his head, tears streaming down his red cheeks. "When I woke up it was dark and I could hear the rats. Then they came with guns again and took me to an office. They started asking questions, and I got scared again. One of them got his gun out and I guess I went a little crazy. That's when they gave me the shot. Before I went to sleep, I remembered the phone number you gave me – the one in Bangkok." He bowed his head. "There it is, buddy. That's all."

He cried softly, his big shoulders heaving, his face in his hands. Kathy Armlin put her arms around him and rocked him gently from side to side. The big fat guy with the frizzy hair and the droopy tangled mustache bawled his eyes out while all around us, members of the smart set picked up their wineglasses and edged away, a little closer to the bar.

The waiter reappeared beside me. "What's the problem here?"

I gave him a long look. "Not a thing, friend. But as you're here, you can bring us another round of beers."

He stood there, his eyes moving back and forth from Freddie to me.

I cleared my throat. "And a couple more corned-beef sandwiches. Right now, if you don't mind."

He nodded and moved off.

Nobody said anything for a while. "What about this?" Kathy Armlin said at last. "If Lorenzo was with Freddie at the motel, then he could testify, couldn't he? I mean, he could tell the police that Freddie didn't do it."

We both stared at her. She blushed.

"Well, I mean, why not? It's the right thing to do, isn't it? Doesn't he have any scruples?"

I coughed quietly. "Kathy, Lorenzo probably thinks that scruples are dried ears or something. He's not going to talk to the police about this. If he did, he'd have to explain what he and Festus were doing there."

She looked at me. "Then what are we going to do? They'll put Freddie back in jail as soon as they get the new indictment. We've just got to think of something."

I gazed deep into my bottle of Anchor Steam, searching for enlightenment. I'm a cautious person. In my line of work you live longer that way. I believe in the harmony of patterns in human affairs; when the pattern is jumbled or unclear, the best solution is often to do nothing. Over the years I'd learned to let events unfold and arrange themselves into a design I could understand. And with understanding often came control. But to achieve control over events I needed to see them clearly, and right now things were about as clear as the bottom of the Marianas Trench at midnight.

What I could see didn't look good at all. Lorenzo and Festus would incriminate themselves if they talked, which meant that neither of them would be coming forward willingly. Freddie could tell his side, of course, but that would pull in Kathy Armlin, Kathy's baby brother, and, eventually, her father. Freddie would lose the only decent woman he'd had since the war, and old man Armlin would lose the election to Delbert Ackroyd. And if Ackroyd got to be state senator, I thought gloomily, I probably ought to consider moving to Burkina Faso.

And that was only half of the story. Ackroyd might or might not make first-degree murder stick, but the way things were going the chances were excellent that Freddie would be seeing a lot of the inside of San Quentin. Lots of guns, lots of metal bars, and not much food. Sooner or later they'd be measuring him for a suit with sleeves that tied together and reserving him a room with padded wallpaper.

And I'd have lost both my best friend and the thirty thousand dollars I'd invested in our business in Mexico. I might wind up in Burkina Faso whether I liked it or not.

"Somebody'd better think of something." Fat Freddie's heavy voice broke the silence. "Cause I'm not goin' back inside, Max. Not ever. I wouldn't last a week in jail; you know that. That hospital was no paradise either."

Something in the back of my head fell into place with a soft click. I put down my beer. "Paradise," I whispered. "My God, that's it. Paradise." I pushed back my chair and got up.

Freddie stared at me. "Where are you going?"

"Telephone call; back in a second." I pushed the plate of extra sandwiches across to him. "Take these."

The phone was in the corner near the restrooms. I fumbled for change, dialed, and was rewarded with a familiar voice. "Homicide, Crake."

"Sergeant Young, please."

A click and a buzz. Canned favorites of yesteryear wafted across the line. I cursed quietly. Ask and ye shall be put on hold. Finally she picked up the phone. "Young."

"Max Donovan, Sergeant. I wonder if you can do me a favor."

"What sort of favor, Mr. Donovan?"

"I've just thought of something important – something connected to Freddie's case. Can you come with me to Berkeley this afternoon? There's somebody at the university I'd like you to talk to."

"I'm just going off duty, Mr. Donovan. I'll refer this to somebody else who can handle it."

"No," I said. "I think it should be you."

"What's this all about?"

46

"I'm not sure yet," I said. "But I think I know where those feathers came from – the ones in the plastic bag on your desk. Can you come?"

She was silent for a moment. "I'll bite," she said at last. "Pick me up in forty-five minutes." She gave me her address on 17th Street. "And, Donovan, this had better be worth my time."

"Bring the feathers," I said.

She hung up.

I went back to our table. "Take care of Freddie," I said to Kathy Armlin. "Keep him with you, and see that he stays out of trouble. The cops will throw him back inside for picking his nose if they catch him at it. I'll call you later."

I laid some money on the table and picked up my jacket. "One question," I said to Freddie. "What happened to the grass in the duffel bag? The cops didn't mention it."

Freddie shifted uncomfortably on his seat. "There's a little problem about that, actually. The cops never saw the bag. I got rid of it on my way to the Bay Bridge. There was this garbage dumpster on Osgood Place, near Broadway. I threw it in there as I drove by."

I nodded. "Well, that's one good thing, anyway."

He looked at me with his sad brown eyes. "Not really, Max. The duffel bag's yours – it's the one you loaned me for the trip to Mexico. It's got your name and address stenciled right on the side."

CHAPTER EIGHT

Sam Young wore a pale blue summer dress that ended just a little above her nicely dimpled knees. Her face was all business. "This had better be good, Mr. Donovan," she said as she climbed out of my car. "I was looking forward to a long afternoon with the travel brochures, planning my vacation. Where are we going?"

"To see a friend of mine," I said. "Someone who might know something about those feathers. Professor Isaac Brown. But we call him Bone."

"Bone Brown? Why do you call him Bone?"

I smiled. "You'll see. His office is in the Anthropology Department, in Kroeber Hall. The quickest way's up Telegraph."

It had turned into a nice afternoon. The sunlight had the clear sparkling quality of a Mediterranean seashore, the air warm with the cool underbite that is Northern California's trademark. Along Telegraph it was business as usual. Hawkers squatted on the sidewalk selling magic charms and hand-carved bongs, while freaks sat cross-legged on the curb and watched the crowds go by. Across the street a magician in a cape decorated with Day-Glo owls stood on a trash can and did tricks for a small knot of Japanese tourists. Incense and the smell of burning leaves drifted through the air.

I accepted a leaflet for the Groucho Marxist Party from a small person dressed in motley and gave a dollar to the thin girl collecting for the People's Clinic. In the doorway of the Bank of America two teenagers lay wrapped in torn blankets, their faces showing the wounds of dreams betrayed and promises unfulfilled. They belonged to the street's underbelly, part of a small army that slept each night in the bushes or under the big houses on fraternity row and nodded through the days, panhandling for food and the daily score. There seemed to be more of them every year.

We stopped for the light on Bancroft, across from Sproul Plaza. On the far curb a group of Hare Krishnas smiled and waved at passersby, their saffron robes brilliant in the sun. A tall blonde with braids three feet long sailed by on roller skates. She was wearing a skintight leotard and wide-stripe leg warmers. Reflecting aviator sunglasses covered her eyes, and stereo earphones in purple fuzz were clamped to her head. She slid deftly past us and swooped on down the street, her rump twitching to a beat only she could hear.

"There she goes!" a voice boomed out just behind my right ear. "The great whore of Babylon!" I turned to see a tiny man perched on top of a wooden box, his face purple with holy fury.

"Jesus," muttered Sam Young. "Welcome to Berkeley."

The little man held a dog-eared leather book in his upraised fist as he chanted in a voice filled with doom and thunder. "When the world ends in fire and destruction and God's Day of Judgment comes, some people are gonna go to heaven, and some people are gonna go to hell!"

I tried to move away, but we were blocked by other pedestrians. They stared straight ahead, refusing to acknowledge the little preacher.

"You wanna know who's gonna go to hell? I'll tell ya who's gonna go to hell! Hippies are gonna go to hell. Black Panthers are gonna go to hell. The faggots are gonna go to hell." He flung his arm out wide. "And all those phony sons of bitches across the street are gonna go to hell too!"

The light changed and the crowd surged toward the Hare Krishnas on the far shore. Drums boomed and bells tinkled in welcome as the first arrivals were presented with flowers and brightly colored pamphlets.

"Ravers," Sam Young said darkly. "Space cadets. No, more than that – galactic commanders. Isn't anybody over here normal?" She grasped my arm. "Your friend Bone's a raver, too, isn't he?"

"Let's find out," I said. "In here."

We entered Kroeber Hall and went past the museum display cases to the elevator. I glanced at the graffiti as we slowly rose. The best one read, 'Berkeley girls are the guys who worked their balls off in high school.' I caught Sam Young smiling at it, and she blushed.

We found Bone Brown in his office, scowling at the heaps of paper that littered his desk. Bone is a large man who compensates for his baldness with a beard. The beard is huge and shiny black and looks like Brillo. It starts high up on his cheeks and disappears down into his shirt without a break. All you can really see of him are his bright intelligent eyes peering out at you from dense underbrush.

But what you really see, of course, is the bone. The one that he wears through his nose.

Some years ago, Bone spent time living with a tribe of people in New Guinea's Western Highlands. They made him an honorary warrior, killed a dozen pigs, and threw a week-long party in his honor. Then they pierced his nasal septum and gave him a cassowary bone to put through it. He still wears his bone and claims it helps get the undivided attention of his students. He has a pair of boar's tusks for formal wear.

He had all of Sam Young's attention as he rose to greet us. She was staring at the bone as he shook her hand, looked her over appraisingly, and nodded at me.

"You said you were bringing a cop, Max," he said. "Miss Young here is certainly an improvement over most I've seen."

She looked around at the genial clutter of books, papers, and strange artifacts that littered the office. She picked up a human skull that had been somehow fashioned into a beer mug, handle and all. Neatly lettered on the side of the skull were the words '*Gaudeamus Igitur, Juvenes Dum Sumus.*'

"'Let Us Be Merry, While We Are Young,'" she read. "God, that's sick."

"Some of my colleagues have a strange sense of humor," said Bone. "It's refreshing, I must say, to meet someone who still reads Latin." He bowed courteously to her. "What can I do for you, my dear?"

She put down the skull and took an envelope from her purse. She opened it and laid a single long blue and white feather on Bone's desk. "For a start, Professor, you can tell me what that is."

Bone peered at it for a long moment, his glasses glinting. He picked it up and twirled it around between his thumb and forefinger. He sniffed at it. Then he laid it back on the desk. "*Pteridophora alberti.*"

"I beg your pardon?" she said.

He ignored her question. "Wherever did you find this?"

Quickly she told Bone the story of the murder and of Fat Freddie's arrest.

When she had finished, Bone shook his head. "Whoever killed that man, Sergeant, it wasn't Freddie Fields. I assume Max has explained all that to you." He picked up the feather again. "Extraordinary. And this is your only clue?"

She nodded. "Do you know what it is?"

Bone raised his bushy eyebrows. "I just told you what it was, my dear. *Pteridophora alberti*, the King of Saxony. It's a bird of paradise. One of the rarest in the world."

"Are you sure?"

"Absolutely. I once did research on them, in fact. I believe I still have a film of this particular species. Would you like to see it?"

"Please."

Moving with the practiced economy of a professional bartender, Bone opened a cabinet behind his desk. He took out a metal box of film reels, pawed through them, and extracted one. Then he burrowed back inside the cabinet and pulled out a small 8mm projector. He threaded the film, then killed the lights and started the projector. A white splash of leader flickered against the wall. The screen cleared, showing jungle foliage, sunlight shafting down through the tree canopy. The sound blipped on, and birdcalls and insect noises filled the darkened room. The camera panned the area slowly.

"I shot this from a blind," said Bone. "Watch. It's coming now."

A flash of color streaked across the screen. The camera tracked quickly to a high branch where a bird had just lighted, and then zoomed in and steadied. The bird was orange and black, with a short tail. From the back of its head swept two magnificent blue and white plumes, easily three times the length of its body. The plumes were identical to the fragment lying on the desk in front of us. Beside me, I heard Sam Young draw her breath in.

The bird remained still for a moment, and then its mouth opened. A harsh hissing sound came from it, rather like escaping steam. Then the bird began to bounce violently up and down on its perch. As it bounced, its neck feathers expanded to form a wide mantle. It bowed its head repeatedly, causing the long plumes to sweep back and forth.

This ritual dance continued for perhaps thirty seconds. Then, without warning, it was over. The bird snapped its head around – perhaps startled by a noise – stood perfectly still for a beat, and then dived off the branch and out of sight.

White leader flashed on the screen. Bone reached over and turned the projector off. No one spoke for a moment, and then Sam Young said in a quiet voice, "That bird – it's absolutely beautiful. Why does it do that? That little dance?"

"It's a mating display," said Bone. "Impressive, isn't it?"

He snapped on the lights. "I shot that film a few years ago up in the Schrader Range as part of a study on human-environment relationships. The natives in those parts use the feathers for trade. In fact, that's when I met Max here – he was flying cargo around to the mountain airstrips in those days."

He picked up the feather. "This is from the King of Saxony, all right; absolutely no doubt about it. No other bird in the world has feathers like that. The King of Saxony bird of paradise lives only in the high montane cloud forests of New Guinea. The species is closely related to the crow, by the way."

Sam Young frowned. "Then what on earth is a bird of paradise doing in San Francisco? And what's it got to do with a murder?"

"Both easy questions, I'm afraid." Bone stood up. "And I'll answer them as soon as I've had my tea. I usually take a cup at this time of the afternoon. There's a new little place a few blocks from here, and I'd be delighted if you'd both join me. My treat, of course."

* * *

Bone took a large and sticky cake from the assortment on the plate and ate it in three precise bites. He smacked his lips and drank half his tea. Then he leaned back and put his pipe – a huge misshapen block of briar – in his mouth.

"I'm not allowed to actually light it, curse them," he said. "But no matter." He turned to Sam Young. "Have you ever heard," he said to her, "of the theory of spheres of exchange?"

She shook her head.

"It's simple, really," he said, helping himself to another cake. "Dreamed up a few years ago by a Norwegian anthropologist, based on some things he'd been observing in a remote part of Africa. The basic idea is that things in one place may be virtually worthless, but extremely valuable in another, because the two economic systems – the spheres of exchange – don't really connect. Now the King of Saxony is found only in one remote corner of the world. In that corner of the world they are plentiful. And because they are plentiful, they are cheap, so to speak. The locals trade them with each other for pigs and shells and things like that." He paused to sip his tea. "But there aren't any birds like that anywhere else in the world. Someone – in California, say – who wanted one, might pay a great deal of money for it."

Her eyes narrowed. "Smuggling?"

Bone nodded. "Smugglers make their money by buying cheap in one sphere and selling dear in the other. That way they can make a killing on the market." He colored. "Oh, dear, I've said something stupid, haven't I? I was forgetting about the dead man."

She leaned forward. "Do you mean to say that a man was murdered because of one of these birds? Don't you think that's pretty far-fetched?"

"Not at all," Bone replied crisply. "There are collectors of rare items all over the world. Some of the rare items are animals. And on the illegal black market, prices are high and profits enormous. All you need is a middleman – someone who can transfer goods out of one exchange system and into another."

Sam Young considered that for a moment. "How much would a bird of paradise be worth?"

Bone shrugged. "I have no idea, my dear. But comparisons can be instructive. For example, Arab traders in West Africa will pay local hunters the equivalent of ten cents for a pair of brightly colored fire finches. Such a pair will sell in Europe or the United States for fifty dollars or more. That's a profit of something like fifty thousand percent. Six months ago, in Hong Kong, customs officers found a suitcase full of drugged Chinese parrots. The birds were estimated to be worth roughly five thousand dollars each."

She gave a low whistle.

"They were neither particularly rare nor beautiful," Bone continued. "It was the difficulty of getting them out of China that made them valuable. The King of Saxony is rare, very beautiful, and I have never heard of one in a private collection here in the United States. To someone interested in such things, I would imagine that the bird would be nearly priceless. Do you want a wild guess? Ten to twenty thousand dollars each. Perhaps much more." He gave a tight smile. "Perhaps enough to kill for."

We sat there quietly for a moment. I slowly became conscious of the canned music in the background, floating just under my consciousness like a mild headache. Bone had noticed it too. He grimaced and got heavily to his feet.

"Excuse me," he said. "I'll just go wash my hands." He wandered off toward the back of the restaurant, looking for all the world like an amiable bear strolling through the woods.

"That's a nice theory," Sam Young said after a moment. "But there's a hole. How could MacKenzie get the birds into the country?"

"Easy," I said. "Dope the birds and pack them in a suitcase."

"What about customs? You couldn't bring in birds in a suitcase without a very high risk of getting caught, right?"

"Wrong," I said. "Didn't Ackroyd say the man was a diplomat? Diplomats have immunity – they don't have to have their bags inspected."

She looked at me. "My God, you're right." Just then there was a crackle of static and a loud pop. The music stopped abruptly. "Thank heavens for that," she muttered. "It was beginning to drive me nutty."

"Thank him," I said, pointing to Bone as he made his way back to our table. "He probably had something to do with it."

"I'm glad you asked them to turn off the music," Sam Young said when he had taken his seat.

Bone winked. "I didn't ask," he said. He opened his jacket to reveal a custom-made waistcoat fitted with pockets containing a variety of pliers, screwdrivers, and other electrician's tools.

She stared open-mouthed at him. "You cut the wires?"

He raised two fingers in a V sign. "Soon the airwaves will be ours," he whispered.

She giggled. "Do you realize that what you just did is illegal? You could be arrested."

Bone grinned. "By you?"

She smiled. "Hardly. Do you do this often?"

"Every chance I get." Bone leaned forward. "Once, my dear, the world was composed of four elemental forces – earth, air, fire, and water. Now we have added a fifth – bullshit. We bombard ourselves with lies, evasions, and half-truths masquerading as the straight dope. We have confused image with reality; worse, we no longer seem to care which is which. Our imaginations grow daily more impoverished, our choices fewer. Those of us with money to buy our way through life are 'consumers' – those of us without are 'clients.' All of us are treated like children."

Bone's eyes were glowing now, a true fanatic's. "The media are the main culprits of course. Television is a farrago of nonsense. It has debased our myths, spoiled all our good stories. As a result we have lost both our code of conduct and our irreplaceable data bank about how the universe really works."

He cleared his throat. "But the worst is what they have done to music. As any musician can tell you, music is quite literally magic. It crosses the divide, you see, between this world and... that one." He waved his hand vaguely into the distance. "All tribal cultures know this as well – it is why they often make their musicians into special people, why they keep the instruments hidden in the forest, why they teach the apprentices in secret."

He sighed. "But all this is now lost. Machine-made music oozes from every crevice – music without soul, without mystery. Music to lull us, to dull our senses. Aural novocain." Bone drew himself up to full height. "I am a crusader, Sergeant, in the endless war against the enemy. I strike swiftly and without warning, at every opportunity."

He glanced at his watch. "And I have a class in fifteen minutes." He stood up, brushing crumbs from his beard with one huge hand. "I trust that I've been of some help to you, Sergeant." He turned to me. "Good to see you back again, Max. Had a chance to see any old friends?"

I shrugged. "Saw Lorenzo yesterday. He's got a new car."

Bone smiled. "Does he really? I hope he takes better care of it than the last one." He took Sam Young's hand. "A pleasure, my dear. Just remember, Freddie Fields didn't murder that man. However he's mixed up in this, it isn't as a killer. Someone else is involved." Bone frowned. "Find that person and you've found your killer."

We walked slowly back to my car.

"That's the first break we've had on this case," said Sam Young. "Now maybe Ackroyd will let me take my vacation on time." She turned to me. "I owe you a favor, Mr. Donovan."

"Tell you what," I said as I opened the car door for her. "You can let me buy you dinner at Spenger's. As a favor."

She thought about it. "You're on, Mr. Donovan. But it'll have to be Dutch treat."

"On one condition," I said.

"Which is?"

"That you call me Max."

She smiled. "If you'll call me Sam."

"Deal. Hop in."

We drove for a couple of blocks in silence. "Max?"

"Yeah?"

"Professor Brown. Does he wear that – bone in his nose all the time?"

I smiled. "I think he takes it out when he has the sniffles."

CHAPTER NINE

"You're a supplier?" she said. "A supplier of what?"

I shrugged. "Just about anything. I can either get it for you or tell you where to find it. I draw the line at drugs, porn, or weapons."

I forked a scallop into my mouth and chewed it. "I supply missing people a lot of the time. There are a lot of lost people in the world, Sam. Some get lost by mistake, some on purpose. Other people sometimes want to find them. I help them do that."

"How?"

"Easy. I think of where somebody might go. Then I go there and look for them. I know most of the good hiding places – the world's back alleys, the places most people wouldn't think of. I look for the accountant who took off with the firm's payroll, the husband who flew into the sunset with his secretary. The kid who went to Nepal and didn't come back. Last year I rescued two French businessmen who'd been taken hostage in Bahrain."

"Was that what you were doing in Thailand? Looking for someone?"

I shook my head. "Nope. This time it was information. I was hired by a British publisher to find out who was pirating their best-sellers."

She frowned. "How can you pirate a book?"

"Simple. You buy a copy the day it comes out, send it east by air courier, and start printing it up on photo-offset equipment in somebody's basement. It's on the street the next day, virtually identical to the real version, but at one quarter the price."

"And you found out who was doing it?"

"Turned out to be several unfriendly gentlemen from Macau who'd set up shop in Bangkok. One of them tried to put a knife through my guts. I was celebrating my survival when Crake called." I took a sip of beer, mentally toasting Joyce Lindsay-Watson's magnificent chest.

Sam shook her head. "I can't believe you do this for a living."

I smiled. "A thing worth doing," I said, "is worth doing for money. But it's dangerous. That's why Freddie and I went into the charter-boat business together. I thought it was time to lower the odds a little. Now I don't know what the hell will happen."

"The charter-boat business?"

"Yeah. See, before the war, Freddie was a boat driver," I said. "One of the best on the West Coast. The man can run almost any kind of rig, from a tugboat to a three-masted schooner. He used to make his living taking motor sailers through the Panama Canal to the Caribbean and back again. Sometimes out to Hawaii. Every now and then he'd get a call to bring one over from the boatyards in Hong Kong or Singapore."

I ate another scallop. "Last year we got the idea of a charter company to take people fishing off Baja, down in Mexico. We got a business permit from the Mexicans and a loan for thirty thousand from the bank. I put in thirty thousand of my own. We bought a trimaran in San Diego and converted it for fishing. Freddie was down there last week, getting the boat ready. I also picked up a used Cessna – I'm supposed to fly our first group of customers down in three weeks."

I looked at her. "You really ought to see this place, Sam. It's like nowhere else on earth. The beaches are pure white, deserted for miles. At night thousands of tiny crabs come out to feed on the phosphorescent plankton washed up by the waves. It's fantastic – you can sit on the sand and imagine you're on another planet."

She smiled. "Maybe I ought to go there for my vacation."

"You could do a lot worse." I frowned. "But I guess we can forget about all that now. Now the only thing is keeping Freddie out of jail. If he goes inside, it'll kill him, Sam, as surely as a bullet between the eyes."

She looked steadily at me. "Maybe I'm out of line here, Max, but let me just ask you one thing, okay?"

I nodded.

"What makes you so sure he didn't kill MacKenzie? Somebody did, after all."

I sighed. "Fair question. Okay, I'll tell you why I'm sure. And then I think you'll understand a little about Freddie. And about me." I pushed my plate aside. "It started when I got shot down and captured."

"You got shot down?"

"My third time, actually. But this time I was in Cong country. I was flying medevacs, and we took an RPG hit on the tail one day. I aimed for a rice paddy, but hit the mud dike instead." I signaled to the waitress for another beer. "They picked me up and sent me up to Long Dinh, a prison camp up near the Cambodian border. When I got there they threw me in the tiger cages. That's where I met Freddie."

"I thought we were the ones who had the tiger cages," Sam murmured.

I gave her a tight smile. "Who do you think we got the idea from? So I spent the next two weeks sitting in my own shit and thinking bad thoughts, and then they put Freddie in next to me. I was in pretty bad shape by that time. Freddie was a Seabee – he'd been drafted and sent out to sort of rearrange the Vietnamese coastline around Cam Ranh Bay. He'd been in the camp more than a year, knew his way around. We started talking. And what he told me saved my life."

I let my eyes unfocus just a little, thinking back to how it had been, letting my mind go all the way back. "They let me out of the cages after a while, but the camp itself wasn't much better," I said at last. "There was one guard who used to make bets with the others about how many times he could make a prisoner spin if he shot him in the ear from ten feet away." My voice sounded far away now, almost as if it didn't belong to me at all. "Another guy liked to put his rifle up against the backs of our heads and pull the trigger. Usually the gun was empty. Every once in a while he'd slip a round into the clip, just for fun."

Sam was silent, looking at me.

"Freddie was the one who got me through it," I said. "He showed me how to separate the physical from the mental – how to maintain my pride and my spirit. They could do anything to my body they wanted, Freddie said, but they could never have my mind unless I let them." I touched her hand on the table, gently. "He showed me how to survive. Later, I showed him how to escape. And we kept helping each other, every day, every way we could, because we were goddamned if we'd die in that country, because of those people, for that cause." My voice was cracking a little so I stopped. "So now I owe him," I said after a few moments. "Can you understand what I'm telling you?"

She nodded.

"Fat Freddie wasn't always fat," I continued. "His nickname started out as a joke in the camp – we were all so thin from dysentery and malnutrition. Freddie was worse than most of us – they'd starve him for weeks at a time. Because he was the leader, you see – the strong one in the camp. There was one guard in particular – Vinh – who was determined to break Freddie. A bunch of the guys were stealing food from the kitchen. We all knew about it of course. One day Vinh lined up five guys in a row and pulled out his pistol. He asked Freddie who was stealing the food. Freddie told him to go fuck himself. Then Vinh shot the first guy in line, right through the forehead."

"My God," said Sam. "Couldn't anyone do anything?"

"Who did you have in mind?" I said. "The attorney general? Anyway, Vinh asked Freddie again, and Freddie told him the same thing. So Vinh shot the second guy. It went on that way until they were all dead." I paused. "Then Vinh made Freddie bury them."

Sam was staring at the tablecloth now.

"It was a different world in the camp, Sam. We had to build our own society there and live by its rules. One of the rules was 'Unity Over Self.' It meant loyalty to friends, at whatever cost. It got us through it... But after the episode with Vinh, Freddie started to lose his grip. I knew then that I had to get him out of there. So I figured out a way to escape and took him with me."

I sipped my beer. "The Cong never broke him," I said. "But America did. It just took longer, that's all." I paused, trying to get the words just right. "I think Freddie used up most of his energy getting us through it, keeping all of us alive. He took care of me and the rest of the guys for a couple of years – looked out for us, worried over us, counseled us. Stood up for us, with Vinh and the others. He was our mentor and protector, you see, and to do his job he had to use part of himself up."

I sipped beer and held the taste in my mouth for a moment. "And when Freddie finally got back home, he found a country that couldn't deal with who he was and where he'd been. He found an indifferent society, and I guess he couldn't give anything but indifference back." I reached across the table and gripped her hand. "You know what he said to me one time? He said, 'Max, I knew the minute I saw Vietnam that it was gonna be a bitch. But I didn't expect it to be that way back in the World too. I had my head up and my belly down in Nam, but the US just snuck up on me when I didn't expect it.'"

"So what exactly is wrong with him?"

"PTSD," I said. "Post-traumatic stress disorder. Battle fatigue, in other words. It takes different forms in different people. With Freddie it's phobias – he's afraid of the dark, he's afraid of not getting enough to eat, and he doesn't like being confined. He sleeps with the lights on and the windows open. But most of all, he's terrified of guns. He can't stand to look at them, touch them, be in the same room with one. He doesn't even like to see guns on the TV. It's because of what Vinh did."

She nodded. "It makes more sense now," she said. "So what's the prognosis, Max? Will he ever get back to being normal?"

I shrugged. "Ex-POWs have a life expectancy about half that of normal people. Suicides, drugs, alcohol – you name it. The doc who was working with Freddie – before he committed suicide himself, that is – said that Freddie needed to get over the guilt associated with all those deaths in the camp. Freddie thinks he caused those guys to die, Sam, and he worries about it. The doc figured that if Freddie could strike back at Vinh somehow, he might begin to straighten out. But since Vinh's not around, he needs somebody like Vinh – a symbol of evil. The doc told me once that if Freddie could ever bring himself to shoot somebody in a good cause, it would probably do him more good than five years of therapy."

Sam stared at me. "Shoot someone in a good cause? Jesus, Max, how's that going to happen?"

"Right," I said. "So you see where that leaves Freddie."

* * *

It was a warm, starry night, and I had the top down as we went back across the Bay Bridge into San Francisco. The city was lit up like a splendid jewel, beckoning us forward.

"All right," she said at last. "Suppose for a moment that Freddie didn't kill MacKenzie. Where does that leave you? With the prime suspect gone, all we've got left is a body."

I thought for a moment. "Let's start with that, then."

"With what?"

"MacKenzie's body. Is it still in the morgue?"

"As far as I know. Why?"

"Let's take a look at it."

CHAPTER TEN

The basement of the Hall of Justice was practically deserted. At one end a couple of motorcycle policemen stood holding their helmets and chatting quietly, looking strangely unhorsed. They glanced briefly at Sam and me as we walked by, but said nothing.

"Ackroyd'll throw a fit if he finds out about this," said Sam. "But what the hell, I owe you one." She pushed open a door. "In here."

I followed her into a large room that smelled faintly of alcohol and decay. Bright fluorescent bulbs made the stainless steel gleam harshly. It reminded me of my high school cafeteria.

In one corner a tall skinny kid sat picking his zits and studying a copy of *Hustler* with interest. He wore thick Buddy Holly glasses and a TKE pin on his shirt. The shirt was buttoned all the way up to his neck.

He looked up at me, his long nose twitching like a rat's. "Whaddya want?" he said. Then he caught sight of Sam and his face brightened. "Oh, hi, Sergeant. What's up?"

"Get your keys, Snedley," Sam said. "We want a look at one of the guests. Where'd you put MacKenzie?"

"The Australian?" He consulted a list in front of him. "Number seven." He closed his magazine carefully. I glanced at it, saw that it was one of the rare anniversary issues. Snedley caught me looking and grinned. He pulled keys from a drawer and shambled over to a bank of what looked like meat lockers. He unlocked one, pulled out the sliding tray, and stepped back with the air of a magician who's just sawn a lady in half. "Voilà," he said. "Step up and say hello."

I stared down at the dead man. MacKenzie had been in his late fifties, by the look of him. A big man, fit and muscular, handsome in a rugged sort of way. But now he was deflated in death, curiously shrunken, only a waxwork model. Or a Frankenstein's monster, I thought, seeing the crude sutures that closed the thoracic incisions the examiner had made. I stared at him, feeling like an interloper as I did so. The dead have no dignity, I thought, no defense against us.

"Notice the head wound." Snedley was playing tour guide, moving around the corpse like a salesman showing off a new car. "Must have hurt like a bastard, huh?"

I nodded, seeing the deep indentation in the temple. "What did it?"

"Who knows? They found pig grease on the wound," he said, dropping his voice confidentially. "Pig grease, can you believe it? But no weapon." He grinned. "Maybe he got hit with a heavy sausage."

"Jesus, Snedley," said Sam. She looked at me. "Let me know when you've seen enough."

I forced myself to return to the corpse. Apart from the massive head wound and the medical examiner's incisions, the torso was unblemished. Then something on MacKenzie's legs caught my eye, and I leaned forward for a better look.

"Look at those scars," I said, pointing. "All around his ankles."

Sam turned to Snedley. "Have you got the medical examiner's report here?"

"Photocopies," Snedley said. "There's photocopies of everything. Just a sec." He went back to his desk.

I didn't need a medical report to tell me about those scars. They were tropical ulcers, and I'd had a dozen or so of them myself. You get them out in places that are hot, humid, and a long way from medical help. Tiny scratches or mosquito bites quickly blossom into open sores the size of a half-dollar, granulated at the edges, oozing pus and hurting like hell. Untreated, they could persist for months. People who wound up with just scars were the lucky ones; others could suffer amputation, gangrene, even death.

I'd gotten mine in the jungles, hiding from Victor Charles. I wondered how and where MacKenzie had gotten his.

Most of the ulcer scars were old, but there were other marks too — smaller and more recent. Tiny blue-puckered welts, scattered around the instep and lower ankles. I bent forward for a closer look.

"What do you see?" said Sam.

"Leech bites," I said after a moment. "Those are fresh leech bites."

"Leeches leave little tiny scars like that?"

I nodded. "They inject an anticoagulant into the blood to keep the wounds open. The bites aren't painful, but they take a long time to heal. MacKenzie must have been walking around somewhere where there are lots of leeches. Not long ago, either."

"I never heard of any leeches around here," Sam said doubtfully. "Do they have them in Australia?"

"I don't know," I said. "Let's take a look at that file." I took the thick manila folder from Snedley and began to leaf through it. There were photographs of the scene of the crime — MacKenzie lying flat on the floor, his head at an odd angle, some blood on the rug. Not a lot of blood, I saw; death must have been instantaneous. There were photographs of the contents of his pockets: some American money, some multicolored Australian bills, some small change, including a couple of big silver coins with holes in the middle.

I looked up at Sam. "Did he have a passport on him?"

She nodded. "Two passports, in fact. Photocopies of both of them should be in there."

I turned back to the file. There were the passports, each page clearly photocopied. The first, an ordinary Australian passport, had several entry stamps for Hong Kong, one for Singapore, and one for London. The London stamp was over two years old.

I flipped over the pages. Here was the second passport, a diplomatic one this time, identifying its owner as a United Nations technical expert and requesting foreign governments to allow said expert to pass without let or hindrance, etc.

Unlike the other passport, this one had been heavily used. There were half a dozen recent stamps into and out of Papua New Guinea, all within the last year. There were several entries into Fiji, and four immigration stamps from the United States – all from San Francisco, all within the past six months.

"Quite the traveler," I said finally. "Somebody's checking all this out, I assume?"

"Luther Crake's telexed Canberra," said Sam. "Also the UN headquarters in New York. Somebody else is going through the airport records here right now. But it's really just routine. They don't expect to find anything."

I turned over pages. There were photographs of the handkerchief in MacKenzie's pocket, the pens in his suit, the Rolex on his wrist. Twenty pages of photocopies were devoted to a painstaking view of the contents of his wallet, from traveler's checks – front and back – to credit cards and scraps of paper.

I held up a photocopy of a small color snapshot. It showed MacKenzie and two other men standing on a beach, arms around each other's shoulders. MacKenzie smiled broadly into the camera, his head thrown back, his teeth gleaming white in the strong sunlight.

The second man was younger. Slimmer and darker, he gave an impression of catlike grace and fluidity. He wore an Errol Flynn mustache and longish blond hair that came nearly to his shoulders. A small earring gleamed beside his smile, and he wore a necklace of what looked like coral chips. Gay? Somehow, I didn't think so.

The third man was a shambling wreck – an emaciated, undernourished goblin of a man who squinted his eyes and hunched over, escaping the sun's glare. Even his smile looked tentative and somehow fearful. The overall impression was of two rich brothers, one conservative and one a playboy, who had posed for a picture with a Skid Row bum.

I passed the picture to Sam. "Who are they?"

"We've no idea," she said. "It was in his wallet. Luther put a facsimile of it on the wire to Canberra this morning, but we don't expect much. The picture could have been taken anywhere, really."

I looked again at the picture, staring at the long shadow of the photographer on the sand in front of the men and at the palm trees in front of the building in the background. It could have been anywhere, I thought, excitement building in me, but it wasn't. It was somewhere very specific, and I knew it well.

It was the balcony of the bar at the Royal Papua Yacht Club. In Port Moresby. In New Guinea.

Well, goddamn, I thought.

There was no doubt at all about it. I had spent too many happy hours at the Yacht Club, drunk and sober, to ever forget the way it looked. There were the broad mahogany railings that I used to lean on and watch the harbor lights at night. There were the decorative lifebuoys hanging at intervals from the rails. There were the wide doors leading into the bar, and off the bar the club coat of arms over the lintel. To the right, the large windows of the dining room. Inside there would be white tablecloths and bare-chested waiters moving slowly under the turning fans. And yes, there was the flagpole, from which the club pennant flew every Saturday during the racing season, with the sleek hulls spanking the waters of the bay out to the reef and back, beers to celebrate their safe return and a curry lunch to top it off.

"What's wrong?" Sam was looking at me. "You've broken out in goosebumps."

I tore my eyes away from the photograph and forced a small laugh. "Nothing," I muttered. "This place is getting to me, I guess." I turned to Snedley. "I don't see how you can work down here, to tell you the truth."

Snedley smiled. "Hey, man, I like it," he said. "Like Lawrence of Arabia said about the desert, you know? It's clean."

I pointed behind him. "Clean? Then what's that rat doing there?"

Sam and Snedley both spun around. "Where?" said Snedley. "I don't see any goddamn rat."

"In the corner there." I quietly detached the copy of the photograph and slipped it into my pocket. "A rat just ran past there. Or maybe it was a big mouse."

Snedley turned and gave me a beady look. "There's no rats in here, man. No mice, either. You need your eyes examined, I think."

I shrugged. "Could be. Maybe this place is just giving me hallucinations." I could feel the photocopy safe in my jacket pocket. I nodded at Sam. "Okay, I've seen enough. Can we get out of here?"

"I thought you'd never ask." She turned to Snedley. "Lock it up."

"This case is practically closed, the way I hear it," Snedley said in a confidential tone as he slid MacKenzie back into the freezer. "The scuttlebutt is the DA's got a crazy marked down for this one."

Sam looked at him. "Nobody's been marked down for anything. There'll be a trial, remember?"

Snedley shrugged and spread his hands. "Hey, sure, Sarge. What do I know, right? But we got an election coming up, and the DA's gotta look good. Upstairs needs a suspect, and the crazy got nominated. The way I figure it, it's in the bag."

In the bag. His last words hit me like a slap in the face. "Uh-oh," I said.

Sam looked at me. "What now? More rats?"

"No. I just remembered something," I said, starting toward the door. In the bag, I thought. Oh my God, the bag. The duffel bag, containing a hundred pounds of high-grade sinsemilla. The bag with my name on it. Sitting in a dumpster. Oh, Jesus, I thought, I'd forgotten all about it.

I pulled a ten from my pocket and folded it into Sam's hand. "Gotta go," I said. "Dinner was great, seriously. Take a cab home, okay? I'll call you later."

She had her mouth open to say something, but I was already out the door. I pointed my car toward the Bay Bridge and gunned it. Somewhere around Osgood Place, Freddie had said – near the Broadway ramp. I roared into the darkness, hoping I wasn't too late.

CHAPTER ELEVEN

I parked the car in a deserted alley between Montgomery and Kearny, in the shadow of a warehouse. Above me and to my right the concrete wall of the bridge ramp cut into the night sky, looming up like a mountain wall. I could hear the whiz of the traffic on it from where I sat and see the winking red taillights of the stream of cars as they rose and curved off toward the elegant jeweled spiderweb of the Bay Bridge, gleaming in the still night air.

It was a good night for prowling. I opened the glove compartment and took out the gloves and flashlight that I'd used when I robbed Lorenzo's office. The Nixon mask was still there too. On impulse, I stuffed it in my pocket.

The street was silent and deserted, but I felt foolish and exposed. Just find the goddamned dumpster, I told myself. Find it and hope the bag's still inside. Then you can go home.

Whistling through my teeth, I ambled down to the end of the street and turned right, toward the ramp. Pay attention now, I told myself; it's around here somewhere. Freddie would have come down Columbus in his truck, running away from the motel. Right around here he'd turned off Columbus onto Broadway, ditched the duffle bag, and kept going toward Embarcadero and the ramp to the Bay Bridge. Somewhere between here and there was the dumpster. You hope. And if you find the dumpster, you'll find the grass.

You hope.

I was starting to sweat. Nearly down to the end of the first block now. No dumpster in sight. A cat watched me silently from a narrow alley, its yellow eyes blinking slowly in the sodium streetlight.

On the second block now. Still nothing. I cursed quietly to myself. Had Freddie been wrong about its location? Had it been picked up already?

No. There it was, ahead of me, halfway down a side street, partially hidden in the shadows. A large green dumpster, its heavy metal pitted with scaling rust, the words 'BARLOW BROS' stenciled in harsh yellow paint on the side.

I looked up and down the street as I approached it. Three blocks away a car was approaching along Pacific. I turned into Osgood Place, melting into the shadows, and let it pass. I crouched low in a doorway, not looking up until the car had purred by and the street was empty once more.

Now for the prize, I thought, wetting my lips. I moved to the dumpster, grabbed the top lip, and hoisted myself up. A cat squalled and erupted from the opening, nearly tipping me off. Balanced on the edge, I turned and eased myself down into the blackness inside, crunching gingerly down onto a mass of construction debris. Careful, I told myself; cats are only the beginning – there could be anything down here. Taking out my pocket flashlight, I began to check out my surroundings.

It was like exploring an Egyptian tomb. The inside of the dumpster was practically room size and full of just about everything. There were split and ripped two-by-four studs, with wicked-looking rusty nails poking from them. Bricks and fragments of cinder blocks littered the floor. Chunks of Sheetrock were packed together with an impressive collection of roofing shingles. And to top it all off, the local residents had been using the dumpster as a garbage can. Half a dozen plastic bags squished under my feet, some of them ripped open by cats, stinking of fish and rotted meat.

Holding my flashlight in one hand, I began to sift slowly through the rubble, trying to keep clear of the nails and sharp metal edges. The duffel bag, I remembered, had been dark green. Almost the same color as a garbage bag, I thought disgustedly, as I unearthed a bag containing what must have been a week's collection of disposable diapers.

Five minutes later I struck it rich. There it was, buried solidly under some six-by-six ceiling beams – my duffel bag. I breathed a silent prayer of thanks and began to dig it out, pushing aside the heavy timbers one by one. They made a dull booming noise as they fell against the side of the dumpster.

One last beam to go. I raised it up and tossed it with a grunt off to the side. I was bathed in sweat and breathing heavily. The air inside the dumpster was foul, and I was choking in the dust and funk of rotten garbage. "Come to papa," I whispered as I bent to pick up the bag.

A powerful light stabbed down into the darkness. "Freeze, buddy," rasped a voice. "Police."

I froze. If you can't run away, always do what you're told. I stayed hunched over, my face out of sight, back to the night sky. The cop's flashlight played across my back for a moment, flicked to the contents of the dumpster and back to me.

"Okay, out," said the voice above me. "Throw the bag out first. Then you. Hands up, in plain sight where I can see 'em. Let's go, move it." I heard his feet hit the ground outside.

Don't panic, I told myself. Just figure out how to get away. I snatched the Nixon mask from my pocket and put it on. Then I hoisted the bag to the top of the dumpster and balanced it there. I grasped the lip and levered myself up and out the hatch. The cop's flashlight moved to my face and stayed there as I slowly emerged from the dumpster.

"What the fuck," breathed the cop.

He was young and wiry and a little scared, holding his gun with both hands the way they teach you in the academy. His eyes were wide open and moving from side to side, as if he were expecting dark forces to spring at him from the shadows. I'd have felt the same way, meeting Richard Nixon at night in a dark alley.

His black-and-white patrol car was stopped in the middle of the street, engine ticking over, the radio inside growling quietly to itself. And it was empty. He was by himself, praise be to God.

Maybe he'd heard my noise, seen my flashlight. Maybe a neighbor had called. I sighed. It didn't really matter. All that really mattered now was getting out of this in one piece. I raised my hands above my head and spoke slowly and distinctly. "I am not a crook."

The cop glared at me, his gun aimed directly at my chest. "Sure," he said. "Let's discuss it down at the station. How about you start by getting down here. Right now."

"You got it," I said, and hopped off the edge of the dumpster. I caught him with my boots on the upper chest, knocking him down and back, flat on the pavement. He gave a mighty whoosh as the air emptied from his lungs. I reached down and grabbed his arm and twisted hard. He grunted and the gun came loose. I scooped it up and threw it as far into the darkness as I could.

I had about five seconds to decide what to do with him. He was getting his wind back, mad as hell, and his humiliation and anger might push him into doing something stupid that would get both of us in trouble.

I flipped him over and unclipped his handcuffs. I thought momentarily of hooking him up to the side of the dumpster with his cuffs, but rejected it as too dangerous. In this neighborhood the kinds of people that might come by would be quick to take advantage of a helpless cop.

There was a much simpler way, I decided. I could just steal his car. The black-and-white stood not five feet from me, motor running. I clicked the cuffs around his wrists and stood up. I picked up my duffel bag and heaved it into the front seat of the car. Then I hopped in, slammed the door, and locked it.

He struggled to his feet, roaring in fury. I smiled at him through the mask, gave him the V-for-victory sign, and put the car in gear. As I drove away, I glimpsed him in the rearview mirror. He was on his hands and knees, searching the darkness for his revolver.

I abandoned the black-and-white four blocks away, in the alley where I'd left my own car. Then I got the hell out of the neighborhood, dumping the gloves and Nixon mask down a drain at the first intersection I came to. The cop might somehow have managed to call the station by now, I figured, but they'd be looking for the black-and-white, not for me. It was still a good idea to leave the area and so I did, driving down Battery to First Street and the ramp toward the Bay Bridge and home.

As I crossed the bridge, I thought about how to get rid of the grass. There were storage lockers at the bus and train stations, but they were checked every few days, so that was no good. There were rental storage units where you could stash trunks and furniture, but they were too big. Or, I thought, I could just pull over and dump the goddamn stuff into the Bay right now. I shook my head. With my luck, I'd probably be seen and arrested. Or the bag would float. Or drop onto a passing ship.

What the hell, I decided; the stuff could stay in the trunk for now. I'd figure out how to get rid of it tomorrow.

Fifteen minutes later I pulled into my garage and killed the lights. My hands were still shaking, but my breathing had steadied. I wiped sweat from my forehead, thinking about a large glass of bourbon and a soft bed. But first, I thought, I needed to call Sam and apologize for leaving her at the morgue.

Whistling quietly, thinking about how she'd looked in her summer dress, I put my key in the lock and opened the side door to the house. I reached for the light switch, then stopped.

I wasn't alone. There was someone else in the house with me.

"Welcome home, asshole," whispered Lorenzo from somewhere in the darkness.

Then Festus hit me behind the ear.

CHAPTER TWELVE

I sat hunched over in a corner of the airport lounge, nursing a double bourbon and brooding. The bourbon stung the inside of my mouth where the loose teeth were, but I didn't care. I intended to be as numb as a zombie by the time the plane took off, and something as chickenshit as a couple of loose teeth wasn't going to stop me.

Festus had only beaten on me for about ten minutes, I reckoned. It just felt like hours. The man was good, I had to hand it to him. Aside from a few bruises on my face and some scraped knuckles, I looked fine. But my insides felt like the turf on the home stretch at Golden Gate Park.

Don't let anyone tell you they're resistant to pain – it's a crock. Everybody has a threshold, most of us have a low threshold, and any competent sadist can find it in five minutes. From that point on you might as well be strawberry jam.

I had one advantage – I'd been there before. So when round one ended and Lorenzo asked me where the money was, I didn't say something dumb like 'What money?' I told him. Then I threw up all over my hall rug. And when I was finished, I asked him a question of my own.

"How'd you know it was me?"

Lorenzo's face shimmered at me from above, through my tears. He smiled, an evil Santa Claus elf. "You're a dumb fuck, Donovan, you know that? It was the dogshit, of course."

I looked up from my knees, wiping drool off my chin. "What dogshit?"

"The dogshit you tracked all over the goddamn place. Those boots you've got leave a nice distinctive print. Your fuckin' footprints was all over the fuckin' office, man, in the goddamn dogshit." He nodded, his eyes bright. "Give him some more, Festus. Harder this time."

Round two went on a little longer. I could hear Festus grunting with effort, smell his anger. This sonofabitch will kill me if Lorenzo doesn't watch him, I thought. Then I blacked out.

The next thing I knew, Lorenzo had me by the hair. He yanked me into a sitting position and put his face close to mine. I could smell beer and onions on his breath.

"You listening, shitbird?"

I nodded weakly.

"Here it is, then. You owe me ten fucking thousand. I'm gonna let you pay it back in pieces, just like my other customers. But for you, we got a special rate. Four points a week. That's four hundred bucks. Every Monday. You're already behind with your first payment, so you owe eight hundred next Monday. You got all that?"

I nodded again, fighting to keep conscious.

"Eight hundred, Monday. You don't pay, we'll come back. Only this time we won't fart around like tonight. Festus is pissed at you, Donovan. In the interests of his morale I think I might let him take you out alone for a ride on Monday night. He'd like that, I know."

I could hear Festus stir beside me. "Lookin' forward," he said.

Lorenzo stood up. "See you Monday." He put his hand on Festus's arm. "No more right now. You'll get another chance."

I stayed on the floor for another twenty minutes or so pulling myself back together. The worst thing about being beaten isn't always the pain. It's the humiliation, the shock and outrage and guilt at having been mastered, invaded, beaten. It's an aspect of torture that the professionals know well and use to their advantage. Properly done, a simple slap on the face can do as much psychological damage to a man as a two-hour session with the electrodes and hot pokers.

So I took a little time to reconstruct my ego. Admit it, I told myself, Lorenzo's right. You are a dumb shit. You were too busy worrying to do any planning. Too hung up on what to do tomorrow to cover your ass for today. And you were thinking about pretty cops when you should have been noticing that you had nighttime visitors.

I talked with myself along those general lines for a while. Then I spent a little more time getting to my feet and into the bathroom, where I spewed up the rest of what was in my stomach. When I'd finished doing that, I opened the medicine chest and shook out some Demerol from an unmarked bottle that I kept there for just such festive occasions as this.

I took the pills and inspected the various portions of my anatomy for major damage. I peered at myself in the mirror. At least Festus hasn't broken any teeth, I thought. And he hasn't left too many visible marks.

The Demerol was taking effect now, making me feel light-headed and floaty. Look on the bright side, I told myself. They haven't killed me, and they haven't broken my arms or legs. And I haven't told them about the marijuana, which is what started this whole fucking thing.

Why, shit, I thought as I passed out on the bed, it's practically a victory.

* * *

So now I was huddled far back in the lounge, in the shadows, my back to the wall. The large plate-glass windows in front of me gave me a nice view of the big jets wheeling back and forth on the concrete apron below, their green and red navigation lights strobing out into the darkness over San Francisco Bay. Mantovani whispered from the sound system, and cowboys and Indians waged silent warfare on the wide-screen TV over in the corner.

I was headed out again. For Port Moresby, on the far edge of the Southwest Pacific. Partly because I'd decided I didn't care to see Festus again anytime soon, but mainly because it seemed to be the next step. I'd hit a blank wall in San Francisco, and all the signs pointed toward New Guinea. I didn't know what I was looking for over the horizon, but whatever it was, I wouldn't find it here.

MacKenzie'd had half a dozen entry and exit stamps from Papua New Guinea, and the King of Saxony bird of paradise came only from the highland mountain ranges of that country. MacKenzie could have gotten his leech bites in a dozen different places, but Jimmy the Greek and I would both lay odds he'd picked them up somewhere in those very same mountain ranges.

Now I was going to find out where.

And then there was the picture. I pulled out my stolen photocopy, unfolded it, and looked again. No doubt about it, it was the Royal Papua Yacht Club, plain as day.

So wherever the trail led, it began in Port Moresby.

The canned music died suddenly with a crackle and a hiss. The bartender swore softly under his breath and turned, fiddling with the tape player on the shelf behind him. I looked over and saw Bone Brown coming through the door to the lounge, a smile on his face.

"You're late," I said.

"Freeway traffic," he grunted. "Plus it took me a couple of minutes to find the leads to the speakers. I've always wanted to do this place, actually." He glanced up at the oversize TV. "I'm working on a way to deal with those, too, but it's still on the drawing board. I called Freddie an hour ago. He's fine and wishes you luck." He paused. "You okay, Max? You don't look so hot, if you don't mind my saying so."

"I'll survive," I said. "Did you bring my money?"

He nodded, pulling an envelope from his jacket. He tossed it on the table. "Two thousand and change; think it'll be enough?"

I nodded. It was all I had left in my account.

Bone took a pen from his pocket and wrote a name and telephone number on a napkin. "Here," he said as he passed me the napkin. "Sarei Badu's the director of the Port Moresby museum and a good friend of mine. I sent him a cable this afternoon. Give him a call when you arrive; he might have some useful advice for you."

I nodded. "Thanks," I said. "I need all the advice I can get."

I bent down, moving like an old man, and tucked the napkin into the side pocket of my flight bag. When I straightened up again Sam Young was standing beside the table.

I got to my feet, pain washing over me in waves. "Sam, I'm sorry about last night," I began. "I wanted to call later and—"

"Don't apologize," she said. "I rang your house, and when I couldn't reach you, I began to worry. I telephoned Professor Brown and he told me what happened. Are you all right?"

"More or less," I said. "Nice of you to come." I pulled out a chair for her. "What's happening down at the Hall of justice?"

"The usual madness." She sat down, brushing her hair back with long slim fingers. "Would you believe, one of our patrolmen swears he saw Richard Nixon climbing out of a garbage dumpster last night."

"Maybe he's starting a comeback," I suggested.

She grinned. "Anything's possible in this town, I guess. Is the flight on time?"

I looked at my watch. "Boarding in about twenty minutes. You don't have to stay, though."

She and Bone exchanged glances. "Ah, Miss Young didn't come out here to kiss you goodbye, Max," he said. "She's going to Port Moresby with you."

* * *

I was finishing my first drink and listening on my Walkman to Gracie Slick singing about sexy witches and sons of bitches, when Sam sat down beside me.

She was carrying something I recognized. Fresh double bourbons, one in each hand. I looked from her to the drinks and back again. She held one out to me. "Want company?"

I thought for perhaps five eighths of a second, nodded, and took off the earphones.

"I thought it might be time to share what I found out today," she said, sitting down beside me. "And to tell you why I came along."

Outside, the Pacific night slipped by, thousands of empty miles of ocean waiting in the darkness.

"There's been a couple of interesting developments today that you should know about," she said, reaching into her handbag for a sheaf of papers. "These are copies of some telexes that came from Australia this morning, and guess what? MacKenzie's diplomatic passport is a forgery. And he's got a criminal record. A long one."

I sipped bourbon as I glanced at the sheets. "So Ackroyd sent you to check it out?"

"Nope." Her mouth went tight. "Ackroyd suspended me this morning – took me off the case indefinitely. That asshole Snedley told him I'd let you into the morgue last night. Then somebody went through the file and found a photograph missing." Her eyes met mine. "The one I figure you stole."

"I guess I messed up your vacation, huh?"

"Forget it. I'd been booked to Greece, but what the hell. The plane fare was almost the same. Besides, I figured it was important to keep on this thing. Something's wrong downtown."

"Wrong? How?"

She shook her head. "I'm not sure, but something just doesn't feel right. Ackroyd is really on edge. He gave me about a half hour of fury this morning before he suspended me. Then Luther came while I was clearing out my locker and handed me these." She tapped the photocopies. "'Just don't let Ackroyd know,' he said. Then I tried to call you."

"Crake gave these to you? Where does he figure in all this? Is he on the level?"

"Luther? He's the best cop I know. Absolutely honest." She paused. "He showed me the telexes because Ackroyd had told him to get rid of them, and Luther just doesn't work that way. According to Luther, Ackroyd told him that it didn't matter whether MacKenzie had forged papers and a previous record; it wasn't worth following up on. He said the case against Fields would go ahead as planned. MacKenzie could be God or the Devil, Ackroyd said – he was dead now, and Fields had killed him."

Her eyes met mine. "So I think something stinks. I don't know what it is, but I can smell it.… And there's something else, Max. I believe you now. I don't think Freddie Fields murdered that man." She smiled thinly. "So we'd better plan on getting along with each other from now on, don't you think?"

A Qantas steward came down the aisle and I stopped him. "Two more double bourbons," I said.

"Right you are, mate," he said, and sailed off.

Sam eyed my near-empty glass. "How many's that?"

"Who's counting?" I said. "Besides, where is it written that I can't get plastered? I've had the shit beat out of me, remember?"

The steward came back and set out fresh drinks on the folding tray. I reached for mine, but Sam moved it away.

"Listen to me for a second," she said. "There's more. I don't want you passing out before I tell you this." She held up the photocopies. "MacKenzie's been arrested a dozen times, convicted twice. Once for mail fraud, once for running a confidence racket. Before that he ran a whorehouse in the Cook Islands. There's also a letter in there from the chief of police of Suva, in Fiji, declaring him persona non grata."

She picked up one of the papers. "But this is the topper. Two years ago MacKenzie was arrested in Darwin in connection with an Aborigine cattle drover who'd been beaten to death with an ax handle. Witnesses said MacKenzie'd done it. Someone had been selling illegal moonshine to the drunks in an Aboriginal reserve outside of town, and after three people had died of side effects, the cattleman decided to confront MacKenzie. Three of them went to MacKenzie's camp that night. One was found dead in a drainage ditch the next morning, his face beaten to a pulp."

"Ugly. What happened to MacKenzie?"

"Nothing. His lawyer apparently managed to cast doubt on the character of the two other Aboriginals, who were pretty heavy into the sauce themselves at the time. MacKenzie was acquitted." She touched the papers. "It's all in here if you want to read it."

I sat back and closed my eyes, letting MacKenzie's image form in my mind. I could picture Mr. MacKenzie very well indeed, for I'd seen many like him. Twentieth-century pirates, hiding out in the backwaters of the Third World. They were the big ones sitting in the back of the bar, up against the wall. The ones with the sharp bright light in their eyes and the edge in their voices, who drank good whisky when they could afford it and anything at all when they couldn't.

They were roguish and charming and smart. Like Scheherazade, they could tell you a different fable every night for a year or more if you cared to listen. They made marvelous friends and terrifying enemies, men who would lend you their last dime one night and break your kneecaps the next in a filthy alley in Hong Kong because you'd cheated at cards.

They were sharks in turbid water — thorough, fast, and brutal — and you gave them a wide berth when they were feeding. Oh yes, Mr. MacKenzie, I thought, I know you. I do indeed, even if we've not been properly introduced.

I opened my eyes. "Do you have anything else on him?"

She shuffled the papers. "Not much. He grew up in the Northern Territory, in a place called Rum Jungle. Can you imagine a place called Rum Jungle? He finished high school and then went in the army. He spent two years in the Royal Pacific Islands Regiment up in New Guinea, when it was an Australian colony, in Port Moresby."

"Where he got the tropical ulcers," I murmured.

"He had a disciplinary record in the army – drunken fights, accusations of theft. He got a dishonorable discharge when he was twenty-one."

I nodded. "And now he's dead on account of birds. Birds he smuggled into the US in his suitcase, with a forged UN passport to get him through customs."

"And he got the birds in New Guinea," she said. "Max, what are we going to do when we get there? I mean, I had to look Port Moresby up on the map."

I took a bite of my drink. "I don't know what you're going to do, Sam, but I'll do what I usually do."

"Which is?"

"Take a stick and stir up the bushes a little. See what jumps out."

CHAPTER THIRTEEN

I figured that Captain Barry Sears of the Royal Papua New Guinea Constabulary was probably one of the last white officers on the police force. He ran his hand through his thick white hair, smoothed the front of his powder-blue uniform shirt, and lit a Cambridge with an ancient Zippo lighter. Behind him the air conditioner wheezed in protest. It didn't seem to be making a dent in the humidity, which must have been somewhere in the mid-nineties.

Sam and I had arrived in Port Moresby that morning on the early Qantas flight from Brisbane. We'd flown into Jacksons Airport, caught a taxi to the Islander Hotel on Waigani Drive, and taken two rooms. When Sam had complained about how much the rooms cost, I teased her, pointing out that if we shared a room we could save money. She'd just looked at me, made a face, and closed her door on my nose.

After a rest I rented a Holden sedan and we drove to police headquarters in the suburb of Boroko. On the way I decided that Port Moresby hadn't really changed very much. No amount of bougainvillea could disguise the fact that the place was still basically a frontier settlement. Prefabricated houses on stilts were everywhere, poking up out of the raw red earth and the *kunai* grass, most of them with chain-link fences and 'No Gat Wok' signs warning off the rascals and the unemployed. Painted on the window of a Chinese trade store in Tabari Place was the notice 'No Checks Accepted for Purchase of Suitcases.'

It was that kind of town, and it had always been that kind of town. The kind of place a man like Brian MacKenzie would like.

Port Moresby was still a small town. Like all small towns, its people knew each other too well and noticed strangers. If MacKenzie had spent time here, someone would remember him. 'Stir up the bushes and see what jumps out' was what I'd said to Sam on the plane. Three double bourbons had given it just the right macho sound, but now I wasn't so sure. In a place like this it would be easy to stir up trouble. And hard to find a place to hide once it got started.

So I sat and watched Captain Sears puff on his cigarette and wondered if it had been a mistake to come to the cops. It had been Sam's idea, of course. I'd agreed, but only on condition that she keep her own identity quiet. In my experience cops were usually part of the problem, rarely part of the solution.

Sears blew smoke out and squinted at me through the haze. "Let's run through it one more time, Mr. Donovan, if you please," he said. "There's a Mr. Fields in San Francisco who's been charged with the murder of an Australian citizen, and you've come out here looking for some information. Right so far?"

I nodded, smiling. "Fields is a friend of mine. Like I told you."

He nodded. "Like you told me." His eyes flicked to Sam. "And Miss Young here is your girlfriend, right?"

Beside me I could sense Sam tensing. "She's a friend of mine, yes."

Sears sat back in his swivel chair and folded his big hands across his stomach. He gave me a broad smile. "All right. The question then is, what can I do for you?"

I gave him the background as briefly as I could. As I talked, I tried to size him up. Sears was a grizzled old warhorse in his early sixties, and in spite of his paunch, his body was tough and hard and had seen some use. His hands were the size of large pork chops, the skin on his massive arms burned to the color and texture of saddle leather. His face seemed to be composed of broad wedges. One formed his nose, another his chin, and a third made up his wide, high forehead.

He had a full head of white hair and a droopy mustache that gave him the air of a benevolent uncle, but his cop's eyes were flat and deadly serious. As I spoke they flicked quickly between Sam and myself. Behind them you could almost hear the whirring of finely tuned machinery.

"So we thought," I concluded, "that since you're head of the Customs and Immigration Police, you might have information on the dead man. MacKenzie's passed through here several times in the last six months."

Sears stubbed his cigarette out. "Dead, you say? In San Francisco? I haven't heard a bloody thing about this. My God, man, do you realize how many Australians come in and out of this town in a month?"

I reached into my pocket and pulled out the picture I'd stolen from the San Francisco morgue. "Take a look at this," I said, pushing it across the desk. "MacKenzie's the big one, on the right."

Sears left the photo on the desk, stared at it a moment, and then nodded. "Where did you get this, mate?"

Sam and I looked at each other.

"From a friend in the district attorney's office," I said. "They found it in MacKenzie's wallet. They're trying to identify the other people in the picture."

Sears looked up from the picture. "What's your plan here, exactly?"

I shrugged. "Not sure yet. I thought I'd ask around a little in town, see if anyone recognizes the other two men."

He nodded. "Well, I can save you a little time on one of them." He pointed to the man on the left, the slim Errol Flynn look-alike. "That bloke there's Binky Dunham. Used to be a helicopter pilot out of Mount Hagen."

"What's he doing these days?"

"These days he's dead, Mr. Donovan. He pranged his helicopter three weeks ago, up on the side of the Schrader Range. No wife, no kids. Not even a girlfriend as far as I know. I took a drink with him from time to time over at the Germania Club, but I hardly knew the bugger, really." He peered again at the picture. "As far as the other one's concerned, I've never laid eyes on him before. That's the balcony of the Yacht Club, isn't it?"

I nodded, taking the picture as he pushed it back across the table at me. Well, it's a start, I told myself. And we've gone through the motions of paying our respects to the law. Now it was time to get out on the street. Having the dead pilot's name would help, but we had a long way to go. I put the picture back into my shirt pocket and took out the scrap of paper that Bone had given me in the airport.

"Can I use your telephone, Captain?" I said.

Sears indicated the receiver on a small table across the room. "Go for your life, mate," he said.

I dialed and listened to the ringing as I glanced idly at the photographs hanging on the wall. There was a diploma from a police academy in Australia, a framed snapshot of Sears on a fishing boat holding a large marlin, and a group photograph of men in uniform labeled 'Pacific Islands Regiment, Taurama Barracks, 1954.'

"It's a beautiful view from here," Sam was saying, pointing out the window. "The mountains and all."

Sears snorted. "Not if you've been looking at it for twenty-eight bloody years, miss. I came up here in the army, over thirty years ago, and joined the police when I demobilized. I'm one of the last white men on the force now. I retire in six months, and it can't come too soon to suit me."

My telephone connection burped, gave a small squeak, and then cut off.

"Try it again," Sears advised. "Bloody phone system's buggered as well, these days." He sighed. "No, it's definitely time to leave. This was a good place in the old days – easy for a man to get things done." He lowered his voice. "Since independence nothing's the bloody same. Take a look out there, for example."

I paused in my dialing to glance out the window to the yard of the police barracks where he pointed. The compound was filled with cars, some of them wrecked, others burned. Only a few looked as if they were still drivable.

"Stolen cars," said Sears. "We get dozens of the damned things every week. Crime's out of control these days. Bloody kanakas are stealing three or four a night. They drive 'em around for a while, then smash 'em up or set fire to 'em. There's only half a dozen or so vehicles down there that run, I reckon."

The ringing at the other end of the line stopped and a voice said, "*Husat istap?*"

"*Apinun*," I said, summoning my rusty Pidgin. "*Yu save toktok long Inglis?*"

"Of course I can speak English," the voice said. "Who is this?"

"My name is Max Donovan. A friend of Professor Isaac Brown at Berkeley. I'm looking for" – I glanced at the paper Bone had given me – "I'm looking for Sarei Badu."

"Ah, Mr. Donovan. I've been expecting you to call. I'm Sarei Badu. Bone cabled me yesterday, said you'd be getting in touch."

Good old Bone, I thought. "That's right." I glanced over at Sears. "I'd like to talk to you sometime soon if you can spare the time. As soon as possible, in fact."

"How about this evening? I'm having a get-together for some of the university crowd. We could talk then."

"If you're sure it wouldn't be an imposition," I said. "I'm, ah, with someone."

"Miss Young, is it? Bone mentioned her. By all means, bring her. Let me show you both a little island hospitality. Informal dress, just a little food and some cold beer. Will that be all right?"

"Fine," I said. "What time and where?"

"I live out behind Hanuabada village, on the road to Gerehu. Number one twenty-four Raku Terrace. Anytime after six o'clock."

"One twenty-four Raku Terrace," I repeated. "Anytime after six. See you then." I hung up and turned to Sam. "We're invited to a party this evening."

Sears cleared his throat. "No need to be telling this to an old hand like you, Mr. Donovan, but I'd watch my step if I were you. Parties where the locals get to drinking sometimes turn a little wild."

"I can handle myself, Captain," I said evenly.

Sears spread his large hands. "No offense, mate. Just some friendly advice." He smiled then, but his eyes stayed flat and watchful.

As we were going out the door, he put a hand on my shoulder. "I meant what I said about being careful around the locals, Mr. Donovan." His voice was soft. "Things have changed since you were last here. Don't take matters into your own hands. I'll check Mr. MacKenzie through our files if you like, let you know if anything turns up."

The pressure on my shoulder increased, almost painful now. "But if you find anything out, Mr. Donovan, bring it straight to me. Don't play policeman on my turf."

He gave my shoulder a final hard squeeze. "You got that, mate?"

"Got it." I left without looking back.

CHAPTER FOURTEEN

It was nearly six thirty and the light was beginning to fade when we piled into our huge, rented Holden and set off along the Hubert Murray Highway for Sarei Badu's house. Local driving hadn't improved any since I'd been away. There was really only one rule of the road in Port Moresby, and it could be summarized in three short words: get in front. Once you understood that, everything happening on the highway made sense.

I drove slowly down Three Mile Hill through Badili and Koki and along Ela Beach, listening to a Slim Dusty record on the radio, glad to be back in the Southwest Pacific after all this time. The sun was low over the harbor, giving the water a coppery sheen. Bougainvillea, flamboyants, and hibiscus flowers turned the roadside into a surreal rainbow of color, and the big rain trees towered gracefully above us as we approached the center of town.

"It's beautiful," said Sam. "I see now what they mean about the South Seas being a paradise."

I grunted noncommittally. It's beautiful, I thought, but only as long as you look only at the surface. Paradise perhaps, but dangerous for the unwary. Things with fangs and stingers lived in among the flowers and vines, and beneath the calm waters of the harbor swam huge hammerheads, hungry for their next meal.

I turned up Musgrave Street, passed the Papuan Hotel, and swung right onto Champion Parade. There was the usual crowd of early evening drinkers on the veranda of the Moresby Hotel. Farther down some kids in ragged shorts were practicing kung fu kicks in front of a Chinese store, raising little puffs of dust.

We drove past Hanuabada village, a cluster of tin-roofed houses on stilts, their walkways extending out into the harbor like long bony fingers. In between the tightly packed houses small pigs and dogs trotted along the narrow boardwalks. Below them double-hulled fishing canoes and kitchen garbage bobbed gently up and down in the dirty water.

Raku Terrace was choked with cars and motorcycles. Sam and I parked the Holden on the main road and walked through the gathering darkness, following the sounds of music.

"I didn't think anyone played Neil Diamond anymore," said Sam. "Especially not that really old stuff."

"You're in a time warp," I said. "Just imagine it's the sixties."

"As long as it's a good party," she said. "I love parties."

Number one twenty-four was like all the others, a prefabricated asbestos-cement box on stilts, the kind public servants here call an A-23. Close up, the music was heavy, almost deafening. Kegs of beer had been set up on the wide veranda, and a large group crowded around them, paper cups in hand. Here and there I could see a few European faces, but it was mainly a local crowd.

We climbed up the stairs to the veranda, threading our way carefully through the packed crowd. Through the open French doors beyond I could see a knot of people dancing inside the house, while a horde of others pressed up against a buffet table at the side. The smell of beer, sweat, and cigarette smoke was everywhere.

"Excuse me," I said to a dark-skinned man blocking our path.

He didn't move.

"Excuse me," I said again.

He turned slowly to look at me with frog-like eyes. "What the fuck are you doing here?" he said. He didn't move.

I looked him over as I considered my reply. Whoever he was, he wasn't a local. His accent was wrong, for one thing, and he looked more like a South Asian than a Melanesian. He was broad and heavy, with skin the color of a chocolate milkshake and a bristly spade beard. He wore a printed lap-lap and rubber sandals, and except for a gold medallion, his chest was bare. I leaned forward to look at the medallion. It was a bust of Lenin.

I decided to take the low road. "We're guests," I said in a quiet voice. "Guests of Sarei Badu. Do you know where he is?"

He ignored my question. "We don't want any more white exploiters here," he said. "Got enough already." His breath stank of beer. "Now why don't you go the fuck back to Australia or wherever it is you came from?"

He had collected an audience now, students from the look of them. They stood grinning and clutching cups of beer, waiting to see what would come next.

The man's gaze shifted to Sam. He smiled, showing little peg-like teeth. "You can stay if you want. Can always use more women at a party, even if they're Kong-Kong women. You feel like dancing, darlin'?"

I laid a hand on his beefy arm, only to have it slapped away. "Don't touch me, white boy," he growled.

He moved toward Sam. "What's the matter with you, babe, you too stuck up for the working class?"

Sam stared evenly at him, saying nothing. Behind us the onlookers snickered.

I sighed and planted my feet, figuring the angle. His gut was enormous but it looked soft. If I hit him hard enough, I could probably drop him on the spot. I dipped my shoulder and drew back.

"Das, what the hell are you doing?"

Everybody turned. An enormous Papuan, well over six feet tall, was pushing his way through the crowd. He sported a Kaiser Wilhelm mustache, and his eyes were dark and dangerous as he glared at the man in front of me. "I'm talking to you, Das. What's going on?"

"Nothin' going on, Mr. Badu, sir." Das's eyes had narrowed to slits. "Just gettin' to know these nice folks. Man says he got a special invitation from you." His voice had slipped into a sarcastic vaudeville parody. I stepped back a pace.

The big Papuan turned. He wore a necklace of dog's teeth around his neck, and his hair was teased out to a huge fluffy bush into which were stuck six or seven cigarettes. "Then you must be–"

"Max Donovan," I said. "And this is Sam Young."

"Delighted. Had a drink yet? Come on inside." Without waiting for a reply, he turned. We followed as he pushed a path through the crowd and into the kitchen. He scooped two bottles of South Pacific Lager from a large ice chest and opened them. "Greenies okay?"

I nodded.

He handed over the beers. Then he smiled and held out a huge hand. "Nice to meet you, Max. You too, Miss Young. Do they really call you Sam?"

"They really do," she said.

Outside the kitchen someone started singing loudly, and from somewhere under the house came the sound of a heavy object falling over.

Sarei Badu grinned, exposing betel-stained teeth. "It'll get worse before it gets better," he said. "I do a bash twice a year for the crowd from the museum and the university. Everybody gets pissed and has a lot to eat." His eyes twinkled and the tips of his mustache quivered. "They might also settle a few old scores, but what the hell. That's the Melanesian way, right?"

I grinned. I liked this man. "Doesn't sound like much has changed."

"You were here, what, four or five years ago? No, not too much has changed. Things are a little more political now, maybe. The rich have gotten richer and the poor – well, the poor have got spokesmen now." His eyes went serious. "Like Das – the guy you ran into outside. Sorry about that, by the way."

"No harm done," I said. "Who is he? He doesn't look like he's from around here."

Sarei Badu shook his head. "He's a Guyanese Asian, name's Mohinder Das. He lectures in political science at the university, the house radical. Very big on Black Power at the moment. He showed up here three years ago. Almost got himself deported last year. He's a stirrer, Max. His politics are strictly self-interest, but he makes a big show of being anti-white and anti-Western. Naturally, the students love it." He put his hand on my shoulder. "Forget about Das, my friend. He's a piece of rubbish."

Somebody had put the Rolling Stones' *Brown Sugar* on the stereo and cranked up the volume. Sam looked at me, eyes bright. "Feel like dancing?"

"I thought you'd never ask," I said. "But I want to talk to Sarei for a few minutes. You go ahead."

She stuck her tongue out at me and moved off.

Sarei plucked two more beers from the cooler. "Let's talk in the study," he said. "I can't hear myself think in here." He started off down the hallway.

The study was cooler and quieter. We sat at a wide desk and drank the beers while I explained why we'd come to Port Moresby and what we were looking for. When I'd finished, he shook his head.

"Birds of paradise? That's a new one. Doesn't really surprise me, though. Smuggling's a big business these days, Max. They use helicopters, seaplanes, fast boats, and they can get damned near everywhere on the island now. Take what they want and get out – we never know a thing.

There's just too much coastline to patrol – too many small valleys to hide in. We've confiscated crates of stolen artifacts over the years, but it's only a fraction of what's going out now." He shook his head. "Now birds? Christ."

My beer was empty. I stood up. "Another?"

He nodded, and I went back down the hall to the kitchen. The din from the party was deafening. I poked my head into the living room and saw Sam dancing by with a tall knobbly Australian with long hair and a bad sunburn. He was saying to her, "Of course the Coconut's the only real nightclub we've got in this town."

"How fascinating," Sam said brightly. "You mean the others aren't real?" She caught sight of me and smiled. "Hi, sweetie. Eat your heart out."

She danced away before I could think of something snappy to say.

I went back into the study and handed Sarei Badu his beer. Then I pulled out the picture and laid it on the desk between us. "Recognize any of these guys?" I said.

He nodded. "Sure. That's the helicopter pilot who died last month. I saw it in the paper. He crashed up in the Highlands, somewhere north of Mount Hagen." He looked up. "You think he was involved in this?"

I shrugged. "Could be." I pointed to the other man, the one who looked like a Bowery bum. "What about him?"

He leaned forward. "He's familiar all right," he said after a moment. "I don't know who he is, but I've seen him around somewhere." He scratched his head. "Damn. It'll come to me, sooner or later." He handed the picture back. "So what are you planning to do next?"

I walked over to the map on the wall. "I need to start tracing this thing back," I said at last. "Follow the string, see where it might lead." I turned to him. "Can you still charter a plane up into the mountains?"

Sarei whistled softly. "Sure, you can get a charter out of Hagen, Goroka, or any of the Highlands towns. All it takes is money. But it's rough country, Max. Where exactly are you thinking of going?"

I looked at the map, tracing the outlines of the Schrader Range, following the contours as they dipped and plunged in drunken arabesques. "I'm not sure yet," I said. "Where the pilot went down, maybe. It's a place to start, anyway." I held up the picture. "I'll be gone a few days. In the meantime see if you can remember who the old guy is. If we can identify him, we've got all three."

Sarei shook his head. "No, Max. There's a fourth."

"A fourth?"

"The bloke who took the picture." Sarei's eyes were serious. "Don't forget about him."

There was a loud crash from outside in the main room, and the music stopped abruptly.

"Uh-oh," said Sarei. "Silence is always a bad sign. We'd better see what's going on." He crossed to the door and opened it.

Everyone in the main room was standing very still, frozen in place as if for musical chairs. The tall Australian that Sam had been dancing with a moment ago was flat on his back underneath the stereo, shaking his head groggily. Blood welled from a gash on his forehead.

Sam stood facing Mohinder Das, the man who'd stopped us on the veranda. Das clutched a beer bottle, which he'd obviously just used as a club.

Sam spoke with deadly intensity in the silent room. "I've already told you I don't want to dance with you. Put the bottle down, dammit, now."

She was using a cop's command voice, but Das was too drunk to notice. He swayed and emitted a long belch. "Slant-eyed bitch," he growled. He grabbed Sam roughly by the arm. "Let's go outside and talk, baby."

As I started forward Sarei Badu whispered, "Careful — he's tougher than he looks."

"So's she," I said.

I strode to the center of the room, feeling like I'd just walked onstage at the elementary school play. The crowd edged back against the wall, waiting for the next moves to be made. Das didn't even see me. I came up behind him and tapped him on the shoulder. "A moment of your time, squire," I murmured.

He spun around, his lips drawn back in a snarl. Just as his beefy hand came up to swat at me, Sam reached over and yanked his beard. Hard. His head jerked sideways as he yelped in pain and surprise.

"Get out of my way, Donovan," Sam said.

I stepped back as she spun Das around like a square dancer, locking his wrists behind him, high up on the small of his back. She pushed forward and Das grunted with pain, bouncing up on his tiptoes.

She turned to me. "If you want to make yourself useful," she said, "you might open the door to the veranda."

"My pleasure." I took four quick steps and opened the wide double screen doors.

Sam pulled Das's wrists higher. "Up," she said. "Up high on tippy-toes. Higher." He grunted with pain as he stretched. "Good. Exactly right." She shoved him forward. "Now move, asshole!"

Das headed across the floor, tripping as lightly as a ballerina, Sam holding his wrists firmly behind him. She ran him straight out through the veranda doors, picking up speed fast, and over the low balcony rail. There was a loud crash and a shriek as he hit the bougainvillea ten feet below.

"*Em nau*," said somebody in the watching crowd. Then everyone burst into applause.

Sarei Badu came and looked over the rail. "Nice work," he said soberly. "Some people around here have been wanting to do that for a long time." He glanced back at the crowd, which was already beginning to reassemble around the beer kegs. "You two could probably use a quiet drink

97

at this point, but I wouldn't recommend having it here. Things are probably going to go downhill from now on."

I nodded. "We'll head back to the hotel. I'll call you when I get back from the Highlands."

"Highlands?" said Sam. "You didn't mention this."

"Tell you later," I said.

We said goodbye to Sarei and went down the veranda steps. At the bottom a dozen students dressed in lap-laps and University of Papua New Guinea T-shirts sat on the grass drinking warm beer straight from the carton. A bleary-eyed Papuan with a hibiscus flower in his hair looked up at me and belched loudly, nodding in satisfaction. Beside him someone else was on his hands and knees, throwing up into the flower beds. The odor of beer and sweat was heavy, and underneath it the sharp tang of fresh betel nut.

"This has been an honest-to-God horror show," murmured Sam.

"A horror show to you, maybe," I said. "But as far as most people here are concerned, it's a typical fun-filled Port Moresby Saturday night. I think that's what Bone calls 'cultural relativism.'"

* * *

We took the back way to the hotel, through the hills. A few miles ahead lay the suburb of Gerehu and the university campus, and beyond it the hotel. We were about halfway there, on a deserted and isolated stretch of road, and I was trying once more to convince Sam to give up her room at the Islander and move in with me.

She didn't even seem to be paying attention to me as she sat staring out the side window of the Holden. Finally she turned around. "Listen," she said. "Are you through with all that for the moment?"

"For the moment, yes," I said. "Why?"

"Because somebody's following us, that's why."

I looked in the mirror and saw headlights a hundred yards behind us, holding steady. "You sure?"

"They got behind us a minute or so after we left the party," she said. "And they've stayed there ever since. I've been watching them in the side mirror. You're not going fast, and there have been plenty of straight stretches where someone could pass. We're being followed."

I jammed the accelerator down and the Holden jumped forward. Behind us the headlights kept pace. "What the hell do you suppose they want?"

We found out sooner than I expected. One moment the car was behind us, and the next it shot alongside, motor screaming. Sam gasped as I swung the wheel and tried to drop back. As the headlights of the other car swung across in front of us, I realized that they were going to run us straight off the road. I glanced sideways, seeing the flimsy guardrails and the ledge beyond.

A grinding shock jolted me forward, and I heard our tires scream as we were pushed sideways across the road. I fought the wheel and almost had us straightened out again when we were hit a second time. I heard a tire blow. The rear end of the Holden broke loose now, and we started to fishtail. "Hang on!" I yelled as I fought to bring the car under control.

I never had a chance. The other car crashed into us again, and the wheel jerked in my hands as another tire shredded and we began to skid wildly across the road. Sam screamed as we hit the guardrails. The tarmac disappeared underneath us, and then we were over the edge and falling, bouncing hard, noise and panic everywhere.

We must have rolled over half a dozen times before we came to a sliding, grinding halt at the bottom of the ravine. My mouth was open and full of crushed glass. By some miracle our headlights were still on. The stench of raw gasoline stung my nose, and I could make out wisps of smoke leaking out from under the hood.

Our seat belts had saved us. I clawed at mine, finally locating the release. Sam already had hers off. The doors were buckled, and so I went to work on the shattered windshield with my boots, kicking out the rest of the broken glass and clearing a hole for us to escape through.

Flames were already starting to lick up through the hood from somewhere underneath the engine. "Get going," gasped Sam as she pulled me through. "The tank'll blow any second."

We made it with less than a minute to spare. We were scrambling up the side of the ravine when the car lit up like a Halloween pumpkin and gently blew apart. In seconds, flames enveloped the front seat, where we had been.

We crawled cautiously up out of the ravine onto the main road and crouched in the bushes, watching and listening for any sign of the car that had pushed us over. The road was deserted, the night quiet save for the crackling of flames below us and the rok-rok-rok of a bevy of swamp frogs in the bush beyond.

Sam looked at the burning car, her face streaked and sweaty in the flickering light. "Great. Just great. What the hell do we do now?"

I looked up and down the empty road. "We walk," I said. "It's about three miles to the hotel. We can be there in an hour if we push it."

She looked down at her high-heeled party shoes. "Well, shit," she said, and kicked them off into the bush. "What are we waiting for?"

We'd been walking for about five minutes when she spoke. "I've been thinking," she said.

"About what?"

"About our sleeping arrangements. Is it too late to cancel that other room? I'd feel better if we were together from now on. All of a sudden I don't like the looks of this."

I took her arm. "That makes two of us," I said.
"There's just one thing, though."
"What's that?"
"Do you snore?"

CHAPTER FIFTEEN

"Binky Dunham?" The Australian pilot behind the Talair
desk put down his sheaf of cargo manifests and looked up
at me. "He a friend of yours, sport?"

I had perhaps three seconds to get it right. I searched
his eyes for clues, and finding none, I pulled out my
money, peeled off fifty kina and laid the notes on the
counter between us. He watched me carefully. "No, not a
friend," I said. "I never knew him. But Dunham knew
somebody I know."

"And?" His eyes were steady, a clear gray.

"And that somebody burned a good friend of mine.
I'm trying to find out what happened – and why."

The pilot looked at the money, then at Sam and me.
"You a copper?" he said finally.

"Do I look like one, for God's sake?" I rubbed my
hand across my face. I'd spent the night on the floor of my
room at the Islander, with air-conditioning that was too
cold and a pillow that felt like a bag full of dead mice.
We'd awakened before dawn and taxied out to Jacksons
Airport to catch the early morning flight to Mount Hagen.
It had been a two-hour climb in an aging Fokker
Friendship, up over the Owen Stanley Range, and Air
Niugini apparently didn't believe in breakfast for its
passengers.

Stepping off the plane at Hagen airport, I felt that I was
finally back in the country I'd remembered. The sun was

bright and the light was crystal sharp, the air smelling faintly of woodsmoke. A group of Jiga clansmen dressed in arse-grass were squatting on the tarmac, waiting to unload the baggage. One of them puffed a foot-long cigarette made of newspaper and twist tobacco, and when I waved at him he grinned back and spat out a bright red wad of betel.

We'd carried our rucksacks straight across the tarmac to the nearest air charter office. I was tired, I was sore, and I needed a cup of coffee. If this jerk won't tell me about Binky Dunham, I thought, I'll pick up my money and find somebody else who will.

It must have showed in my face. The pilot reached across and covered the money with a large grimy hand. Then he smiled, showing crooked teeth. "Just asking, sport," he said. "This friend of yours – how'd he get burnt, if you don't mind my asking?"

"He's in jail. On a murder charge."

"Because of something Binky Dunham did?"

"Maybe. That's what I came here to find out."

The pilot thought about that for a long minute. "All right," he said finally. "This is all I know, fair dinkum. Binky Dunham came out here about three years ago from somewheres up north – Sulawesi, I think it was. He got a job with Talair, running a chopper up into the mining camp in the Star Mountains. Parked it right out there," he said, pointing out the dirty office window to an empty stretch of tarmac. "He ran mail and supplies up, and brought reports and empty beer bottles back. He'd leave here around midmorning if the weather was clear, have lunch at the camp, and come back in the early afternoon. A right lurk of a job, if you ask me. He did Mondays to Friday, and then he went to Moresby for the weekends."

"What'd he do in Port Moresby?"

The pilot snorted softly, stealing a glance at Sam. "What does anybody bloody well do in Moresby, mate? He went there to get snockered and dip the old wickeroo. You ever get a look at some of the local women they've got around here? There's some Moresby bints aren't too bad, if they take a bath and put some of them nice hibiscus flowers in their hair, but the Marys up around these parts are bush through and through. Smell of pig grease and woodsmoke, got bodies like a baked potato."

"Who'd he stay with in Moresby? A girlfriend?"

The pilot shook his head. "Naw, not that I know of. He took a room, usually at the Papuan Hotel. Had a sort of a mate there, in fact. Our Binky liked his drop, see. Used to spend his time with some old dried-up bastard, drinking in the bars. The fucking local bars, for Christ's sake." He nodded at Sam. "Pardon me, miss."

I took out the picture and laid it on the desk between us. I pointed to the third man, the one who looked like a derelict. "This the one?"

He leaned forward to look. "Yeah, that's him. Blue. That's what they called him, on account of his hair. Never knew his real name, though." He shook his head. "Only white man I ever knew who drank regularly in the local bar, a real ratbag."

"The place where Dunham crashed the chopper," I said, "was it far from here?"

"As the crow flies, no. Could have been on the bleedin' moon, though, for all the good it did Binky." He brought out an old map from under the counter and spread it out. "Here's Hagen, see, and here's the way Binky flew up to the camp in the Star Mountains." He traced the route northwest with a dirty finger. Then he stabbed a point to the east. "But there's where he pranged it."

I leaned forward. The crash site was about thirty miles north-northeast of Mount Hagen, up against the side of the Schrader Range. That section of the map was largely blank, the words 'Relief Data Incomplete' overprinted on it.

"Looks like he was way off course," I said. "Was he lost?"

"Binky? Lost? He wasn't lost, mate. He was one of the best pilots they had. The day was as clear and nice up here as you'd ever hope to see. No, whatever happened to him, he wasn't lost."

"Then what was he doing fifty miles off his flight path?" I said.

He looked at me carefully. He knew what I was asking. Pilots are a clannish breed, and he hadn't yet decided whether I could be trusted. I laid another fifty kina on the counter and watched his eyes change. He'd just decided that it didn't matter whether he could trust me or not.

"Just a guess, mind you, sport, all right?"

I nodded.

"At a guess, I'd say money. I'd say our friend Binky was using a little company time to do business in. It wouldn't have been hard. He usually flew alone – just him and the clobber he was carting up to the mine. He could go just a little bit out of his way to do a few errands, like, and no one would be the wiser."

"What kinds of errands?" I had some ideas of my own, but I wanted to see what the pilot knew. Or felt like telling me.

The pilot shrugged. "Anybody's guess, sport," he said. "Like picking something up or dropping something off, maybe. Whatever it was, I'll bet it was worth a lot of money. If they ever found out that old Binky was playing silly buggers with the company's chopper, he'd get the sack."

I nodded. "How'd they find him after he went down?"

"His automatic distress signal kicked on, and one of the mail-run pilots spotted the wreck. But locating the bugger was the easiest part of it all. I know, cos I helped bring him out. He'd come down bang on top of this great huge piece of rock, see, sticking a couple hundred feet up out of the jungle. The lads from Rescue flew around up there for a couple of hours while they tried to think of what to do. Finally they called me to bring up the big Chinook they keep down at Jacksons. I brought it up over the wreck and sent a couple of the lads down on the winch."

He nodded, enjoying the telling of it. "He was a right mess, of course; they put him in a box and shipped him down to Queensland the next day. We left the chopper there – it was nothing but scrap, really."

"So what caused the crash?"

He looked at me, his eyes screwed up. "Well now that was the funny thing, you know? The investigators decided it must have been a bird strike."

"Bird strike?"

"That's right, mate, a bloody bird strike." He leaned across the counter. "They found bird feathers, see, all around the seat where Binky was strapped in, and more on the ground. All different colors – blue-and-white-striped, red and yellow, all sorts. Fuckin' rainbow, the crewman said. So they figured he must've hit a flock of bloody parrots or something."

"And you believe that?"

He shrugged. "Choppers are funny that way. Birds, updrafts, who knows. Maybe he flew too close to the trees, clipped a rotor." He looked at me, his eyes serious. "I'm sure of only one thing, mate. He was up to something, was our Binky. And I'm betting there was money in it – lots of money."

"Why lots?"

"Stands to reason, mate – he got himself killed for it, didn't he?"

* * *

"God was in a pretty good mood when he made most of New Guinea, but he lost his temper for sure when he got to this part." The pilot's voice crackled through on my earphones, clear and loud over the thunder of the props and the bone-rattling vibration of the airframe.

We were ten minutes out of Mount Hagen airport, five thousand feet above the jagged savageness of the Western

Highlands, and already it looked like dinosaur country. Our pilot kept one finger on the wheel and hummed tunelessly as he pushed the aging Cessna higher up toward the purple ramparts of the Schraders, straight ahead.

Thank God for money, I thought. Another hundred kina had persuaded the Talair clerk to take us up into the Schraders before lunch, to the Tavi Mission station. Tavi Mission was the closest point to where Dunham had come down, he said, and ten minutes later we were airborne and on our way.

It was a mere fifteen-minute flight, but a few thousand years into the past as far as most everything else seemed to be concerned, and Sam's eyes were wide as she stared out the window at the scenery. The ground below was a vast green carpet, folded in impossibly jumbled waves, each reaching higher into the mountains beyond. Every few miles a dozen or so low huts crouched in a ragged clearing beside small gardens of taro and sweet potato. Here and there an avalanche had slashed a red-earth wound across the face of the bush. In the deep-shadowed valleys rivers gleamed like secret pools of quicksilver. It was beautiful and awe-inspiring, but right now I was thinking about other things, such as money and good ideas. I was fast running out of both.

The mountain peaks were closer now, turning from purple to dark green as we came closer. Clouds with dark bellies were spilling up behind them. In a few hours, I knew, it would start to rain.

The pilot caught my glance and nodded. "Rain," he said into the earphones. "Every bloody day up here, more or less exactly about one o'clock. It'll piss down for an hour or so, and then stop just like they closed the tap. You might want to hang about a bit at the mission before you get out on the trail."

I shifted on the hard seat. "Tell me about the mission," I said.

He touched the controls and we banked sharply, coming around the end of a mountain spur and starting up into a narrow valley. "Tavi Mission? It's a half-assed strip on a mountain side, like a hundred others up here. The missionary's a Yank like yourself, only he talks different. Soft-spoken, but built like a cement outhouse. He's got a church, a nice house all by himself, couple of sway-backed mules, and some chickens. Oh, and the old Beechcraft he bought last year. I come in here every week or so on a regular run with the mail and whatever supplies he asks for. Doesn't seem to need much, though. His name's Fairley – Pastor Fairley."

"He's all by himself, you say?"

"Yep. Strange old bird. He's doing all right, though, near as I can see. Nice house, plane, everything he wants, and he runs an area the size of a small country."

Sam leaned forward. "Runs it? What do you mean?"

"Out here, ma'am, the missions are sort of in charge of things. There's no government officer for over thirty miles, and in this country that's two or three days walk. There's no real way in or out of here except by plane. The pastor calls in every day or two to tell everybody he's alive, otherwise we wouldn't know. There's a couple of thousand square miles of jungle down there with a few thousand locals living somewhere inside it, and more up and down than a man could count in three lifetimes. So the mission runs things – keeps the books, so to speak. The locals up here don't know the difference between the church and the government anyway, so when Fairley speaks they all listen. Hell's bells, this place wasn't even discovered until 1964, can you credit that?"

He started fiddling with the controls as we rounded another spur of the mountain range. "Coming up," he grunted. "Just ahead now."

He thumbed the microphone. "Papa Tango Oscar to Tavi Mission, requesting permission to land."

A moment later a voice came back into the earphones, pure Texas, raspy with static. "Tavi Mission here, come on in. Praise the Lord."

The pilot clicked off. "Praise the bloody Lord is right. Flying into Tavi'll make a believer out of you if nothing else will. This strip's a pisser, my oath it is."

Glancing up, I saw what he meant. The strip was a narrow corridor of grass hacked out of the ridge, sloping sharply upward and turning slightly to the left. At the end of the strip was a broad church made of thatch and a couple of outbuildings. Then a steep hill, rising dramatically up beyond the strip, and on top of it the mission house, broad verandas and shiny new tin roofing gleaming in the morning sun. You had one chance, if you were a pilot, to get a plane in or out of here. I tightened my grip on the edges of my seat.

"This is insane," whispered Sam. "We'll never be able to land down there."

The pilot trimmed the flaps some more and cut the throttle all the way back, subtly changing the engine's pitch and the angle of the aircraft. We felt almost weightless now, drifting down smoothly through wispy patches of mist. Sam's knuckles were white on the back of my seat.

He made final adjustments. "Hang on, here we go."

We dropped like an express elevator, and Sam let out a squeak of surprise. A thump, and water splashed up from the wheels on either side of the cockpit. The pilot gunned the motors hard and the Cessna bumped and lumbered along the grass, up the hill to the church at the end of the strip, toward the single figure walking down toward us.

The engines died, leaving only humid silence. The pilot flipped open the door, letting the smell of woodsmoke and rotting vegetation into the cabin. "Tavi Mission," he said. "That'll be Fairley coming now." He pointed at the tall figure walking slowly down the hill toward the strip, a battered brown hat pushed back on his head.

I hopped down and pulled our rucksacks from the cargo bay. The pilot leaned over and shouted out the cockpit door, "You really going up in there to where Dunham bought it?"

I nodded. "Yeah. I really am."

"Is it far?" asked Sam.

The pilot laughed. "No more'n five or six miles, miss, but most of it's straight up. Hope your legs are in decent nick. You'll get your exercise, that's for sure."

"At least we'll get to see some local color that way," she said.

The pilot snorted. "Local color? Aye, plenty of that about. And it'll all be brown and nasty." He turned to me, his face serious now. "I forgot to ask you before. Got a gun?"

"Do I need one?"

"Hard to say. The locals aren't too friendly up here, and there's a hell of a lot of forest to get lost in. The first rain that comes will fill your footprints, and you can walk from here to buggery before you'll find a way out. So mind how you go."

He shut the cockpit door and gave me the V sign. Then he gunned the engine, skidded the Cessna around on the grass, and headed back down the runway.

CHAPTER SIXTEEN

We stood and watched the Cessna dwindle to a black speck in the vast blue sky, its drone growing faint as it drifted away across the ranges. The light was clear and crystal sharp, and the air was sweet and fresh. You could almost believe the world was young.

The tall man coming toward us across the grass wasn't young, though. Under a Harry Truman hat, his long face was deeply tanned, crow's-feet and wrinkles radiating out from his watery brown eyes. With his long pendulous earlobes, he resembled an old hound dog. He wore khaki trousers, a Sears work shirt, and ankle-length boots. Then I noticed his arms. They were knotted with muscle, the veins prominent, and there was dirt under his fingernails.

He stopped a few feet away and inspected us, his eyes darting quickly from side to side. I'd seen that kind of glance before, I realized. Professional bodyguards scanned their surroundings in just the same way, eyes alert, never stopping.

He took off his hat, took a big step forward, and thrust out a wide leathery hand. I shook it. It was as tough as a piece of old hide, and underneath the skin his muscles were lean and hard. "Praise the Lord," he said.

I thought about that for a second. "Likewise," I replied.

He opened his mouth wide in a delighted guffaw, revealing large store-bought teeth. "Well, now," he said. "I'm Pastor Fairley." He winked. "Not a great name, not a bad name. Just a 'fairly' good 'un."

He grinned again. "Not tourists, though, are you? Folks come up here, they come for a reason. Whatever it is, I'm always glad to have company. Come up on the porch and have some lemonade and we'll talk."

* * *

Pastor Fairley listened quietly while Sam and I explained why we'd come. When we were through, he nodded. "You were lucky to get in here, Mr. Donovan. The weather's usually not so obliging." He pointed down the hill to a low building at the edge of the airstrip. "I got my own plane awhile back, but I can't fly the darned thing half the time on account of the clouds."

I saw an old Beechcraft parked inside a hangar made of native materials. Beside it stood several drums of fuel. "I wouldn't have thought you needed a plane, Pastor," I said.

Fairley grinned. "I do the Lord's work here, Mr. Donovan, and when he calls, I go. He who travels alone travels fastest, I've found." He set his glass of lemonade down and wiped his mouth with the back of his hand.

"Now, about this man Dunham," he said. "Can't tell you folks much, I'm afraid. I only saw him a time or two. He put in here once to make a small repair. Another time, I saw him drunk in Mount Hagen. It doesn't much surprise me that he might have got mixed up in something." He turned his wet eyes on me. "What exactly are you lookin' for up there, Mr. Donovan? Don't seem to me like there'd be much left. They winched the body out, after all."

I nodded. "I don't know exactly what I'm looking for," I admitted. "I guess I'll know it when I see it. Everything we've found out about MacKenzie and the business he was involved in leads back here. There's got to be a clue somewhere."

"Well, the crash site's up outside of one of the local Ginta villages. About five miles from here and two thousand feet farther up. That's rough territory – pretty much half a day's walk for a fit man." He looked at us. "Or woman. You two look like you can handle that, so let me ask you another question. Either of you know anything about the Ginta people?"

"Not a thing," I said.

Sam shook her head.

"Then let me enlighten you a little. They're a lot like children in some ways – they can be kind and generous, but they get mad awful quick, and they don't much believe in compromise. For most of 'em life runs along a set of pretty straight lines. If something – or someone – gets in the way, they just knock it over and keep on going. Now, you look like you can handle yourself, but there's something else. The Ginta aren't Christian. I've been working with 'em for years and hardly made a dent. They have a mushroom cult, Mr. Donovan. Every few days they'll cook up a mess of mushrooms and eat 'em. Makes 'em *long-long* – crazy. They're apt to run amok then. I'd sure hate for you and Miss Young to get mixed up with that." His hound-dog eyes brimmed with concern.

He stood up. "So I better go on up there with you. Time they heard another sermon again, anyway, I reckon." He grinned. "Help yourself to more lemonade. I'll check the weather report on the radio and throw a few things in my sack. Be right back."

When he returned a few minutes later he was strapping on an ugly-looking automatic pistol. Sam looked at it suspiciously. "Is that really necessary, Mr. Fairley?"

"Shucks," said Fairley. "I've been carrying this thing around with me up here for years. Hardly notice it anymore. Don't weigh anywheres near what it looks like," he said, patting the heavy web belt. "This here's a Colt 1911A1. Thirty-nine ounces when it's empty, which this one is not."

"Is it that dangerous, to have to walk around with a loaded gun?" Sam said.

Fairley nodded, a little quick movement like a bird's head. "You betcha it's dangerous, little lady. This place used to be a restricted area until 1975. You couldn't get in here without government permission, and you had to be armed at all times."

"But you're a missionary," Sam said. "Surely they wouldn't hurt you."

Pastor Fairley smiled, showing me teeth and a quick gleam of something else, far back inside his eyes. "The Lord takes care of them that takes care of themselves." He hitched up his trousers and looked at the sky. "Gonna rain in a couple of hours. Time we were going."

* * *

In the movies the jungle is always noisy. In a real-life jungle the animals, birds, and insects hardly make a sound. Not when there are three humans huffing and puffing their way through their backyard like a pack of steam locomotives.

The trail wound through the thick forest, climbing steeply as it left the mission. All of us were quickly soaked with sweat and covered with insect bites as we slipped and slid up the narrow muddy track. The tree canopy blocked most of the sunlight, creating a humid shadowland on the forest floor. Insects flew back and forth across the path, keeping our hands busy as we tried to bat them away from our perspiring faces. Now and then I caught sight of small groups of colorful butterflies. Once Sam grabbed my arm and pointed, and I caught a glimpse of the King of Saxony himself, perched on a branch high above us.

The rain began promptly at one o'clock. Gently, and then, in the space of a minute or so, steadily. What had been a soft patter became a roar, as the heavens opened up. The trail turned to mud in short order, and soon, all of us were soaked through. I heard a sound like thunder nearby as a huge tree came down.

"The rain does that," said Fairley. "Some of them trees are nearly two hundred feet high, all covered with that spongy moss stuff. Get a couple of good rains in here, the trees'll soak up tons of water. Tips 'em right over. The locals won't walk around in the forest while it's raining." He grinned. "They leave that to fools like us." He brushed water off his forehead. "Another two miles," he said. "Not long now."

* * *

We stood and stared at the Gintas, and they stared back at us. The rain had stopped, but we were still soaking wet and covered with mud, obviously facts of enormous but silent interest to some twenty or thirty villagers who faced us across the clearing.

113

The men wore arse-grass leaves on their buttocks and pig's tusks through their noses. They stared intently at us, their steel axes and bush knives held at the ready. The women were small and round and kept their hands folded modestly over their bellies. They were dressed in simple loincloths, their faces, breasts, and buttocks decorated with lines of white, orange, and red pigment. They all wore woven string bags folded neatly on their heads. Some of them cradled small naked babies at their hips.

I counted roughly equal numbers of men, women, children, and pigs. They were standing up to their ankles in the thick red mud that covered the central village clearing. Behind them, at the edge of the clearing, a large longhouse on stilts rose up dramatically. Behind it wisps of smoke rose from a squalid cluster of low huts made of pit-pit stalks and pandanus leaves. Dogs growled and yapped in the distance, punctuating the steady drone of flies from a nearby rubbish heap. I would give anything, I thought, to be able to make Bone Brown appear in front of me right now.

"Not exactly tripping over each other to say hello, are they?" I said.

"The Gintas don't like strangers," Pastor Fairley said in a low voice. "They think outsiders bring evil spirits and unhappiness to the village."

Sam looked around. "They might be right," she murmured. "I can't see much joy around, can you?"

I looked up at the sky. The rain was over, and the sun was coming out again. I checked my watch: four o'clock. More than two hours of daylight left. I couldn't see standing around like this for the rest of the afternoon, so I said, "How far is it to where Dunham came down?"

Fairley looked surprised. "Not far. About half a mile. You want to keep going?"

"Might as well," I said. "Doesn't look like anyone's going to ask us in for tea."

Fairley spoke a few words in the local language to one of the men, and the crowd drew back. The Gintas watched us silently as we walked slowly along the narrow muddy corridor, through the wretched settlement, and out the other side. From between two of the huts a dog appeared, baring its fangs and growling. One of the men leaned forward and struck it with the flat of his ax, hard. It yelped once, convulsed, and lay still on the path, blood oozing from its open mouth. No one said anything as we carefully stepped over it and walked into the jungle.

* * *

The trail wound steeply up through rocks and mud, presenting only minimal hand- and footholds. I watched my feet and was very careful where I put them. Accidents now could be worse than dangerous, I realized; they could be fatal. We had no radio, the mission was miles away, and it would take hours to fly someone out to get medical help.

Half an hour later Fairley raised his hand for a halt. He took out a red-checked bandanna and wiped his forehead. "There she is," he said, pointing straight up. "Right up on top of that outcrop there. You really gonna try to climb up that thing?"

I glanced up at the rock wall. The rock rose straight up beside the trail, the top at least two hundred feet above us. I could see nothing but blue sky at the edge. "Unless you know an easier way to get on top."

He gave a short barking laugh. "Son, you've got more guts than I do, I'll say that." He looked at his watch. "You better get busy, then. There's about ninety minutes of good light left. Gets dark pretty fast around here, once the sun goes behind the ranges. You'll want to be off the rock by then."

Sam frowned. "Do you really think you can get up there, Max? It looks like it goes straight up."

"I'll be fine," I said, boosting myself up to the first set of holds. "Piece of cake."

Fairley nodded. "And may the Good Lord have mercy on your soul."

CHAPTER SEVENTEEN

I lay flattened like a snake against the rock, my fingers searching desperately for a hold. Sheer friction was all that was holding me on the face right now. The trail was a couple of hundred feet below, and if I didn't find something to hang on to pretty soon, it would be a hard landing. My fingertips found and caught a tiny crack in the rock face, and I locked on and pulled. Now for the next.

I inched upward, moving with agonizing slowness across the nearly vertical rock face. Piece of cake, my ass. It was a lot more fun years ago in college, I thought. Friction climbing observed from below resembled a ballet in extremely slow motion – the climbers seemed to flow across the rock, never stopping, never ceasing their upward probing. A joy to watch.

Less of a joy, however, to do. Especially in the jungle at eight thousand feet, with sweaty palms and insect bites that itched like hell. I glanced back down at Sam and Pastor Fairley. They were mere blobs on the trail, their upturned faces pale against the deep green of the forest. I wiped sweat from my forehead, brushed a large mosquito away from my ear, and hauled myself up another few inches.

It settled into a routine. Reach, pull. Reverse, push. Reach again. Missed it. Find another, quickly. Don't step back, don't break the flow. Got it. Pull, change hands, reach, pull again, hard now. Up, keep going up. Find the holds and keep moving. Breathe in, don't look down, keep going, dammit. Then I edged up over the lip, my free hand scrabbling for a hold.

I found a wide crack, jammed my fingers into it hard, and hauled myself up and over, using my elbows, knees, and gut. Bad climbing form, but screw that for a laugh, I thought as I flipped onto safe, level ground. I was breathing like a locomotive and pouring sweat as I waited for my heart to stop trying to jump out of my chest. Piece of bloody cake, oh yes.

After a few minutes I sat up to look around. The top of the rock outcrop was reasonably level and seemed to be large; a sort of tabletop. I was nearly three hundred feet above the trail, I calculated. I gazed out over the canopy of trees to where the Bismarck Range loomed in the middle distance, its peaks retreating away from me toward the west and south. Small birds circled here and there above the treetops, reveling in the late afternoon sunlight and the cool breezes that swept upland from the coast some fifty miles away. I could see no roads, no buildings, no campfire smoke – nothing, in fact, to show that humans had ever been here at all.

Except for what lay a hundred yards away.

The jagged skeleton of Binky Dunham's copter sat silently in the bright sunlight, its shattered and twisted ribs reaching to the sky. An ancient reptile carcass, bleaching slowly in the Mesozoic heat. I got up and began to walk slowly toward it. So this was how Binky had finished, I thought as I approached the wreck.

There is a time – a long time, for most of us – when we believe that we are immortal. We know of death, but we do not believe in it. Not for ourselves. Death is something that happens to others, to people not as clever as we. Later, with experience, we begin to make death's acquaintance, first in small ways, and then – eventually, inevitably – we glimpse its face. We stare death in the face and then we know. Not now, death says; not this time. Enjoy yourself. I'll be back. But we know beyond a shadow of a doubt. The days are numbered, the countdown begun.

And here was where time had run out for Binky Dunham. He was dead and gone, smashed like an egg across a high rock far from home. Gone to wherever good pilots and clever crooks go, and we wouldn't be seeing him again. Now what was important was to find whatever he'd left behind him. Whatever could give me a clue – no matter how small – to what the hell was going on that connected the people up here in the jungle with a dead man in a sleazy motel room in San Francisco.

I swept the helicopter with my eyes, top to bottom, stopping as something caught my eye. I moved closer, bent, and looked closely at the chopper's tires. It had rained every day since the crash, washing most everything clean, but down in the grooves of the tires, I could still see mud. Thick red mud. Mud that shouldn't be there. I closed my eyes, trying to remember what the pilot had said about Dunham's route. Leave Mount Hagen at midmorning, he'd said, fly straight to the camp. But here he was, more than sixty miles off course, with red mud on his wheels.

Somewhere between Mount Hagen and here, Dunham had set down. The question was, where?

I stood up, thinking of the Ginta village below. The clearing in front of the longhouse was more than adequate for a chopper this size. And it was covered with the same red mud.

But if he'd landed in the village, I thought, what was he doing there?

I bent over and crawled into the cargo hold. Already vines and creepers had infiltrated the wrecked machine, and driver ants and termites had set up housekeeping in the cracks and crevices.

The copter had been carrying the usual assortment of junk when it came down. I poked through it, not really expecting to find anything. Six kegs of nails, their sides split by the impact of the crash. A dozen cartons of South Pacific Lager, worth their weight in cigarettes up in the remote mining camps of the Star Mountains. The rest of it was machinery – small boxes of spare parts, some crates of chain-link drive, crated ball bearings. No trace of anything the least bit out of the ordinary.

I moved into the cockpit.

There were dark stains on the pilot's seat and a crumpled flying glove on the floor. I picked it up and looked at it, trying to imagine what Binky Dunham had been like in those last few seconds when he'd seen death again and known that this time it was going to stick. He might have been a bastard, but crash-landing an aircraft is a lousy way to go. I could certainly vouch for that.

Flies buzzed around my head as I poked through the wreckage, searching for something, anything, that would give me a clue as to what the hell had happened. There was a half pack of Cambridge cigarettes beside Dunham's seat, faded and dried from the sun. A pair of silver-faced sunglasses lay smashed in a corner. I picked them up and looked for a moment at my reflection in the one good lens.

Had Dunham been the victim of deliberate sabotage or just bad luck? What had he been doing up here, miles off his normal flight path? And why the hell hadn't the man had the common decency to at least leave me some clues? It was hot inside the chopper and I was growing dizzy, dripping sweat.

Then I noticed the boxes behind the pilot's seat. Small cages, really, made of bamboo strips. I picked one up; it was empty. There were four of them. And below them a pile of small bones.

I got down on my hands and knees. There were a dozen or so tiny bones scattered about the metal floor of the cockpit. Beside them some scraps of feather. I picked one up and peered at it, feeling my heart begin to pound as I recognized the distinctive blue-and-white pattern. The King of Saxony.

I stood up, a smile spreading across my face. Dunham, you old rascal, I thought. Up from Hagen, land in the mining camp, eat lunch, start back to Hagen in the early afternoon. Do a little dogleg on the way, land in the Ginta village, pick up the birds. Home before the rain hit.

I nodded. It made a lot of sense. I picked up three or four of the feathers and put them in my shirt pocket. I'd wanted evidence, and I'd gotten it. I glanced at my watch – time to be going. It would be dark within the hour. That we were going to have to spend the night in the Ginta village was bad enough, but I didn't intend to spend it on the rock face.

One last look around. I peered inside the first aid kit, checked the compartment where the flight logs and maps were kept. All empty. Whoever had picked up Dunham's body would have taken the paperwork with them. I was about to call it a day when something occurred to me. If Dunham had had something to hide – something small, for example – where would he have hidden it? Not in his crash kit, certainly, and not inside the pocket of his logbook.

I knew just the place. I got down flat on the floor and peered up at the underside of the seat. Pilots in Vietnam had kept their stash taped under the seat all the time; it was so common as to be practically a joke. I grunted and moved in closer, running my hand over the metal springs of the seat.

My hand touched something smooth and hard, and I edged forward on my back, trying to see what it was. Well, well, I thought as I spotted the tiny leather address book wedged into one of the seat springs. Well, well.

I pulled it free and sat up, opening the tiny book and scanning the pages. They were addresses, mostly of women. Some contained tiny notes. 'Jennifer Greenwood, Cairns,' I read. 'Two-pot screamer.' 'Linda Ansett, stew from Brisbane. Nice legs, snores.'

Somebody should tell Jennifer and Linda not to hold their breath waiting for Dunham to show up again, I thought, riffling through the pages of the book. More of the same, plus some notations here and there about bets

Dunham had apparently been in the habit of placing at various Australian racetracks through a bookie in Port Moresby. On the back cover the word 'Blue' and a string of numbers and letters – 1463230E851S. Hadn't the Talair pilot mentioned that Binky Dunham's drinking partner was called Blue?

Just below that I saw something that made my heart start to pound again. Last month's date, a colon, the word 'MacKenzie' and a string of telephone numbers. I drew my breath in sharply.

The area code for all the numbers was the same: 415. San Francisco.

I walked back to the edge of the cliff, figuring the times and schedules. Say two days to get ourselves back to Moresby. Then the early morning flight to Sydney, with connections later that same day on a flight out to San Francisco. Call it twenty hours across the Pacific. Four days, give or take, and there was the date line to deal with, but four days anyhow. I could call Bone from Moresby and give him the telephone numbers and that would save a little time.

All right.

I yelled over the edge, and a moment later I saw Pastor Fairley's face appear on the trail far below. I waved the address book. "Jackpot!" I yelled. "I'm coming down!"

Fifteen minutes later I hit the ground. Pastor Fairley was waiting for me. He had his pistol out and pointed at my chest. "Give me the notebook, Donovan."

I opened my mouth, closed it again, and handed over what I had found. "I don't get it," I said finally. "You're a missionary."

Fairley smiled, his hound-dog face crinkling in amusement. "Don't confuse God and Mammon, Mr. Donovan." He jerked the pistol up the trail. "I had to kinda tie Miss Young up a little, but she's just fine. Let's get moving. It'll be dark pretty soon."

CHAPTER EIGHTEEN

The inside of the hut was cramped and uncomfortable, and being tied up didn't help. Sam and I sat on the hard dirt floor with our backs to the pit-pit wall. Pastor Fairley sat on a folding chair in front of us, sipping hot tea. I had a headache and my lower back ached, but those were the least of my worries right now.

The night pulsed with sound. Out in the forest the tree frogs were warming up the orchestra, tuning their vocal cords to a fine pitch. Sometimes one would solo, stopping to give way to another. Once in a while they'd do a duet, one frog's strident tone working in counterpoint to the other's. But mostly it was the entire percussion section, flat out, at full volume.

In the village a different sort of performance was beginning. The Gintas were eating mushrooms and getting noisily high, preparing to commit ritual mayhem.

A gecko clucked with impatience from high up on the wall of the hut. It had remained rigidly still for the last ten minutes, waiting patiently for insects to fly toward the Petromax lamp set on the earth floor.

"And that's how I wound up out here," Pastor Fairley was saying. "I'd had a good run for my money out in Oklahoma, but things were getting just a little too narrow." He held the pistol easily in his hand, like an old friend. I had no doubt in the world that he'd blow my head off in a split second if he had to.

"I'd always thought of myself as a decent man, actually. I didn't mean to kill that bank guard in Muskogee, but once a man's dead, he's dead." He smiled, a kindly old uncle. "I killed a few more on the way out of town that were dumb enough to try to stop me."

He took another sip of tea and gestured to the plate of beans and the teapot beside him. "I'd offer you some, but it wouldn't be much use you eating. Pure waste of food." He looked like an old-time cowpuncher squatting there near the fire, his enamel mug held up close to his lips. Except that this wasn't West Texas, it was New Guinea. And those weren't cattle lowing out there, either.

He shifted his legs, pulling up his trousers. "Anyway, I killed me another three or four gettin' down to Mexico. I stayed down in Chiapas for about six months, holed up in a place I knew about. When I thought things had blown over a little, I snuck back across the border to take a look around."

He shook his head. "It was bad, Mr. Donovan. Not only were they still looking for me, they'd upped the reward money. There was only one thing to do. I'd had time to think about it, and I figured this was the only way." He smiled. "I heard the call and became one of the Lord's missionaries. And here I am today."

"Didn't anybody find that strange?" I said.

"Why, hell, boy, people were glad to see me. Those puckerbrush churches are always happy to welcome another damned fool. Especially one who's so interested in spreading the word to the heathen. It didn't take me but a few months before I was overseas." He winked. "Course it also took a few doctored papers – certificates of divinity school and such – but that was child's play."

He forked beans into his mouth and chewed for a moment before he spoke again. "My first post was down in Costa Rica. With an old fart, name of Pastor Collier. Half deaf, blind in one eye, and gimpy. Been in church work all his life. Lived way out in the jungle, all alone. He had a local woman to do stuff for him. Cooking, washing, and so forth."

"How long did you wait?" I asked.

Fairley cocked a bright bird's eye at me and nodded appreciatively. "You catch on quick, Mr. Donovan. That's good; I like to see that in a man. I waited a year, as a matter of fact. I wanted to let the trail in the US go nice and cold. In the meantime I got rid of the woman, made the old bastard dependent on me for everything that happened around there. I read the mission literature and checked out a few things, and when the time was ripe I made my move."

"You killed the old man."

"Humanely, Mr. Donovan. Humanely. I don't believe in causing pain unless it's deserved." Something moved in his eyes then, making them gleam strangely for a moment. "You two, for example, are going to suffer pain, lots of it. And you deserve it, far as I'm concerned. Never should have come snooping around up here in the first place."

"Tell me how you killed the old man," I said quietly.

"Oh, that was easy. I just crept into his room one night and put a pillow up against his face. He heard me come in. He never slept much at night, I think. Too old, and too much going through his mind. I sometimes thought he'd figured me out, but if he had, he never let on. 'James?' he said. 'That you, James?' 'It's me, Pastor,' I said. 'Now don't you worry.' Then I put the pillow against his mouth and nose and held it there. He twitched a bit, that's all. The next day I told the villagers that he'd died in his sleep."

He finished the tea and put his mug down. "I'd been setting things up for months, of course. Typed letters from him to the Central Board of Missions extolling the virtues of Brother Fairley. Letters in support of Brother Fairley's application to join the Southwest Pacific Outreach Mission, for posting to New Guinea." He smiled. "It worked like a charm. I'd figured out from the start that I needed somewhere alone, where I could more or less be myself."

"Looks like you got it," I said.

He nodded. "I got it, Mr. Donovan. I've been here for almost six years, and I've got just about everything a man might need. More money than I can spend, my own private aircraft, and a piece of property about the size of Rhode Island. Not much company, but I don't mind. Never cared much for women, to tell you the truth. Nor for men either, come to that. Up here, Mr. Donovan, I'm judge, jury, paymaster, policeman, and teacher. What I say goes. Me and nobody else. And that's just the way I want it."

"Tell me about the birds," I said.

"The birds? Well, that was MacKenzie's idea. I met him two years ago down in Port Moresby, and we sort of hit it off. We started with artifacts – masks and statues and all that. I got them from the Gintas, Dunham flew them out, and MacKenzie sold them.

"Six months ago he had the idea about the birds. I'd seen the birds, of course, here in the forest. Even figured they might be worth money to someone. MacKenzie said he knew people who'd buy them. I got him one lot and he sold them in Hong Kong, made a pile. So we did it again. Then MacKenzie said we ought to try these people he'd heard about in San Francisco. They were rich, he said. So I got some more birds for him, and he took them." He spat into the fire. "Shit-fire, now you tell me he's dead."

"Who was MacKenzie going to sell the birds to?"

Fairley smiled. "Go to hell, Donovan. I don't know, and I wouldn't tell you if I did. Each of us operated independently. That's the way MacKenzie and I wanted it."

He leaned forward. "Let's talk about you two instead. Hear that noise outside? The Gintas are getting ready. They're painting their faces and sharpening their spears. About an hour ago the men sat down in the longhouse and passed around the mushrooms. Cream-colored tops with little gold spots; they grow out in the forest, under ferns and big leaves. Makes 'em wild, Donovan. I've seen them do it a dozen times. They all eat the mushrooms, and then they see God, and then they go on the rampage. They're out for blood tonight."

Sam spoke. "But why us? We've done nothing to these people."

Fairley picked up the teapot and poured his mug half full. "Let me explain something to you," he said. "As far as the Gintas are concerned, nothing ever happens by accident. If a tree falls in the forest and kills Uncle Charlie, we say it was just bad luck he happened to be under it at the time. The Gintas don't see it that way. Why that tree, at that time, and how come Uncle Charlie was right underneath? No accident; somebody set it up. Witchcraft. So they start looking for the culprit, the witch. If they can't find him in the village, they raid one of the neighboring groups. They find the witch and kill him. Just like they're going to kill you tonight."

Fairley spread his big hands. "Very biblical, don't you think? An eye for an eye. They had a good deal here, you see, selling birds of paradise to Dunham and me. I set the deal up, Dunham came dropping out of the sky and showered them with cash, and then he flew away again until the next time."

He sipped his tea. "No more 'next time' now. The big bird crashed, and that was the end of the money. And the Gintas want to know why. For weeks they've been asking me who made the helicopter crash, and finally, this afternoon, I had an answer for them."

"We're the witches," I said.

Fairley beamed. "Like I said, you catch on quick. I explained everything to the Gintas earlier, after I brought you back to the village. You're witches, both of you. You came back to the scene to make sure Dunham was dead, and to eat any bones that might have remained."

"Ugh," said Sam.

"Witches eat people around here, Miss Young," said Fairley. "It's a relatively civilized practice compared to some of what goes on, believe me. That's why they stuck you out

126

in this hut, away from the rest of the village – they don't want you anywhere near them. When they're ready they'll come and drag you out. By killing you they'll avenge Dunham, and maybe even bring back the good times again."

I nodded. It made perfect sense in its own crazy way. Why not? "How are they going to kill us?" I asked him.

He stood up. "Well, sometimes they tie witches up to a pole in the center of the village and have the men practice throwing spears at them. Other times they just bash their heads in with stone axes." He went to the door of the hut and peered out. "They'll do it however they feel like, I reckon. And they'll do it soon. They're pretty crazy right now. Won't be much longer."

"How are you going to explain this afterwards?" said Sam. "Somebody's going to realize we're missing, you know. They'll come looking for us, sooner or later."

Fairley shrugged. "You two came to the mission, and against my advice you insisted on going into the forest. You seen the size of the trees we got around here? They fall over when they get wet – you heard 'em yourself, this afternoon. I reckon that's the way you got it. You must have wandered off the main trail and had an accident. Sure as hell nobody around here saw you. Nobody at all."

He stretched, put his gun into its holster, and tugged up his trousers. "Think I'll go and see how things are coming along." He winked. "Don't go anywhere, now." He stooped and went out the door, into the rising din outside.

* * *

"Come here," I said quietly. "I want you to do something for me."

Sam pushed herself along the dirt floor until we were side by side.

"Lie down," I said.

We lay face to face. She smelled of woodsmoke and sweat. I was sure I smelled worse. "What do you want me to do?" she said.

"My GI can opener," I said. "Fairley searched us for weapons, but he missed the can opener. It's around my neck, on a piece of rawhide. You've got to bite through it. Once you do that, you can cut me loose."

She nodded. "How much time do you think we have?"

"Five minutes," I said. "Maybe less."

She nodded and bent to her task.

It was almost erotic, having a beautiful woman nuzzling your neck, but I was too busy being scared to death to enjoy it. I had to be free before Fairley got back, or else Sam and I would die. It was as simple as that. And as the man said, the prospect of death concentrates the mind wonderfully.

Sam bit my neck. "Ouch."

"You're moving," she muttered. "Hold still or I'll bite you again."

Thirty seconds later I felt the rawhide part. "Turn around," I said to Sam. "Take the opener in your hands and open the blade. Good. Now back up against me and cut through the rope. Careful, for God's sake. Don't cut my wrists."

"Oh, shut up," she hissed. "Raise your hands a little. There. Now hold still."

She sawed awkwardly at the nylon cord for several long minutes, and then suddenly I was free. I got up, massaging my wrists. I bent and freed Sam's hands and brought her to her feet. Then I kissed her, hard.

She took a deep breath. Just then Pastor Fairley showed up.

He came straight through the low door of the hut, bent over, eyes down. I hit him on the back of the neck as hard as I could, and it seemed to do the job. He went down like a cement sack being pushed off the back of a pickup truck, and lay still on the ground.

"Watch the door," I said to Sam. Outside, the noise of the Gintas seemed to have increased. Whatever they were planning was going to happen within the next few minutes. I didn't intend to be there for the kickoff.

I quickly hog-tied Fairley, making the knots as tight as I could. Then I went through his pockets. I took the notebook I'd found in the chopper, his gun, keys, and a book of matches. Then I looked around the hut. Walls of pit-pit, floor of dirt. Our rucksacks against one wall. Next to them a low cupboard. I opened the cupboard. Inside were five or six bottles of drinking water, some canned food, and a five-gallon can of gasoline for the Petromax. I emptied two of the water bottles and opened the cap on the gasoline.

Sam peered out into the night through the hut's tiny window. "You ought to see this, Max," she said. "They're really raving."

"Just tell me if they start moving this way," I said. "I'm looking for something to make a fuse with." I pawed through the rucksacks, pulling out a pair of pink lace panties. "I believe I've found just what we need."

"Put those back," Sam protested. "They're my last clean pair."

"Sorry," I said. "You've just donated them to the cause, my friend."

I tore the panties in half, twisting each half to make a wick, then I splashed fuel on each wick before stuffing them into the mouths of the gasoline-filled bottles.

Now all we needed was a target.

Just then Fairley woke up. "What the hell—"

"Evening, Pastor." I bent down and put the muzzle of the gun into his ear and pushed, hard. "Does that hurt a little? Good. Now listen up. Don't even think about calling for help. One peep out of you and your brains'll be strawberry jam on the wall."

Fairley's lip curled back, like a cornered dog's. "You'll never make it out of here alive, Donovan. The Gintas are as whipped up as I've ever seen them. They're out for blood, boy. You're not going to get away from them."

I smiled. "Just watch us, Pastor. You have a good evening, now." I hit him just behind the ear and eased him to the ground.

We slipped unnoticed into the shadows cast by the huge bonfire that the Gintas had made in the clearing. I carried the gun. Sam carried the gasoline bombs.

"If we create a diversion, we can slip away before they notice," I whispered. "It's about five miles to the mission station. We might make it."

She leaned over and kissed me lightly. "Let's get going, then."

We wormed our way around the village on our bellies until we were twenty feet from the side of the longhouse at the edge of the clearing. We lay hidden in the tall grass, watching the spectacle unfolding before us.

Fifty or sixty men stood in a long line before the fire, swaying and stamping their feet. The rest of the village stood in a semicircle, watching with somber, serious faces. The dancers were naked except for short loincloths. Their faces and chests were painted in white, red, and yellow designs. They had rattles of some kind fixed to their ankles, so that as they stamped their feet a metallic crash echoed through the clearing. Each man had a long black-palm spear in his hand.

The bonfire spat and crackled, throwing grotesque shadows onto their contorted faces. The men leaped and capered in the firelight, waving their spears and shouting hoarsely. Every now and then one of them would stop, bend over, and vomit copiously. The singing and shouting were growing louder and more frenzied. Soon the climax would come. With a roar, the Ginta warriors would charge Fairley's hut and drag us out.

Except that we wouldn't be there.

"These guys're ripped to the gills," I whispered to Sam. "I'm surprised they can still stand up. I'm going to throw one of the bottles. Get ready to run."

"What about Fairley?"

"He'll be all right. The wind's blowing away from his hut. But we ought to be able to burn the longhouse down, don't you think?" I gave her the gun. "Cover me."

Pulling Fairley's matches out from my shirt pocket, I struck one and lit the wick of a cocktail. "Get set," I said. "Don't wait to see the fireworks." I waited until the wick was burning well. Then I ran forward and chucked it underhand, like a big softball, toward the front of the longhouse.

The bottle hit the doorpost and shattered. A brilliant orange glow lit up the night, accompanied by a loud, sharp thud.

Everyone froze. The Gintas stopped dancing and shouting, and all eyes turned toward the longhouse. Already the walls were aflame, tongues of fire climbing rapidly up toward the thatch on the roof. The first screams erupted from the crowd.

"That's it," I hissed to Sam as I stuffed the second gasoline bomb into my pack. "Let's get out of here."

We turned and raced for the trail at the edge of the village. I looked back once, just before we entered the forest. The longhouse was a solid wall of flame. The fire had spread to the other huts now, and the Gintas were running in all directions, panicked. Sooner or later one of them would find Pastor Fairley, but they had other things to worry about right now.

Sam was ten feet ahead of me and moving fast. I pulled alongside her, breathing hard. "You set a fast pace."

"I was women's cross-country champion in college," she said, hardly missing a beat. "I'll bet I can run you into the ground."

"You're on," I panted. "But what if the Gintas are faster than either of us?"

"Shut up and keep running."

CHAPTER NINETEEN

We stumbled through the forest in near-total darkness, crashing against branches and tripping over vines. Sam kept up a brutal pace, proving her claim to have been a cross-country champion. I managed to match her, but only just. I was covered with insect bites as I lurched along the muddy trail, cursing every bottle of Mekhong whisky I'd ever laid eyes on and expecting to feel a Ginta spear between my shoulders any second.

Finally I put my hand on Sam's shoulder, bringing her to a stop. "Enough," I croaked. "Can't do any more."

She was bent over, breathing heavily. Both of us were dripping sweat. Far down the trail in the darkness, I heard something like a pack of yapping dogs. The hairs on the back of my neck rose, and I shivered in the forest heat.

"The Gintas," she gasped between deep breaths. "They're right behind us. We've—" she paused for more air "—we've got to keep going, Max."

"No," I said. "We'll never outrun them. That's clear now. We've got to try something else."

"What?"

I gulped in air. "We'll hide. Go off the trail and hide. Let them pass us."

She looked doubtful. "I don't know, Max. I think it's better to—"

We heard the dog yelps again, closer this time. I grabbed her arm. "Come on." We plunged into the pitch-black jungle and took cover under a fallen tree trunk.

"Yuck," whispered Sam as we wormed our way underneath it. "It's all slimy. I'll bet there are bugs too."

"Count on it," I said. "And keep your mouth shut no matter what starts crawling up your leg. The Gintas know all the forest noises. If you get ants in your pants, keep it to yourself."

She dug me viciously with her thumb. "I don't have any pants," she said. "You used them for the Molotov cocktails, remember? And why the hell are you still carrying the one you didn't use? It's heavy, and all it does is slow us down."

"I've got a feeling it's going to be useful," I said. "Now scrunch down and shut up. Here they come."

We huddled in the damp rotting debris and listened as the Gintas ran past, their curious doglike whoopings echoing back at them from the thick tree canopy overhead. I counted fifteen of them, blobs of blackness flitting down the path. Then they were gone, swallowed up by the night, their whoops growing fainter.

I found Sam's hand in the darkness and squeezed it. "Let's wait another ten minutes, just to be sure," I said.

We waited in silence, but no one passed by on the trail. Soon the night noises of the forest crept back – the singing whine of the mosquitoes, the chirping of various strange cricket-like insects, sleepy birdcalls from time to time, and from somewhere nearby the intermittent croaks of courting tree frogs.

Sam's teeth glowed softly in the dark. "Just like a Tarzan movie, huh, Donovan?"

"Yeah," I said, crawling out of our hiding place and brushing the dirt from my clothes. "Complete with unfriendly natives. Let's get going."

* * *

We crouched in the tall *kunai* grass above the mission and listened. The Gintas were out there somewhere, but I was damned if I could hear them. Fairley's church reared up in the moonlight like some kind of Third World haunted house, but I wasn't interested in that.

133

I was watching the grass-roofed hangar. Where Fairley kept his plane.

I'd been watching it for some time now, and I hadn't seen any movement. Either the Gintas were inside the hangar waiting for us, or outside it, watching it just as we were.

Of course, I thought, I could be wrong. Maybe the Gintas figured we weren't particularly interested in the plane. Maybe they were looking for us somewhere else.

Rule that one out, I decided. The Gintas might be short and ugly, but they certainly weren't stupid.

So it was back to playing parlor games in my head. The one where you have to tell what you're most afraid of. If asked, I might say something like, 'The scariest thing? Oh, maybe trying to escape from a bunch of homicidal drug-crazed witch doctors by flying a light plane out of the jungle in the middle of the night.'

And then the leader of the game would say, 'In that case, that's what you're going to have to do.'

That's what I was going to have to do, all right, and I'd been thinking about it hard. We didn't really have any other options. There was the radio in the pastor's house, of course, but we'd have to start the generator to power it, and in any case the mission strip had no landing lights. So even if we could raise someone on the radio in Mount Hagen, there'd be no way they could get us out before morning.

We didn't have that long.

Getting into the hangar is only the first step, I thought. No guarantee that Fairley'd left any fuel in the plane. And if there was fuel, no guarantee there'd be enough to get us to Mount Hagen.

In fact, I thought, no guarantee the damned plane will even start.

About all we had going for us, I decided, was the fact that the Gintas were probably still pretty high on the mushrooms they'd gobbled earlier in the evening. It might interfere with their reactions just enough to give us a fighting chance at getting away.

Sure. It might also make them able to see in the dark and leap tall buildings at a single bound.

There was only one way to find out. I felt to make sure the last gasoline bomb was still in my knapsack and took a tighter grip on Fairley's pistol.

"Let's go," I whispered to Sam.

"What's the plan?"

I stared at her. "How the hell should I know? This is strictly improvisation." I began to slither through the grass like a crippled snake.

We crept into the hangar through a break in the back wall. Once inside, we froze, backs against the wall, and stayed that way for nearly five minutes while our eyes grew accustomed to the dark.

The hangar was silent. Too silent for my taste, I decided. There ought to be mice skittering about in the darkness, and a pigeon or two rustling quietly in the eaves. Instead, the place was like the bottom of a mineshaft, minus the dripping water.

Fairley's Beechcraft loomed a few feet away, a patch of blackness against the now lighter background. Ahead the open doorway of the hangar allowed some of the moonlight to enter for a few feet. At least we weren't going to have to haul the doors open.

If I can start this thing, I thought, every Ginta in the country'll come running the first time the engine fires. We'll have maybe sixty seconds to get the plane rolling. So the sooner I get started, the better.

Holding the pistol at the ready, I opened the cockpit door. "Inside," I whispered. "Quick. Sit in the far seat and strap yourself in."

Sam nodded and climbed in. I hoisted myself up and into the pilot's seat. I reached over and closed the door, pushing the handle down to lock it, then I took Fairley's keys from my pocket and located the one I wanted. I ran my fingertips over the control panel. It's not the same as the planes I was used to, but I can handle it, I thought. Just as long as there's power in the battery and fuel in the tanks. Pray for both, I thought as I inserted the key and turned.

The panel lights came on and the fuel needles snapped to full. Then Sam screamed.

I turned to see a Ginta behind her, inside the cockpit with us. He had Sam by the hair and was pulling her head back, exposing her neck. In his other hand a long and wicked-looking knife was coming up fast.

I swung the heavy .45, hitting him on the bridge of the nose. There was the sound of cartilage breaking, and the Ginta fell back screaming. I heard a thump from outside and the sound of feet scuffling in the darkness.

I scrabbled for the wing lights. If there were more of the bastards, I wanted to see them. The outside landing lights blazed on to reveal the hangar crawling with Gintas. Sam yelled again, and I turned. Another Ginta was coming at us through the cargo hatch. He held a long palm-wood spear, and his lips were drawn back in a snarl.

I cursed. The bastards had been waiting for us all the time. I should have checked the cargo hatch before we got in. I raised the pistol and fired at the Ginta crawling toward us. A thunderclap boomed through the tiny cockpit as a large hole appeared in the airframe beside the hatch. I'd missed. Before I could fire again the Ginta dropped back out of sight.

I glanced at the one I'd hit in the face, still unconscious on the floor. "Get him out and get the goddamn hatch shut!" I yelled at Sam. "Hurry!"

As she moved to the back of the plane, I could hear thumps and thuds as the Gintas outside hammered on the fuselage with their spears and axes. If we were going to take off, it had to be in the next few seconds. After that there wouldn't be enough left of the plane to matter.

I adjusted the throttles and ground the starter, counting the seconds in my head… five, six, seven, eight. The port engine caught with a roar and a belch of smoke. The Gintas backed away from the scything prop, screaming. I gunned it hard, pumping up the pressure as high as I dared, feeling the airframe tremble under me.

I flipped the starter on the starboard engine. It caught almost immediately and I let out a rebel yell. "Thirty seconds!" I shouted. "Get that gasoline bomb out of my pack and then strap in. We're moving out!"

Sam gripped my arm. "Max, look. What are they doing out there?"

In front of the hangar a group of Gintas were busy pulling over fuel drums and piercing them with their spears. High-octane aviation gas was gushing out, forming a wide puddle in front of us. As I watched one of the Gintas came running up carrying a handful of burning grass.

"Oh, shit." I opened the small cockpit window, aimed Fairley's .45 at the man, and pulled the trigger. There was a dry click. The gun was jammed.

He dropped the burning grass and a wall of flame roared up in front of us. The Gintas drew back with excited yells and shrieks, waving their weapons in the air.

"Hang on," I muttered to Sam as I released the brakes and pushed the throttles ahead full.

Slewing wildly, the plane shot ahead, through the flames and out onto the strip beyond. Behind us the hangar had started to burn, lighting up the entire area. I could see Gintas converging on us from all directions, weapons held high.

We tore up to the end of the strip, bouncing uncontrollably. The Gintas ran alongside, keeping pace easily. Spears and axes thudded against the sides of the plane. I turned to Sam as we neared the end of the strip.

"I'm turning around up here," I said. "When I do, light the gasoline bomb and throw it at the buggers. Think you can do that?"

She nodded, her expression grim.

I reached the end of the runway and skidded the plane around, pivoting smartly on the brakes and stopping.

"Now!" I said to Sam.

She was ready. Lighting the wick we had improvised from her underwear, she threw the bomb out the cargo hatch, smashing it on the ground. There was a flash and a billow of flames.

I revved the engines as high as I dared and released the brakes. We shot off into the darkness careening and bumping down the grass strip like a nightmare roller coaster.

I gripped the wheel and prayed. We had one chance to get off, and anything could happen in the next thirty seconds. I watched the airspeed indicator climb slowly. We were approaching the point at which there isn't enough airspeed for takeoff and not enough room left on the runway to abort. Aborting takeoff here would mean falling down the cliff.

I had no idea how much runway we had left, but at this point it was academic. Now or never. I hauled back hard on the wheel.

The nose came up and the wheels left the ground and then we were airborne, not a second too soon. The downdraft from the cliff face hit us and we dipped, but we were out over the valley and soaring now, the burning mission station behind us and receding fast. We were safe, on our way to Mount Hagen and civilization.

Sam put her arms around my neck and kissed me. "Congratulations. For a has-been pilot, you didn't do too bad."

I kissed her back. "Exciting vacation, huh?" My hands were trembling on the wheel.

"Next time," she said, "I'll go somewhere safer. Weren't you telling me about Mexico – about the beach at moonlight?"

"The crabs come out by the thousands," I said. "You've never seen anything like it. Oh, shit."

"What's wrong?"

Something on the instrument panel had caught my eye. The gauge for the main fuel tank, to be exact. The needle had shown nearly full a moment ago. Now it was at two-thirds full. And dropping.

"We're losing fuel," I said. "One of those spears must have pierced the tank."

"How serious is it?"

I thought about that for a moment. It was the middle of the night, we were flying through unfamiliar mountain territory, losing fuel. Maybe the spare tank had a few gallons in it. Maybe not.

I smiled at her. "Be an angel," I said. "Go in the back there and see if Pastor Fairley might have stashed a couple of parachutes somewhere."

CHAPTER TWENTY

Barry Sears glared at us across his desk as he ran up the score on his fingers. "One rental car, one cyclone fence, one private aircraft—"

"The plane's not a complete write-off," I said. "Anyway, I'd have been all right if someone had turned the field lights on."

"It was two o'clock in the morning, for Christ's sake." Sears bit the words off, the ends of his mustache vibrating with anger. "Why on earth were you trying to land an aircraft at Mount Hagen airport at two o'clock in the morning?"

"It's a long story," I said.

Sears nodded. "I'm sure it is, Mr. Donovan." He resumed his count. "One rental car, one cyclone fence, one private aircraft, and one prefabricated storage hangar."

I nodded. "A shame about the hangar, I agree. Planes are hard to control once they start to slide. I've had it happen a couple of times."

Sears ignored me, picking up a typed sheet. "There are also reports of fire in a native village north of Mount Hagen. What do you know about that?"

I looked him straight in the eye. "Nothing, sir. It's true that the locals were a little excited when we left, but Pastor Fairley said that was normal. You'd have to ask him about the fire."

Sears snorted. "I've been trying to. Fairley hasn't been heard from in two days. Not since you went up there, in fact." He laid his meaty hands flat on the desk and leaned forward. "I had my doubts about you right from the start, Donovan. I'd have you – and your girlfriend – in the lockup right now if I could. We're sending a man up to Tavi Mission tomorrow morning. If Fairley wants to make a complaint, it'll be my pleasure to sort you out, boyo."

He let his breath out. "Right now, however, you're free to go, more's the pity. Just understand one thing, mate. I want you to stop doing whatever you've been doing, you understand? No more mucking about. I hear you've been stirring again, I'll have your balls for beads."

I stood up. "Is that all?"

His eyes narrowed. "Not quite. There's going to be money owing for the damage you've caused. Quite a bit of money, I imagine. So stay close to town, and don't plan on leaving the island until you've settled your account. Do we understand each other?"

"Perfectly."

Sears stood up. "Then I'll not keep you," he said.

* * *

"Those are the numbers," I said into the phone. "Find out who they belong to and see if there's some connection."

Bone Brown's voice was clear but distant on the overseas line. "Will do. How are things going out there?"

"Hard to explain," I said. "But definitely interesting. There's a lot more to this than meets the eye. How's Freddie doing?"

"So-so. The hearing's next week, and he's worried about going back to jail. His girlfriend's a gem, but she's had a tough time keeping his spirits up. He keeps asking for you, Max. When are you coming back to San Francisco?"

I sighed. "I need another few days, Bone. I'll be back as soon as I can – tell him that. In the meantime, work on those telephone numbers I gave you, okay? It's the best lead we've had so far."

When I hung up, I felt depressed. If the telephone numbers didn't turn something up, we were finished. There was nothing more to go on. The trail that had led to the Ginta village had petered out suddenly. It was a lurid tale of corruption and greed in the jungle, good for a couple of column inches in the local papers, but it led nowhere, and none of it would help Freddie very much. And if the hearing was next week, time was running out.

I flipped idly through Dunham's small notebook. Once again I saw the word 'Blue.' The old derelict, I thought. The third man in the photograph. What had the pilot said? He lived at the Papuan Hotel, drank in the local bars.

Sam came out of the bathroom, her hair done up in a towel. "I'm exhausted," she said. "But clean, finally. And ready for bed. What about you?"

I stood up. "Not yet," I said. "I think I'll go out for a quick drink."

She stared at me. "Are you serious?"

I nodded. "Get some rest," I said. "I'll be back before you know it."

It didn't turn out quite that way.

* * *

Musgrave Street in downtown Port Moresby is short and contains only five things of note: the Papuan Cinema, the Papuan Hotel, the Moresby Hotel, the Steamships Trading Co., and Burns Philp Ltd. The Papuan Hotel, for all its pretensions, had always been a dump, and it didn't look any different now to how it had eight years ago, which was the last time I'd set foot in the place. An overweight Motuan with his hair done in a Little Richard pompadour sat behind the registration desk and raised his eyebrows as I walked over.

I smiled to show I was nice. "I'm looking for one of your guests. A man called Blue. Can you give me his room number?"

The Motuan spat betel juice into a coffee can beside him.

"Blue Thompson? Blue's not a guest, sport, he's an employee. He sleeps out back in the spare room, but he's not in right now." His small eyes looked me up and down. "He's boozing. At the usual place, most likely."

I smiled again. "Here in the hotel?"

The Motuan's lip curled a millimeter. "You don't shit where you eat, mate." His fat thumb jerked over his shoulder. "Down the street at the Moresby's where he usually lies up."

I was halfway out the door when he called to me. "Tell him he's got to get the bloody kitchen mopped out early tomorrow morning. Tell him that."

The Moresby Hotel, of marginally better standard, was a hundred feet down the street. I had a pretty good idea of how this was going to go by now, so I didn't bother with the lounge bar upstairs. I went straight into the public bar, in the basement.

The noise and the smell hit me the moment I walked through the door. Do-gooders often criticize New Guinea's drinking code, which stipulates that females are categorically not allowed in public bars. There was a reason for this, and it was spread out before me in all its glory.

Men sat or lay on the floor in small groups, beer bottles stacked in front of them, as they argued, sang, and shouted in a wild cacophony of noise. The floor crunched with shards of broken glass, and under the strong tang of spilled beer and cigarette smoke, I caught the heavier odor of bitter vomit.

I was the only white man in the place. Or nearly so.

Blue Thompson slumped against a table at the back, rolling a cigarette from a bag of Bugler tobacco. The table in front of him was littered with beer bottles. As I watched he finished building the cigarette and pawed the tabletop for matches, knocking over two empty bottles in the process. No one in the bar took the slightest bit of notice.

It was him, all right. The seamed and ruined face at the table matched the one in the photograph perfectly. Under his thin and greasy red hair, Blue's eyes were shell craters. He looked like a desiccated Danny Kaye, and in a few years, if his liver held out, he'd be straining hair tonic through Italian bread for his morning pick-me-up.

He looked up and saw me standing in front of his table. "What the bloody hell do you want?" He didn't say it nastily. It was just his way of opening a conversation.

I shrugged. "Thought I might join you, if you don't mind."

Blue smiled, showing me teeth like timbers from a shipwreck. "Scared of the locals, are we? Starve the lizards, boyo, these drongos here are too drunk to do a body much harm. But take a pew, by all means." He half rose to his feet, bumping the table in the process. Another beer bottle smashed on the concrete floor. He wasn't drunk yet, but he would be soon.

"I'm Johnnie Thompson," he said. "They call me Blue on account of the hair."

"Max Donovan," I said. We shook hands.

He peered at me. "You're not from around here." It wasn't a question.

"San Francisco." I waited to see his reaction, but nothing showed in his face. So I pushed it a little. "I'm flying helicopters for the mining company. One of their regulars got killed awhile back. Guy named Binky Dunham."

His eyes grew somber, seeming to sink back farther into his head. He stared at me for a long while. "Dunham was my mate," he said finally. "Him and me was in business together. In a manner of speaking."

"Yeah? What sort of business?"

His face snapped shut like a trapdoor. "Nosy bugger, aren't you? What the hell you doing here, anyway?"

I shrugged. "The beer's cheaper here than upstairs."

It was the right thing to say. "Right you are, mate. Right you are." He nodded sagely, draining his bottle of South Pacific Green.

I knew just what to do. "Don't get up," I said. "It's my shout."

Blue's smile widened. "Decent of you, mate."

I went to the bar and brought back two beers.

"Thanks, son," said Blue. He raised the fresh beer bottle and drained it, his prominent Adam's apple working furiously. "Lord, I'm as dry as a year-old cheese."

He set the beer bottle down and belched explosively. Then he glared at the drunks around him. "Y'know, son, the Territory used to be a good place, before independence. Now it's a bloody dog's breakfast. Look at 'em. Stupid bloody no-hopers, all of 'em. Pay night's open slather in places like this." He swung his ruined eyes to me. "You'd better stick with me, lad, if you're going to be tasting the amber tonight." He peered at the empty beer bottle. "And there's better places than this to drink in. Feel like moving on?"

* * *

"Came up here during the war," Blue was saying. "Was in the Pacific Islands Regiment, right over there in

144

Taurama Barracks." He waved his hand vaguely toward the darkness.

I nodded wearily, wondering how much more beer Blue could possibly drink and how much money I had left in my pocket.

We were sitting in the outside – or 'garden' – bar of the Boroko Hotel. There hadn't been a garden anywhere near the spot for over fifty years, I estimated. If the public bar of the Moresby Hotel rated one on a scale of ten, the garden bar of the Boroko Hotel went far into the minus numbers.

About two hundred locals were grouped around the immovable concrete tables and benches, singing, shouting, and being sick. A string-band record played from somewhere, barely audible against the roar of the crowd. Against the cinder-block wall was a cage of thick steel bars. Inside it three sweating bartenders dispensed beer in paper cups.

Given the circumstances, it wasn't a bad system. The furniture was bolted in place – it couldn't be broken, burned, or thrown. No bottles to throw, either – no broken glass to fall on or to use as a weapon. Clean the floor with a hose in the morning and you were ready for another fun-filled evening of excitement.

"After the war," Blue was saying, "I hung around. So did some of my mates. There was three of us stayed, and another come back later. Four of us in all." He peered at me craftily. "We'd've done all right, too, if it hadn't of been for that bloody storm."

"What storm?"

"The one what sank the fuckin' boat, of course," he said patiently. "It was Binky who put me onto it, see – him and another bloke named MacKenzie. You don't know Brian MacKenzie, of course – he's another one of my mates from army days."

I sat up a little straighter. "Tell me about the boat, Blue," I said softly.

He looked around and lowered his voice. "It was a few months ago, now. We was onto a good lurk, me an' the others. Mates, we are – we help each other out. We was down at the Yacht Club one day, an' Binky asked if my old lorry still ran. Course it ran, I told him. So he said they needed a job done up the coast. We was gonna make our bloody fortunes, he said."

"And?"

He grimaced. "Buggered, that's what. Know the trade winds here on the south coast, what the locals call the *lahara*? Well, a great bleeding storm came up just as I was waitin' in the truck, on the beach, just this side of Delena. Boat was a mile or so offshore, trying to find its way through the reef. I could see her runnin' lights an' all. She hit the reef square."

"And sank?"

"Course she sank, you daft bugger. Went down like a sack of shit, right there in front of me. Crew jumped, but they never found a soul. All drowned, I reckon."

He shook his head. "That was when it all began to go bad. MacKenzie left, and then Binky went and pranged himself up in the jungle somewheres." He looked at me, his eyes cloudy with faded hopes. "That was my chance to make it, laddie. And the bloody boat went down, not half a mile off Mauro Point over on Yule Island."

He was slurring badly now, hardly able to hold his head up. Nothing to lose now with a direct question. "What were you carrying, Blue? What was the boat supposed to pick up?"

He stared at me. "Carrying? I was carrying sweet fuck-all, mate. I was picking something up, not sending something off."

I leaned forward and grasped his arm. "What was it, Blue? What was on the boat?"

He shook free. "Don't know, and that's the truth. Never knew what it was. Boxes, Binky said, wooden boxes. Heavy." His arm swept out and tipped over the last of his beer. "Whatever it was, it was worth a lot of money, I'll tell you that for free."

He stood up, weaving unsteadily. "Half a sec," he said. "She'll be right." Then he bent forward and vomited onto his shoes.

* * *

I had the large map of Papua New Guinea spread out on the floor and Binky Dunham's notebook in my hand. What had Blue said? Mauro Point, just off Yule Island. That's where the boat had gone down.

I looked again at the numbers scribbled in the notebook: 'Blue – 1463230E851S.' With my finger I traced the lines on the map. Longitude one forty-six degrees, thirty-two minutes and thirty seconds east of Greenwich. Latitude eight degrees and fifty-one minutes south of the equator.

Just off Yule Island.

"Bingo," I said softly.

CHAPTER TWENTY-ONE

We left Port Moresby on the morning tide, heading south by southwest through the Basilisk Passage. Daugo Island slipped by on the starboard side, followed by the smaller islands of Haidana and Idihi. Soon we were crossing the outer reef, the laurabada trade wind in our face.

It was a dinkum day, as the Australians say. The *Kokoda Lass* cut smartly through the water, her twin hulls slapping the waves solidly. The sun was strong and bright, tempered by the breeze and the sea spray, and the colors of the water seemed to vibrate. We passed a large pua-pua full of fishermen, who waved and shouted greetings in Motu.

An early morning call to Barry Sears at police headquarters had elicited the information that for diving and deep-sea fishing, Ron Purvis was the only man to have. What Purvis didn't know about the reefs and islands up and down the coast, from Daru to Milne Bay, wasn't worth knowing, according to Sears. A call to Purvis and some negotiation over a beer at nine o'clock, plus most of our remaining cash, had set us on our way an hour later.

Clouds were massing over the tops of the Owen Stanley Range inland. I stood at the rail and watched them, sniffing the salt air and recovering from my hangover. When we had cleared the reef I walked forward to where Sam was talking to Purvis in the wheelhouse.

"And what's the gun for, Mr. Purvis?" she was saying as I came up the ladder. I looked and saw a businesslike .30-30 rifle clipped upright beside the wheel.

Purvis smiled, showing large white teeth, startling against his deep tan. He was a large man in his late fifties, built like an oaken cask and burned to mahogany by years on the open water. He was dressed in white duck shorts, flip-flops, and a battered terry-cloth cap with a picture of a beer bottle and the words '*Mi laik wanpela moa*' on it.

"Sharks, miss," he said. "Lots of people like to go out over the reef, snorkel a bit in the shallows." He patted the gun. "I keep a lookout with this."

"In the shallows?" said Sam. "Surely there's not much danger there?"

Purvis's smile widened and his eyes narrowed to slits. "Round here, miss, anytime you're in water over yer ankles, you're in trouble. We got just about everything that's nasty in these waters." He waved his hand out over the waves. "Sea snakes, for example. Most venomous creature in the world. Sea wasps. Moray eels. Barracuda. And sharks."

He adjusted his sunglasses, his expression serious. "Including the great white itself. So I keep a full magazine in the gun and my eyes open all the time anyone's in the water."

Sam shivered. "I'm terrified of sharks," she said. "Suppose you're underwater? What do you do then?"

"You don't need to panic," I said, moving up beside Sam and putting my arm lightly on her shoulder. "Sharks are simply curious most of the time. They'll swim close, take a look, and decide to move off elsewhere."

Purvis looked at me. "Had a bit of experience with sharks, have we, Mr. Donovan?"

"A bit," I said. "In the Caribbean."

Purvis grunted. "Never been there. Sharks are curious, all right. They're sometimes hungry as well. If there's dead fish or offal in the water, they'll get properly worked up. Then you want to get back against something – the hull of the boat, a coral head, anything. Flatten yourself against it.'

He opened a locker and took out what looked like a policeman's nightstick. He passed it to Sam. "And if you have to, miss, you use this on the bugger."

Sam frowned as she turned it over in her hands. "Can you really hit them hard enough to hurt them with that?"

Purvis smiled. "You can hit 'em with it. You can also shoot them with it. It's a shark billy. Look at the end – see that hole there?" He turned the grip around so that she could see the firing ring. "Rotate that ring to arm it. Then press this stud here. It fires a twelve-gauge lead slug."

Sam whistled softly. "That should do the job, shouldn't it?"

Purvis nodded. "It will if you get 'em in the head. And you'd better make sure you do. Only way to stop a shark is to hit 'em in the brain."

"And if you miss?"

Purvis chuckled, a rumbling sound that came deep from his big belly. "There's only one slug in the chamber. Send it wide and you're fish bait, miss. Fish bait."

* * *

Three in the afternoon found us just outside the reef in the narrow passage between Yule Island and the mainland. Mauru Point lay off to port. The tiny village of Delena, where Blue had said he'd brought the truck, sat a mile away on our starboard side.

The sea was holding calm and the wind was low and coming from the southwest. I made Purvis check the coordinates carefully and position the *Kokoda Lass* exactly as Binky Dunham had written it in his notebook.

"Are you looking for something in particular, Mr. Donovan?" Purvis asked as we dropped anchor. "There's better diving off the point there."

"There's a wreck somewhere around here," I said. "They told me about it in Moresby. I thought I'd try and locate it if I could."

Purvis glanced down at the chart he held in front of him. It showed the two curving arms of the coral reef clearly, and the narrow break through which ships could gain access to the calm and shallow lagoon. Beyond the reef the water dropped off sharply into the open sea. We were anchored in the break itself, just inside the reef, in about thirty feet of water.

"Any idea where she might be?" Purvis said.

"Somewhere around here, that's all I know. I'll just have to work both sides of the reef a mile or so in either direction." I glanced at the sun. "There's time for some diving today, in fact."

Purvis nodded. "You're the boss." He looked at Sam. "Just a formality, mind you, but do you both know how to dive?"

"I'm NAUI certified," I said. "And Sam's had ten hours of pool instruction." I didn't mention that it had been in the police pool. "She won't be going down today, though."

"Fair enough. I'll show you where the gear is, then."

The *Kokoda Lass* was fitted out for open-sea operation, both diving and sport fishing. In addition to bunks for six,

Purvis had a well-equipped galley and a small but comfortable lounge with a wet bar. Down below there were refrigerated lockers to store the catch in, as well as large tubs of chum to use as bait for the big fish. A full-sized compressor filled the diving tanks, and Purvis had a wide selection of high-quality diving gear. Barry Sears had been right; Purvis was the man to see if you wanted to dive.

I eased into a wet suit and strapped on my buoyancy compensator with its attached air tank. I tested the regulator and checked my air supply on the gauge.

"I'll need another two tanks," I said to Purvis.

"No worries, mate. Got as many as you want here."

I nodded. "Feel like diving with me? You're more than welcome, if you'd like."

Purvis shook his head. "My diving days are over, Mr. Donovan. Both ears are buggered, and one of my lungs is shot to hell." He chuckled. "Should have taken better care of myself. Today, all I do is watch the other divers." He hefted the gun. "And try to keep 'em safe."

Sam looked suspiciously at the knife I was strapping to my leg. "For sharks?"

I laughed. "For poking at things. And also for cutting myself free of abandoned fishing lines." I pointed to the rack of wet suits. "Sure you don't want to come along?"

She shook her head. I nodded, put on my mask, and rolled backward off the transom.

The water was crystal clear and calm, the visibility excellent. I wasn't sure what I was looking for, but I'd know it when I found it, that was certain. Any boat that could cross the Gulf of Carpentaria at night would have to be a decent size – thirty feet at least. It had gone down less than three months ago, and the currents in this part of the Papuan Gulf weren't that strong. By rights it should be still visible, big enough to stand out on the sloping sandy bottom like a sore thumb.

I worked the bottom in quarter-mile stretches a hundred yards apart, keeping a rough course by my wrist compass and occasional sightings on the headland of the point. I kept my depth shallow to conserve air and energy and to avoid decompression stops. I swam slowly, parallel to the underwater cliff face, the point where the reef shelved off abruptly and dropped down into the real ocean beyond, a thousand feet deep and more. The water over the reef was blue-green and dappled with sunlight. Beyond the cliff it went from deep blue to depthless and infinite black.

Some people are afraid of heights, some of spiders. I was afraid of the deep water and of what lived within it. It was a primal fear, one that no amount of reason or science could dispel. It was rooted in my very genes, and as I gazed into the infinite depths of the water to the side of me, I shivered. Out there was shark country, where the great white was king, knifing soundlessly through the water, head twisting this way and that to catch the scent of blood. All my childhood fears and nightmares seemed to be embodied in that dark depthless stretch of water.

I stifled my fear and moved back over the shallow part of the reef. Sharks could still pose a danger here, but I knew they preferred to hunt in the deeper open water. I drifted above the sandy bottom, breathing slowly and regularly through the regulator, as my eyes searched the bottom for a sign – any sign – of a wreck. Debris, perhaps; a length of anchor chain; spilled cargo. Collections of fish might indicate part of the wreck; several times I dived down briefly to investigate schools of brightly colored fish, only to find them busy devouring a morsel of food.

I labored on through the rest of the afternoon, stopping at six o'clock, just before sundown. I had used up nearly three bottles of air, and I was more tired than I'd thought; Sam had to help me up the ladder into the boat. I was also cold through to the bone. Although tropic waters seem warm at first, they steal heat slowly but surely, and even my wet suit hadn't been protection enough.

* * *

After dinner that night we sat in comfortable deck chairs on the aft platform of the big catamaran, sipping icy-cold bottled lager and staring up at the brilliant starry sky. We were at anchor about a half a mile offshore in sixty feet of water. I estimated that I'd covered less than a mile of the western side of the reef.

I turned my beer bottle slowly in my hands and stared up at the Southern Cross, thinking. Tomorrow would be more of the same. And if, in another day or so, we found nothing, then we might as well give it up. If I was wrong and the boat had foundered on the reef instead of in the channel, she could be anywhere to either side. And if she'd hit the reef, she might have tumbled down the steep cliff into the deep. If that were the case, no one would find her, ever. In effect, I thought, we were looking for a very small needle in a very large haystack.

"Mr. Donovan."

I came back from where my thoughts had taken me, to hear Ron Purvis speaking to me. "Mr. Donovan," he said again.

"Yes, Mr. Purvis?"

"Had enough?"

"Enough what?"

"Enough diving. You did more diving today, Mr. Donovan, than most of my customers do in a month. You planning to dive again tomorrow?"

I smiled. "You can't ever get enough of a good thing, Mr. Purvis." I gestured with my beer bottle. "Tomorrow I'll try the other side of the reef – over more to the east. I'd like to start early, say about eight. That all right with you?"

Purvis nodded. "It's your money, Mr. Donovan," he said. "Although personally, I think you're wasting your time. Even if you find this mysterious ship you think is down there, what do you think you're going to find on board her? Pirate treasure, perhaps?"

I drained my beer. "Perhaps, Mr. Purvis. Perhaps. Let's find the wreck first, shall we?" I stood up. "Eight o'clock, then, if the wind and current are right. I'll need four bottles filled and ready to go."

Purvis looked at me. "They'll be ready. Like I said, Mr. Donovan, it's your money."

CHAPTER TWENTY-TWO

I found the wreck the next day, just after lunch. I was working the east arm of the reef this time, my muscles sore from the unaccustomed labor. I coasted twenty feet below the surface as I patrolled the reef, working out from the shallows to the very edge of the deep.

Just then I spotted her. She lay on her side in forty feet of water, poised on the lip of the reef's edge. I adjusted my buoyancy compensator and dropped down, my heart beating fast as I approached the splintered hull.

She was an oceangoing ketch, fifty feet long. The name on her transom identified her as the *Kumar*, out of Suva. It wasn't hard to see why she had gone down. The hull had been smashed inward, almost certainly by one of the huge coral heads that dotted the area. They rose up like underwater buttes from the main coral bank, towering ten or sometimes twenty feet above the main part of the reef.

Small brightly colored fish had already claimed her as a holiday resort. They pranced in stately fashion in and out of her hull, pausing briefly to examine the various bright anemones and fronds that had sprouted from the crevices. Wrecks attract fish, but they also attract other, less playful inhabitants of the deep. As I approached, a moray eel drew its ugly head back a fraction into its hole under a flat rock.

It lay poised motionless in the water, its tiny bright eyes watching me as I swam slowly by at a respectful distance.

I circled the wreck, peering into the ruined hull and the wheelhouse. I checked my air supply; it was down to three hundred pounds, which meant I should start back up. I cracked the valve on my buoyancy compensator and started slowly for the surface, making a mental list of the things I would need. Ropes, spare air bottles, some mesh collecting sacks, and a big light.

I shivered. The light would be a big help, but I didn't particularly want to go poking around inside the innards of the *Kumar*. I hoped there wouldn't be any bodies.

* * *

An hour later we had the *Kokoda Lass* positioned over the wreck, and I was ready. Back down under the water, it was cool and still and quiet, with only the occasional rippling frond to signal the presence of a weak current. I'd made up a rope sling and thrown it over the side just before diving down. I had a collecting bag clipped to my belt and a large and powerful flashlight slung around my wrist.

The moray slid farther back into its lair as I approached. I balanced the air in my buoyancy compensator so that I was floating eight or ten feet off the bottom, and then I began a slow tour of the *Kumar*. She'd hit on the opposite side of the hull from where the coral head had holed her, and her planks were smashed and gouged. She must have sunk pretty fast, I thought, to hit the bottom that hard.

The ship had carried a crew of from four to six, I guessed – more than enough to run her across the Gulf of Carpentaria and into Papuan waters. If Blue Thompson's guess had been right, they were all dead now. Snapping on my light, I dropped down from the deck and peered inside the gaping hole in the hull, into the hold.

Boxes. Twenty or thirty large wooden crates, jumbled together in a mad pile. Securely fastened with spikes, banded with inch-wide steel straps. The markings on the side had been crudely painted over. I wrestled one out onto the sandy bottom and turned it over, looking for clues as to what it might contain. Even underwater it was heavy.

Sucking hard on my regulator, I looped my makeshift cargo sling around the box and pulled it tight. Then I cracked the valve on my buoyancy compensator and headed for the surface, admiring the silvery wobble of my bubbles as I slowly followed them to the light and the air above.

"Give me a hand," I said to Purvis as I came over the side.

"What did you find?" asked Sam. "What is it?"

"No idea," I grunted, heaving hard on the rope. "Boxes – lots of them. In the hold. Heavy. For all I know, they're full of ball bearings."

But they weren't, and I knew it. Five minutes later I pried the top off the crate with a crowbar, stood up, and let out a deep breath.

Purvis peered forward. "Well, shit my socks," he said in a low voice.

They were M16 rifles, smeared with grease and wrapped in heavy-gauge plastic to keep the water out. There must have been twenty of them in the crate, packed like sardines.

I ripped the plastic off one of the rifles and inspected it. Etched into the stock were US Army identification numbers. "Stolen," I said.

Sam looked at the guns and then at me. "How many more crates are down there?"

"A couple of dozen at least. If they're all like this one, there's enough ordnance there to fight a small war." I turned to Purvis. "I'm going to bring the rest of them up. I'll need those extra bottles."

He nodded. "No problem. We can rig the sling through the winch there – get 'em up for you a lot faster." He turned to Sam. "It might help if you was to go down and lend a hand with the fastening, miss, while I work the winch."

"He's right," I said. "Want to try it?"

"Sure."

Purvis grinned. "That's the spirit. You get her kitted out, Donovan. I'll go call in on the radio and get the weather forecast for the afternoon. Wouldn't do to get caught by a storm."

He stumped off toward the wheelhouse, whistling softly.

* * *

Half an hour later I was back under the water, this time with Sam close at my side, her eyes wide and anxious under the mask. We stayed just below the surface while she got used to breathing through the regulator. Then I took her arm, vented my buoyancy compensator, and we sank down together until we hovered just above the wreck. I pointed to the moray eel glaring at us from under his rock and made a biting motion with my fingers. Sam nodded to show she understood.

Together we began to bring out the crates and stack them on the sandy bottom. It was hard work, and both of us were gulping air as fast as we could. Two tanks of air and half an hour later, we had all the crates out on the sand. There were three different sizes. I guessed that the small ones contained grenades, pistols, ammunition, and plastic explosive, the middle-size ones the M16s. I couldn't decide whether the long flat crates held machine guns or some kind of bazooka.

We'll know soon enough, I thought. We were nearly out of air again, so I switched each of us to a fresh bottle.

Then I attached the first of the crates to the sling and tugged on the end to signal Purvis to start the winch. Almost immediately the crate rose smoothly from the bottom and began to recede away from us toward the surface. I motioned to Sam to help me get the second sling around another crate while we waited for the hook to return.

It was easier work now, and our breathing returned to near normal as we hooked one crate after another to the winch line. I checked my watch, adding my bottom times. At forty feet I could stay underwater for up to one hundred minutes without a decompression stop, and I had nearly reached that limit now.

Three crates to go now. Purvis had asked me to tell him when we were getting near the end. I signaled for Sam to stay where she was and rose up, breaking water a few yards from the boat.

Purvis was standing on the foredeck, his rifle cradled under one arm.

"Three more to go," I shouted.

"Good on ya," he said. "I've got the rest of 'em stacked under the aft awning. And there's cold beer ready for when you finish."

I grinned and gave him the thumbs-up, sliding back under the water.

We finished attaching the last of the crates. I pulled on the line and the winch began to haul. As I gazed upward at the crate receding away from me toward the hull of the *Kokoda Lass*, I saw a disturbance on the surface, toward the stern of the boat. Something had hit the water. As I watched I saw whatever it was break apart and start to slowly sink, a faint pink cloud spreading out around it in the water.

With horror I realized that the stuff in the water was chum – the fish bait Purvis had stored in his freezers. What the hell was going on? I motioned for Sam to stay where she was and headed for the surface fast.

I broke water a dozen feet from the bow. Purvis was nowhere in sight. "There's bait in the water!" I yelled. Nothing moved on deck. "Purvis, can you hear me?"

A shot crashed out, splashing the water inches from my left ear. I turned in the water and saw Purvis coming fast out of the wheelhouse, rifle in hand. He stepped to the rail, raised the gun, and fired again.

I flipped sideways in the water as the second shot hit inches away from my ear. Then I jackknifed and dived under the boat. Looking up, I saw three other bullets drill into the water at the spot where I'd been a second ago. I moved down under the keel, where I knew he couldn't hit me, and hung motionless in the water, trying to figure things out.

Just then the first of the sharks arrived, attracted by the smell of blood in the water. It bore straight in, twisting its head sideways just the merest bit to gulp down a chunk of fish bait. It gave me a flat-eyed stare as it went by. Farther out on the reef I could see two other sharks headed this way, nosing in from the deeps beyond the reef. Another load of fish bait hit the water above me, sending a pink cloud of blood out. The blood would attract more sharks and drive them into a feeding frenzy, where they would snap and rip at anything, even each other.

Hobson's choice, I thought. If we tried to get back on the boat, Purvis would shoot us. If we stayed in the water, the sharks would eat us. I looked down at Sam. She was moving backward slowly, seeking the relative safety of the wreck's hull, her eyes fixed on the circling sharks above.

A big gray shark nosed toward me inquisitively. I took my big flashlight and banged it on its nose, hard. It veered off in search of easier prey. As long as there was fish bait to be devoured, the sharks would stick with that. Once they'd snatched it all up, they'd come after the next course on the menu. Between now and then I had to figure out what the hell to do. I glanced quickly at my pressure gauge and cursed. I was running out of air.

Another load of bait hit the water, this time on the opposite side of the hull. There were half a dozen sharks around the boat now and more on the way. I vented air from my buoyancy compensator and dropped smoothly to the sandy bottom. Sam was flattened back against the hull of the wreck, her shark billy in her hand. Her eyes were wide with terror as she grabbed my hand.

She was breathing hard, hyperventilating. I shook her hand off and looked at her pressure gauge. Two hundred pounds left. She'd be out of air soon as well, ten minutes at the most. But it didn't really matter, I thought – in less time than that, the sharks would take care of us. Soon the water around the *Kokoda Lass* would be so thick with predators that we'd stand no chance of surviving. We had to get out of the water. And that meant somehow taking care of Purvis.

We had to get on the boat.

Purvis would know we were coming – he'd be able to spot the bubbles rising from our regulators. There was no way we could prevent the bubbles from escaping – they were a dead giveaway to our position. Unless, I thought, we stopped using the regulators. I grabbed Sam's hand again and bled air into my buoyancy compensator, pulling her up with me toward the hull of the *Kokoda Lass* above.

We bumped up against one of the twin hulls near the aft end, where the stairs were. Purvis would be expecting me to try and use the stairs, and so I needed to reinforce his guesses about what I'd do. Once I had us positioned so that our bubbles were escaping aft, I pushed Sam up flat beside the short keel. The sharks were getting nosier now, and more aggressive, but if she stayed flat to the hull, they couldn't easily take her.

I took my tank and buoyancy compensator off and fastened them to a strut with the webbing straps. I made signs to Sam that she should release air from my regulator every few seconds. I stripped off my fins and weight belt and watched them drift slowly down toward the bottom.

One of the fins was snatched by a shark less than ten feet after it left my hand. I hit another shark hard on the side of its head with my billy as it veered in toward me.

Then I took a last long gulp of air from my regulator and pushed off, moving down the long hull toward the bow.

Toward where Purvis would least expect me to make an appearance.

I paused at the anchor chain to collect myself. The next step had to happen very fast and very smoothly. I had to climb the anchor chain and get on deck before Purvis could shoot me. I had never been any good at throwing knives, so I left it on my belt. Instead, I took the shark billy and gripped its leather thong between my teeth.

If Purvis was aft, watching Sam's bubbles, I might have a chance. If he were waiting for me in the bow, I had no chance at all. Time to find out.

I came up out of the water fast, feet scrabbling against the sloping sides of the boat as I heaved myself up the anchor chain hand over hand. One pull, two pulls, and I was up at deck level, looking at Purvis's back as he stooped over the railing aft. Three pulls – he heard the noise now and began to turn. Four pulls and I was reaching up with one hand to grasp the railing. Purvis turning all the way around now, the rifle coming up as he realized what was happening.

I flipped myself over the edge onto the boat, moving fast, presenting minimal target area. Purvis fired, splintering the deck inches from my face. I rolled sideways onto my back as I reached for the shark billy.

I cocked my arm back and did a fast sit-up, letting the billy go with all my might. It caught Purvis square in the face. He roared in pain, dropping the rifle as his hands came up and he staggered backward.

I reached Purvis just as he hit the low deck rail and started to fall. I hooked two fingers into his belt and held him balanced over the edge. Both of us looked down at the sharks circling in the clear water. I thought about just letting him go.

"Jesus, mate." His voice was a croak.

"Say the secret word."

"For the love of God, mate."

Then I remembered that Sam was still down under the water. "Your lucky day, Mr. Purvis," I murmured as I pulled him back to safety.

CHAPTER TWENTY-THREE

Too far to swim to shore," I said.

"Definitely too far," Sam said. "And," she added, "there are the sharks."

"There are indeed the sharks."

We were anchored just off a small coral head some three miles out to sea. The chart identified it as Bavo Island, and Port Moresby lay fifteen miles farther east along the coast. Bavo Island was about two hundred yards long and thirty wide, and consisted of beach and a single dried-out palm tree. It also had an inhabitant, who at the moment was hopping from one foot to the other on the hot sand.

"Let's talk it over, Donovan," Purvis said. "Christ, mate, you leave me out here and I'll bloody well starve to death."

"Die of thirst, more likely," I said.

Sam nodded. "You're going to lose water fast, you know, with just that bathing suit on."

"We can make a deal," Purvis said. "Those guns are worth fifty thousand dollars. Bring me back on the boat and we can split the money."

"Why should I split the money with you?" I said. "After all, I've got the guns."

His expression grew crafty. "You've got the guns, sport, but I know who to sell 'em to. Without me, the guns are scrap iron."

"You had a buyer, then?"

"Too right we had a buyer. Cash in hand. Buggered it up for all of us when the damned boat went down. None of the rest of 'em know how to dive, and I can't. Binky was trying to find us a diver who'd keep his mouth shut, but he's dead now, isn't he?" He tried a weak smile. "What d'you say, mate, do we have a deal?"

I went down in the galley and returned a moment later with a carton of canned food and a plastic five-gallon jerrican of fresh water. I tossed the canned food over the rail onto the sand. "You'll need this," I said, "if you're planning on staying out here for a while."

His face grew thick with rage. "What the hell are you playing at, you bastard? I can't eat this – I've got nothing to bloody well open them with! This is no deal!"

"You're right," I said. I pulled a can opener out of my pocket and held it up. "This is the deal, Purvis. This little beauty here for the name of your buyer. And to show you I'm a nice guy, I'll throw in the water as well."

"You rotten–"

"Easy," said Sam, raising the rifle a fraction. "Let's not get abusive. We've had enough unpleasantness for one day, don't you think?"

I let him think about it for a while. Finally he said, "All right. His name's Das. He's not a local, he's an Asian from one of those places in South America. He–"

"Mohinder Das? The university lecturer?"

"He's the one," said Purvis. "He's the buyer. He'll give fifty thousand dollars for the shipment, cash on delivery."

I thought about it. It made as much sense as anything, I reckoned. "How do I know you're telling the truth?" I said finally.

Purvis laughed. "It's Das all right, fair dinkum. If you don't believe me, check it out. I'll still be here when you get back, won't I?"

I threw the can opener and the water to him. "One last question," I said. "Who were your partners? I know about Dunham and Blue Thompson, and about the missionary. Who else was in on it?"

Purvis looked at me, squinting in the glare of the sun.

"Go to buggery, Donovan," he said. "I don't care about Das, but I won't grass on my mates. I'll fry out here first."

He meant it. I started the engines and shifted the *Kokoda Lass* into reverse. As we moved away from Bavo Island I pointed to the lone palm tree. "Try and stay out of the sun," I shouted. "And have a wonderful time!"

* * *

"So what are we going to tell Sears?"

I stopped staring at the beads of sweat on the side of my beer can and looked over at Sam. "Huh?"

"Captain Sears," she repeated. "What are we going to tell him?"

"About what?"

She sighed. "About Purvis, you dummy. And why he's no longer with us."

"We'll think of something," I said, and went back to studying my can of South Pacific Lager.

Sam shook her head with irritation and went below. A moment later I could hear dishes being rattled around in the tiny galley.

Sure we'll think of something, I told myself. But that wasn't what was on my mind right now. Instead, I was thinking of the thirty crates of extremely dangerous implements of murder and destruction that we had salvaged from the wreck of the *Kumar.* For which Ron Purvis had tried to kill us. Accounting for Purvis's whereabouts was the least of our worries right now; he was a closed chapter, a finished story. But the guns, ammunition, and explosives in the crates in front of me were a continuing melodrama, one that wouldn't go away no matter what we did. And that required some creative scheming.

I checked the compass and made a slight course correction. The *Kokoda Lass* was headed slowly back to Port Moresby. I wasn't in that much of a hurry to get there, however, because once we arrived I had to do something. And right now I hadn't a clue as to what it was going to be.

Mohinder Das was involved, but what in hell was a professor of politics doing with so much firepower? There were enough machine guns, M16s, M7A2 antipersonnel mines, Colt pistols, and light and medium mortars to wipe out all of Port Moresby. All of it was US Army standard issue; all of it was in its original casing. The covering paint had flaked on some of the crates, the words 'Oakland Army Depot' clearly visible underneath. I remembered the newspaper story I'd seen about thefts from the armory. It seemed like a century ago.

What linked Das together with Purvis, Blue Thompson, Pastor Fairley, and the late Binky Dunham? How did the weapons figure in all of it? A coup was ridiculous – wasn't it?

I had to get back to Port Moresby, that much was clear. There were still too many unknowns in the equation; I needed a telephone, a car, and a safe place to stay for a couple of days until I figured things out. And all the while, time was running out for Fat Freddie Fields.

I finished the last of my beer and burped gently. Finding a safe place to stay is easier said than done, I thought. No place was safe now. I'd been poking around at the edges of something very big, and whatever it was, it was beginning to stir.

I felt a hand on my shoulder. "Another beer?" said Sam.

I nodded, and she gave me a can of SP Lager.

I squeezed her hand. "Thanks," I said. "Going to keep me company?"

She smiled and plopped down into a deck chair beside me.

I sipped my beer and held the wheel steady with my toes as I savored the feel of the air and the sun on our bodies. I looked around the tiny wheelhouse at the bits and pieces that Purvis had tacked on the walls. Some photographs of men holding up big fish, a year-old calendar from the ANZ Bank in Port Moresby, a charter-boat operator's license, a list of VHF radio call signs for the Central and Milne Bay provinces.

My eyes lingered on a faded framed photograph of Purvis's army unit, the men looking hot and uncomfortable against a backdrop of palms. After a moment I got to my feet, put down my beer, and moved closer to get a better look. I looked at it for a long time. Then I nodded, took a swallow of beer, and moved to the other wall to study the list of VHF radio operators.

"What's going on?" said Sam.

I turned. "Huh?"

"You're whistling. A little soft tune, just under your breath. You did that before, when you matched the coordinates from Dunham's notebook with the chart of the coast." She looked at me suspiciously. "You've just figured something out, haven't you?"

"Naw," I lied. I reached over and picked up my beer. "To tell the truth, I was just thinking about what to have for supper."

"Supper? Well, there's canned food and stuff we could fix down in the galley."

I shook my head. "We'll be in Port Moresby in two hours," I said. "Let's eat out, to celebrate."

She smiled. "What are we celebrating?"

I took her hand and pulled her close. "Being alive," I said.

Then I kissed her. She floated in my arms, weightless, her body heat blending with mine. We stayed that way for a long time. When we broke apart her eyes were bright.

"Come here," she said. It was little more than a whisper. I followed her up to the deck and watched in mute wonder as she stripped off her swimsuit and drew me down on the smooth decking beside her.

We made love with an unexpected silence and passion, broken only at the end by her cry of release, followed closely by my own. We lay a long time beside each other, still coupled, nuzzling and touching with noses and fingertips, celebrating life and each other.

I licked salt from her neck and ears, and then from her cheeks, where wetness lay in flat drops. I drew back and looked at her. "Thinking about this afternoon? Don't. It's over, Sam. We're all right."

She stared back at me defiantly, tears glistening in her eyes. "We're not all right," she said. "And you know it. You're planning something right now, and it's going to be dangerous, isn't it?" She fixed me with her eyes. "Isn't it, Max?"

I nodded. "Maybe. Probably. Oh, shit, Sam, I don't know. What the hell do you want me to do?"

She drew me close. "Make love to me again, Max. Right now. That's what I want you to do."

* * *

We saw the lights at Napa Napa, west of Port Moresby, shortly after dark. We were just outside the reef, running dark, the motor throttled right back. I switched off the engine and silence fell across the water. The stars were magnificent, arcing across the sky in wild, random patterns. The Southern Cross hung high in velvet darkness, and far out to sea a freighter's lights winked unsteadily as it plowed south.

"End of the line," I said. "We'll take the inflatable in from here." I touched her cheek. "And once we're ashore, I'll buy you dinner. How's that sound?"

"Yum. I'll have to put some clothes on." She gestured at her tiny swimsuit. "Give me five minutes to change, okay?"

I nodded, and she disappeared below.

Five minutes was all I needed. I picked up a flashlight and the carry-on that held my clothes and headed for the rear deck. It took me less than a minute to locate one of the crates that held the pistols. I pried it open with my knife and pulled out a .38 automatic. I fished around inside the crate until I found the ammunition and selected two clips. Wiping everything clean with some cotton waste, I hid the pistol and the clips in my bag. I was back in the wheelhouse before Sam came back up the ladder, looking cool and elegant in a light cotton jumpsuit.

"Nice," I said, and kissed her lightly. "My turn to change."

Below decks, I put on tennis shoes, a pair of light slacks, and a loose barong tagalog shirt I'd picked up in Manila last year. I put one of the clips in my pocket and the other in the pistol. Then I shoved the pistol under my belt, in the small of my back. I did a quick check in the mirror while I combed my hair; nothing showed.

It's Saturday night, I thought, and I'm all dressed up with nowhere to go. Time to find some action.

* * *

We scuttled her outside the reef. It was deep out there, at least five hundred feet straight down, and away from the fishing grounds. No one would ever find her and her deadly cargo. The sea was calm and the stars shone with a warm and steady fire. We opened the cocks and stood offside in the inflatable dinghy and watched as the *Kokoda Lass* slid slowly under the water.

As she sank I felt a weight lifting from my shoulders. The stern vanished with a ripple and a gentle burp, and then there was nothing but the ocean and the stars and the warm darkness. I started the outboard motor and turned the dinghy toward the lights of Port Moresby Harbor, a mile away across the water. Sam touched my shoulder. "I'm glad that's over," she said.

I turned to look at her face, lovely in the starlight. "It's not over," I said. "Not till Freddie's free. Not till the fat lady sings."

We slipped quietly into a mooring at the Royal Papua Yacht Club and tied up without attracting attention. Waves lapped sleepily around the hulls of the boats as we walked up the dock. Across the road came sounds of muted revelry from the wide veranda of the clubhouse, where a hundred or so expatriates sweated and clutched cold schooners of beer.

I grunted with effort as I picked up the single crate of M16s I'd saved from the *Kokoda Lass*. I'd wrapped a sheet around it to hide the stenciled markings. Breathing hard, I humped it up to the end of the dock to where Sam had found a waiting taxi.

"The Islander Hotel, please," I gasped as I set the crate down heavily on the backseat.

The Papuan taxi driver hawked a gob of betel juice out the window and started the engine. "Sure thing," he said cheerfully. "What's in the box? Looks bloody heavy."

"Whisky," I said. "Just drive, okay?"

"No worries, mate." The driver slammed his bare foot to the floor and we roared out onto the road just in front of an approaching Toyota utility truck. Ignoring the furious blaring of the Toyota's horn, our taxi careered toward town, using the white line as a rough guide.

Ten minutes later we miraculously pulled up in front of the Islander. Now, I thought, for the tricky part. Inside our room I laid the crate on the bed and wiped the sweat from my forehead. "I need a shower, Sam," I said. "Go on down to the bar and order me a gin and tonic. I'll be there in ten minutes."

"Okay. Where are we going for dinner afterward?" she said.

I winked. "It's a surprise."

She smiled and closed the door.

As soon as she was gone I opened the Port Moresby telephone book, found Mohinder Das's number, and dialed it. This had better work, I thought.

"Who is it?" It was Das.

I waded right in. "Mr. Das, you don't know me, but I'd appreciate a moment of your time. I'm a friend of Ron Purvis."

"Who?" His voice was wary now, guarded.

"Ron Purvis," I repeated. "The skipper of the *Kokoda Lass*. I've got a delivery for you – something you ordered."

"What the fuck is this?"

"What the fuck it is, Mr. Das, is the cargo that was on board the *Kumar* when she went down. That say anything to you?"

There was a long silence on the line. Finally he said, "Who the hell are you?"

"I'm a businessman, Mr. Das. I've got the *Kumar*'s cargo and I'm selling. Interested?"

"Where's Purvis? Put Purvis on the phone."

"Not possible, Mr. Das. Ron Purvis isn't part of the deal anymore. And this is your lucky day, because the price for the cargo just went down. Today only, it'll cost you a mere twenty thousand. You interested?"

"The *Kumar* sank a couple of months ago. That's what Purvis said, anyhow. What the hell are you trying to pull?"

"I'm offering you a deal. I've got her cargo, and I can prove it. Why don't we meet and discuss terms?"

"How do I know you've got anything to sell?"

"I'll bring a sample to our meeting," I said. "You bring the money. Twenty thousand dollars, cash."

There was silence for a moment. Then he said, "Where and when?"

"In half an hour," I said. "You know the lookout point at the top of Burns Peak?"

"I know it," Das growled. "You coming alone?"

"Alone and unarmed," I said. The first part was true anyway. This was nothing for Sam to get involved in. All I had to do now was sneak out past the lobby and find a taxi. "See you in half an hour."

"Wait," said Das. "Who the hell am I talking to? How—"

"How are you going to recognize me? Think about it, Mr. Das," I said. "How many other people are going to be up there at this time of night?"

I hung up.

CHAPTER TWENTY-FOUR

It was fully dark now, the full moon rising above the sea. I heard footsteps approaching up the narrow gravel path. I checked the pistol under my shirt and stood up, trying to quiet my breathing.

It wasn't all nerves. The taxi I'd snagged outside the Islander had been able to take me only partway up the rutted, twisting track to Burns Peak. I'd had to hump the crate of M16s the rest of the way myself, and my muscles were still trembling in protest.

"You look out, *masta*," the taximan had said before driving off. "Plenty rascals around here at night."

Too right, I thought. And I was about to meet one right now. I stepped out from behind the rock, both hands high and in sight, and smiled. "Hello, Das."

He stopped ten feet from me. "You. I remember you. At the party last week." His voice was flat and his breath

171

rasped like a leaky bicycle pump. He was breathing hard, his belly pumping in and out like a bellows.

"I knew you'd be pleased," I said. "How's tricks?"

Das grunted. "You were with that Chinese bitch."

I widened my smile. "Careful, sport. Remember what happened the last time you talked like that?" I took a step forward, listening hard to the night. If he'd brought reinforcements, they were out there somewhere in the dark, not far away.

He made a dismissive gesture with his thick hand. "Never mind that, man. Where's the stuff?"

"Over here." I turned and led him back down the trail to where I'd put the crate. We were high up above Port Moresby Harbor, the lights of the port and the city strung out below us like fairy lights at a cosmic garden party. The air was warm and moist, and from somewhere below the strains of a string band drifted up from the suburbs of Konedobu.

I showed him the crate and stood back a few yards while he poked around inside it. The full moon lit up the peak brilliantly, and I could see the excitement on his face as he pawed through the rifles.

"There's no ammunition," he grunted.

"It's with the rest of it," I said. I pulled a slip of paper out of my shirt. "Thirty crates in all," I said, passing the slip over to him. "Contents of each duly noted."

He peered at the paper, then crumpled it up and stuffed it in a pocket. "I heard the *Kumar* sank. That's what Purvis told me."

"Purvis is out of the picture," I said. "You deal with me from now on."

His tiny eyes watched me. "Suppose I don't. Suppose I just take these and call it even."

I smiled. "Go right ahead. All you've got there is rifles without ammunition. About as useful as a crate of broken eggs. The ammunition's with the other twenty-nine boxes. You ready to deal?"

He wheezed in disgust. "How much?"

"I told you. Twenty thousand. It's a bargain, considering that Purvis wanted fifty."

He stood silent for a moment, considering whether to kill me, tell me to go to hell, or pay me. After giving the matter careful thought, he decided to try and trick me instead. "Twenty thousand, okay. But first you tell me where the rest is."

I shook my head. "First you give me the money, Das. Then I tell you."

He scowled. "Sonofabitch. How about I show it to you, okay? I don't trust you."

"Okay, show."

He nodded. "I'm gonna reach into my pants pocket now," he said, "and pull out an envelope. Don't get any ideas."

I watched him carefully as he extracted a crumpled manila envelope from his baggy trousers. Undoing the metal clasp, he drew out a sheaf of bills and fanned them slowly in my direction. "Twenty thousand, right here," he said.

I peered at the bills. They looked genuine, but it would be easy enough to fake it too. What the hell, I thought; what's life without a little risk?

"Deal," I said. "But first I want answers to a couple of questions."

"Questions? What questions?"

"What are all the guns for? You planning to take over the country?"

He looked surprised for a moment. Then he laughed, a wheezing, throaty sound that seemed to come from deep inside a well. "Not *this* country, friend."

Suddenly it was clear. Of course, I thought, why hadn't I seen it before? "You're with the Free Papua Movement, aren't you?"

Das shook his head. "I'm not with anybody, whitey. But yes, I supply the Organisasi Papua Merdeka. The freedom fighters in West Irian, battling the Indonesian imperialists. They need guns and explosives; I supply them. It's a simple business arrangement."

"Okay," I said. "Next question. Why'd you try to kill us that night after the party? Getting even is one thing, but running our car over a cliff was a little excessive, wasn't it?"

Das glanced sharply at me. "Kill you? What the hell are you talking about? I never tried to kill you."

"He's right, Donovan." A voice spoke from the darkness off to my right. "That was me. I tried to kill you, not Das." Captain Barry Sears stepped out of the shadows, a gun in his hand.

Sears walked over to me, patted me down, and took my pistol from my belt. "Move over there next to Das," he said. "Not too close. There, that's about right."

"What the hell are you doing here?" My mouth was dry and awkward, as if it hadn't been used in a while. I've made a bad mistake, I thought. A very bad mistake.

Sears smiled. "I put a tap on your telephone the day after you arrived, Donovan. Heard every bloody word you said over the blower, including your call to San Francisco the other day." His pistol flicked from side to side like a snake's head. "Thought I'd get in on the fun."

"Sonofabitch." Das's voice was a soft breath of hate, barely audible on the humid night air.

Sears laughed. "Don't take it all so personally, old son. Circumstances change, you know. Wasn't it just last week you were telling me you'd sing like a bird unless I produced the weapons we'd promised you? You threatened to ruin me, you bastard. Well, now you know what it feels like to hold the hot end."

He turned to me. "It was me, Donovan, who ran you off the road that night. The day you showed up I knew you were trouble. Knew I'd have to take care of you somehow. So I took a car from the impound yard at the office and followed you that night."

He grimaced. "You were a little too quick for me that time. Then I sent you up to Fairley thinking he'd do for you, but I was wrong again." He paused. "What's happened to Ron?"

"Purvis? He's safe, out of the way. You were all in it, weren't you?"

Sears nodded. "We were mates, Donovan, all the way back to the barracks. Ronnie and Blue and Brian and I. 'The Four Musketeers' they used to call us in the regiment. Then Brian got sent up on a charge. We were all in on it, mind, but Brian never told, not a word. He took his punishment like a man. He was spoiled for the Army then, of course. He went south, but we stayed mates through it all. Ronnie and Blue stayed up here in the Territory, of course, and so did I."

His voice went up a notch. "We had it all perfect, Donovan, until somebody killed Brian in San Francisco. Then you showed up here, poking your beak into everything." His breathing was ragged with anger. "You buggered up one of the sweetest lurks we ever had, do you know that? And now I'm going to kill you, my oath I am."

I cleared my throat. "You'd better think about this, Sears," I said. "It isn't going to work."

"Isn't it now?" He smiled, his lips drawing back over his large white teeth. "I think it'll work very well indeed, lad. In just a moment I'm going to shoot you, and then I'm going to shoot Das here. I'm going to shoot you with your own gun, Donovan, and when I've done that, I'll kill Das with my own. Then I'll put your gun in Das's hand. The story will practically tell itself. You tried to sell arms to Das, and while you were dealing he shot and killed you. I'd watched the whole thing, intending to arrest both of you. When Das fired I moved in, but then he rounded on me, and I had to return fire in self-defense. Result, two criminals out of the way, and a dangerous gunrunning network smashed."

He nodded. "It'll work, Donovan; it'll work very well indeed. I'll be a bloody hero, in fact." He smiled again. "And twenty thousand dollars richer."

He brought the hand with my gun in it up and leveled the barrel at my chest. "Say goodbye, Donovan."

The noise of the shot was so loud and so totally unexpected that all of us jumped. Sears whirled around as if stung. I dropped flat to the ground.

"Freeze, Sears!" Sam's voice rang out from the darkness. "Drop the gun, now!"

"The hell you say," growled Sears. He crouched low, weaving from side to side like a cornered bear, peering into the shadows for a target.

Beside me, Das moved. His arm was a blur as it came up from under his loose shirt and shot out straight, pointing rigidly toward Sears. I caught the merest glimpse of something thin and bright. Sears grunted with pain, pivoted, and looked down with surprise at the stiletto protruding from between his ribs.

Blood welled up between his clenched teeth as he fired twice, hitting Das once in the neck and once in the forehead. The Guyanese fell over without a sound and thumped heavily on the grass beside me. Sears stared at me defiantly for a moment, and then seemed to fold in upon himself gracefully, ending up as a small inert pile of clothing on the ground.

Sam stepped out of the darkness, pistol at the ready. "Are you all right, Max?"

I nodded. "I think so. How the hell—"

She sighed. "I figured you'd try something like this. I saw you leave the hotel and followed you in another taxi." She looked down at her bare feet. "I'd have been here sooner if I hadn't had those damned heels on."

"You came just in time," I said. "Where'd you get the gun?"

"Same place you got yours, sweetie. I took one from the crate when you weren't looking." She glanced at the bodies. "Are they both dead?"

As far as Das was concerned, the answer was pretty clear. Half of his head had been blown away. I moved over to Sears and felt for a pulse. "Nothing," I said after a moment.

Sam nodded and put down her gun. "Good. He was – they were – bad, horrible men, and I'm– I'm" – she was stuttering now – "I'm glad they're dead." She paused, gulping air. "And, and you – you're a" – she was sobbing now – "you're a damned fool, Max Donovan! You could have been killed!"

And with that she drew her fist back and hit me as hard as she could.

CHAPTER TWENTY-FIVE

"The colors are amazing." Sarei Badu hunched forward in his chair to peer again at my bruised eye. "Does it hurt a lot?"

"Oh, God, I'm so embarrassed," Sam said.

"Stop apologizing," I said to her. "It'll go away in a day or so. We were both a little wired up last night. I don't blame you a bit."

Sam smiled. "Do you mean that?"

"Absolutely." I looked her in the eye. "Just don't hit me again, that's all I ask."

She giggled. "Don't stand me up for dinner again, then."

The waiter came with our drinks. We were sitting in the airport bar at Jacksons waiting for the flight to Sydney to board. The air-conditioning felt good, and so did the nearly twelve hours of sleep we'd both had. When the drinks had been unloaded Sarei Badu raised his glass. "I'm glad to see you both alive."

We all touched glasses. "So are we," I said dryly.

"I'm sure." He looked at me soberly. "You took a hell of a chance, Max, going up there at night with the both of them."

"I didn't count on Sears," I said. "I knew that he had to be involved once I saw that picture on Purvis's boat and realized that he and MacKenzie and Purvis had all been in the same army unit together. But I figured on taking care of Das first. I thought if I could get him to talk, I could get Sears that way. I should have realized the phone was tapped."

"You should have let me help you," said Sam.

Sarei took the morning's *Post-Courier* from his briefcase and spread it on the table. The headline read, 'A Hero's Death.'

"Read it," Sarei said.

Sam and I read the lead story. In fulsome prose it recounted how Captain Sears, longtime stalwart of the Papua New Guinea Constabulary, had selflessly sacrificed his life to apprehend a nefarious arms dealer and political radical. An official funeral was being planned at which the prime minister himself would convey the thanks of a grateful nation, etc., etc.

I shook my head. "They've laid it on a bit thick, haven't they?"

Sarei winked. "More or less on purpose. When you called me last night I got in touch with some friends in the prime minister's office. We all agreed that this was the better way to handle it. There were too many loose ends around; we didn't want a detailed investigation."

"Well, just don't forget to send someone out to Bavo Island. Purvis is probably getting thirsty by now."

"A cutter's on its way, I'm told." He sipped his beer. "It's all worked out well, hasn't it? This way everybody gets what they need. We get rid of Sears and Das and break the major smuggling ring in the country. I heard this morning that they took Pastor Fairley in for questioning. Our relations with Indonesia are intact, and the weapons are nowhere in sight. And best of all, you get to go home. I don't see how we could improve on that, do you?"

"What about the *Kumar*? Did you get the information I wanted?"

Sarei snapped his fingers. "I nearly forgot." He took a piece of paper from his pocket and unfolded it. "The *Kumar* was registered out of Suva, owned by Vellupillai Subramanian, who's apparently a local Hindu copra trader. Her cargo was listed as automobile spare parts, transferred in Suva from another ship, the *Sea Witch*." He looked again at the paper. "Panamanian registry, out of Oakland, California."

I put down my beer. "The *Sea Witch*?"

"Yes, the *Sea Witch*. Why? Do you know it?"

I knew it, all right. The *Sea Witch* had been the name on the cargo manifests I'd seen in Lorenzo's office the night I'd blown his safe.

"My, my," I said softly.

Behind me the public-address system announced boarding for the Sydney flight.

* * *

"Nice shiner, Max," Bone said as he picked up Sam's bag. "It was a door, wasn't it?"

"That's right," I said as I stepped outside into the California air and sunlight. "It's nice to be back." I looked closely at him. "But you've changed somehow. It's the bone, isn't it? Why aren't you wearing your bone?"

"Tell you later," he said. "Here comes Freddie with the car. Let's go."

Bone opened the door, threw the bags inside, and motioned for us to get in. Freddie was driving. Kathy Armlin sat in front with him. Sam and I were jammed in back with Bone. Everybody told everybody else how great it was to see them again for a few minutes while Freddie got us up to cruising speed on the freeway, headed toward the city. Then Bone turned to me.

"Who goes first, me or you?"

"Me," I said.

I spent the next ten minutes telling them about what had happened in New Guinea. It sounded lurid even to my jaded ears. When I was through Bone nodded.

"So you never found out who killed MacKenzie?"

"As a matter of fact, no."

"That's too bad. Because according to Ackroyd, the charge against Freddie will be changed to first-degree murder the day after tomorrow. No bail for murder suspects, so he goes back inside. We've been discussing his options, actually."

"No way I'm going back in," said Freddie from the front seat. "Kathy and I are going to Mexico, Max." He turned partway around. "By the way, that guy who works for Lorenzo has been looking for you everywhere. Word on the street is he's gonna kill you if he sees you. You musta done something really shitty to him, boy."

Bone coughed. "We have one lead left. Do you remember that list of San Francisco telephone numbers you read to me over the telephone from Port Moresby? The ones you found in the pilot's notebook? Well, I did some checking. There were six numbers. Three of them belong to zoos, and three of them to private citizens."

"Zoos?" said Sam.

"Zoos collect animals, my dear. Including birds of paradise. All three zoos had been called by MacKenzie. All three had been offered a pair of birds. All three refused."

"Why?"

Bone smiled. "It's unethical, apparently. One of the zoo officials explained it to me. They get a lot of calls, it turns out, from people with, ah, hot animals to sell. There's a big trade, apparently. Unless they're absolutely

180

sure they're dealing with someone reputable, they turn them down flat."

He paused. "Well, almost flat. One of them admitted that he'd hesitated for a second when he heard they were birds of paradise. There are apparently no King of Saxony birds anywhere on the West Coast."

"What about the other three numbers? The private citizens."

Bone pushed his glasses up on his nose. "Now it gets interesting," he said. "Two of them are dealers in collectibles. Anything rare and expensive. But MacKenzie didn't have much luck, apparently. One dealer's in prison for a customs violation last year. The other one died two months ago."

"What about the third dealer?" I said.

"Ah," said Bone.

"What the hell does 'ah' mean?" I said.

Bone waited for a moment, savoring it. "It means," he said at last, "that the third person wasn't a dealer at all. He was – he is – a private collector. A very rich private collector, in fact. Have you ever heard of someone named James Whitney Eager?"

Sam and I both shook our heads.

Bone bent over and extracted a newspaper from his briefcase. "Read and learn," he said, pushing it toward me.

The society page of the *Examiner* had it as the main header: 'Pacific Heights Executive Hosts City DA's Bid for State Senator.' Underneath, the text detailed how J. Whitney Eager, 'King of Silicon Valley,' would host a thousand-dollar-a-plate kickoff fundraiser on Friday evening for District Attorney Delbert Ackroyd, candidate in the upcoming race for state senator. Current polls put Ackroyd virtually even with Randolph Armlin, local philanthropist. The turnout for the dinner, the article continued, was expected to be heavy among the Bay Area's conservative and wealthy element. Several celebrities were expected to attend. Mrs. Maude Ackroyd, a former student of the opera, would open the speeches with a solo rendition of *The Star-Spangled Banner.*

"Jesus Christ," I said as I passed the paper to Sam. "This guy is a friend of Ackroyd's?"

Bone nodded. "More than a friend. Eager's been a heavy contributor to Ackroyd's campaign. The two are apparently thick as thieves, according to my sources." He coughed discreetly. "No pun intended, of course."

"And he's holding a fundraiser on Friday night," I said. "My God, that's tonight."

Bone smiled hugely. "That's right." He dug into his bulging briefcase and produced a white waiter's jacket. "Here, put this on. I hope you two didn't have anything else planned for this evening."

CHAPTER TWENTY-SIX

"Ow," said Freddie. "Take it easy, will ya? I can't breathe."

"Hush," said Sam. She pulled the cummerbund tight around Freddie's waist and fastened it. "There. Have you ever thought of joining Weight Watchers?"

We were standing with thirty other domestics in the lower reception area of J. Whitney Eager's sprawling Spanish-style mansion. We were part of Costello's Custom Caterers, a small army of men and women especially imported into the Eager homestead for the evening. Bone looked every inch the avuncular bartender, while Freddie and I had donned the white jackets and bow ties of ordinary serving grunts. Sam and Kathy Armlin looked fetching in French-maid uniforms. Sam had already been patted on the backside once by one of the other waiters, and Kathy Armlin was getting the eye from a couple more of them over in the corner.

Bone Brown checked his watch. "They'll be starting any minute now." He turned to me. "What's the plan?"

I thought for a moment. "This guy lives alone, right? He'll be down in the hall when the guests come. Think you can find the burglar alarm and turn it off?"

Bone opened his butler's jacket to reveal his custom-made waistcoat. "Depend on me."

"Good. Once the alarm's out, we've got to search the house. Start with his den or study – wherever he keeps his papers."

"What am I supposed to be looking for?"

I shook my head. "I don't know. Anything that might tie him to MacKenzie or the birds. Or anything. Hell, Bone, find something – it's our last chance."

Hands being clapped together smartly made me start. I turned to see a man who looked like Salvador Dali standing on the landing.

"That's Costello," Bone whispered to me. "The ringmaster. You're supposed to be on loan from another agency, in case he asks you."

"What other agency?" I said, but Bone had moved away.

"Places, everyone," trilled Costello, balancing on the tips of his thin, pointed shoes. He clapped his hands together once more. "Places, please."

Everyone in the room moved into groups, the waitresses on one side, the cooks and sauce-makers in another corner, and the serving waiters and bartenders off to the side. We were left high and dry.

Costello cocked an arch eye in our direction. "The new people, I suppose." He sighed then, waving one elegant paw at Bone. "Go and join the bartenders, my good man. Hurry, now." He peered at Sam and Kathy. "You two are cocktail servers, of course – over there."

He looked at Freddie. "Good God," he muttered. "Stay in the kitchen and help take the trash out. And you," he said, turning to me, "will help me take the guests' coats."

He snapped his fingers pettishly. "Come along, dear boy. They'll be arriving any minute now."

Sam was trying her best to hide an attack of the giggles. I scowled at her and moved slowly up the stairs to where Costello waited, glancing in the mirror to see if Sam's makeup had adequately covered my Technicolor eye. Not perfect, but it would do.

We walked down a wide hallway and into a wide marble foyer flanked by tall windows and crowned with an enormous ornate chandelier. Costello jabbed me hard in the ribs. "Straighten up," he hissed. "There's Mr. Eager."

A large, hairless man in a tuxedo approached across the floor, looking for all the world like W. C. Fields in a penguin costume. His cheeks were bright with grog blossoms above a nose that belonged on a 747's wingtip. Small beady eyes like shotgun loads peered out from the fleshy, pouchy face.

His voice was surprisingly mild. "Ah, Mr. Costello. Our guests should be arriving momentarily. I hope you're properly organized."

"Certainly, Mr. Eager." Costello was unction itself, his smile as practiced as a Subic Bay nightclub hostess. "I've just made a personal inspection. Everything is ready."

"Good." Edgar's eyes swiveled, fixing me like gunsights. "And who is this?"

Costello hesitated.

"Maximilian, sir," I said.

"Maximilian? A rather unusual name in this day and age, isn't it?"

"Maximilian was emperor of Mexico," I said with what I hoped was the right mixture of deference and dignity.

"I know that," Eager said dryly. "You're not Mexican, though, are you?"

"No, sir," I said. "I'm, ah, Norwegian. But my father was fond of history."

Eager looked at me for a moment. "Is that so," he said finally. "Well, you'd better do a good job this evening. We have some very important guests coming. Including my good friend the district attorney."

"Depend on me, sir," I said in a voice straight out of *Jeeves*.

He nodded curtly – Churchill inspecting the troops – and clomped off down the hall.

Costello smiled thinly. "Funny," he said, "you don't look Norwegian, somehow." He peered at my makeup. "How'd you get that black eye?"

I shrugged. "I've got some rough friends," I said.

His eyes glittered briefly. "Really? We must have a chat sometime."

I pointed to the entryway. "Here come the first guests now."

* * *

I spent the next half hour greeting people, taking their coats, and directing them inside to the salon, where the waiters and waitresses – Sam and Kathy among them – stood ready to ply them with strong drink. Freddie stayed prudently out of sight in the kitchen.

Then the Ackroyds arrived in a flashy little two-seater Morgan sports car. Delbert Ackroyd wore a tweed driving cap, leather gloves, and a long coat over his formal clothes. His wife had on an enormous pink ballroom gown, matching her complexion almost exactly. The Morgan was a bright red, polished to brilliance, with heavy chrome bumpers and a set of ahooga horns that went all the way down the hood. The steering wheel was on the right, of course. It must have set Ackroyd back plenty, I thought.

The Ackroyds extricated themselves from the tiny seats with difficulty and started toward the entrance. "Excuse me," I said to Costello. "I'd better make some space in the cloakroom for Mr. Ackroyd's things."

Costello's joyful cries of greeting were muffled as I burrowed back into the coats.

From behind a Burberry, I watched Delbert shepherd his huge wife through the foyer, shake hands with Eager, accept a drink from Kathy's tray, and sail on into the main room to scattered applause. I'll have to stay out of sight from now on, I thought.

Costello peered into the cloakroom. "What are you doing back there, Maximilian? Here, put Mr. Ackroyd's coat away, will you? You can go out afterward and collect the car keys from the boy in the parking lot. By God, did you get a look at that woman? They say she's actually going to sing after dinner, just before the speeches start."

"Is she any good?"

He pursed his lips. "If you ask me," he said, dropping his voice, "she has all the musical ability of a warthog throwing up into a garbage can." He sniffed and drew himself up. "But that's just my opinion, of course."

I nodded as I took the topcoat, my mind on other things.

Now that Ackroyd was here, attention would focus on him. It was time to find Bone. As soon as Costello had turned away, I headed for the back of the house.

In the kitchen Sam and Freddie were staring at a huge plate of hors d'oeuvres.

"Oh, gross," Sam said. "Somebody took a bite out of this one and put it back."

Freddie scratched the end of his nose thoughtfully. "Well, maybe it wasn't very good, Sam."

Bone came through the door, a smile on his face. "Jackpot," he said quietly. He took a manila file from under his bartender's jacket. "I found this in the desk upstairs," he said. "The drawer was locked, but I picked it." He opened the file, took out a sheaf of canceled checks, and fanned them out before us like a magician at a birthday party. "Take a look at these."

All of them were made out to Delbert Ackroyd and signed by Eager. "Jeepers," said Kathy Armlin as she went through them. "If these are campaign contributions, they're way over the limit."

"There's also a note," said Bone. "It was in with the checks." He passed it to me.

> *I've put the investigation on hold and as soon as we charge Fields your worries are over. That should be worth a little extra, don't you think?*

Sam looked over my shoulder. "I'll be damned," she breathed. "That's Ackroyd's handwriting."

"Then we've got him," I said.

She shook her head. "Not exactly. This note was obtained by theft. I doubt that it would stand up in court. You'll need something more, I think."

"Then let's find it," I said. I turned to the others. "Eager's still busy glad-handing the guests. Bone, you and Kathy go back upstairs. Try not to make a mess, but search every room. Freddie, you and Sam do the downstairs here. Be discreet but thorough, and for God's sake, don't get caught. You're looking for anything that can connect Eager to either MacKenzie or to Ackroyd. Everybody take it slow and easy – no risks. We'll meet back here in an hour to compare notes."

Bone nodded. "Fine with me. But what are you going to do while we're busy searching things? Max, are you listening to me?"

I was staring out the window at Ackroyd's red sports car in the parking lot, an idea forming in my mind. "What am I going to do?" I said finally. "Well, for a start, I thought I'd go for a little drive."

* * *

Ackroyd's car drove like oiled silk, barely making a noise as I slid through the city. I felt like I could drive it forever. No one had given me a second glance as I'd wheeled it out of the parking lot at Eager's and onto the street.

I parked the Morgan a block from my house. Slipping into the garage through the back window, I took the duffel bag with the sinsemilla out of the trunk of my own car, where I'd left it before my trip to Port Moresby. Going into the kitchen, I put three extra-strength garbage bags one inside the other, zipped open the duffel bag, and transferred its contents into the garbage bags. I hefted it. Heavy, but manageable. So far, so good. Now, I thought, for the phone call. I dialed. Please let him be there, I prayed.

"Yeah?"

For the first time in my life, I was glad to hear Lorenzo's voice. "Hi, buddy," I said. "Glad I caught you in. I've got a business proposition for you."

"Who is this? Donovan? That you, Donovan, you bastard?"

"Hey, it's nice to know friends care," I said. "Let me tell you about my proposition."

"Fuck your proposition, shitbag. You owe me ten thousand bucks, remember?"

"That's what I'm calling about. I've, ah, been out of town on a little business that turned out better than I expected. So I thought I'd call and square accounts. Remember the bag of weed you were going to buy from Fat Freddie?"

"I remember. So what?"

"Still want to buy it?"

There was a pause. "What the fuck you sayin', Donovan? Spell it out for me."

"Okay. I've got the weed now, over one hundred pounds of prime sinsemilla. You were going to pay ten thousand for it. It's yours on special offer, today only, for free. Provided you'll let bygones be bygones." I paused. "What do you say?"

"You serious? How'd you get ahold of the weed?"

"Details, Lorenzo. What about the deal? You on? Today only, right now, in fact. Otherwise I sell to somebody else for more money and come pay you later. You're getting a bargain, man."

"Maybe," Lorenzo said. His voice was wary now. "But I got to see it first. Me an' Festus. You fuck us around, Festus'll blow your head off."

"We've had our little differences, Lorenzo," I said, "but I wouldn't mess around with you on this. Especially not with Festus after me."

"Bet your ass," Lorenzo grunted. "Okay, Donovan. Bring the shit over here and I'll take a look at it."

"No way," I said. "We meet on neutral territory. You know where the Conservatory of Flowers is in Golden Gate Park? See you there in half an hour." I hung up the phone before he could reply.

I leaned back in my chair, feeling my heart thudding. This had better work, I thought.

CHAPTER TWENTY-SEVEN

Lorenzo's Cadillac cruised slowly into sight, coming down JFK Drive. Festus was at the wheel. I ducked down low behind the wall to make sure he didn't see me and watched as the car moved out of sight. When there was no chance they'd spot me, I hopped over the low wall and jogged after them, whistling between my teeth. I watched as they turned up Pompei Circle toward the Conservatory. This was a dead-end street – they'd either find a place to park or have to come back. Either way, I had them boxed.

I saw them a hundred yards down the road, getting out of the Caddy. I ducked into the woods and waited until they went by. Festus hunched over slightly as he walked, as if he were carrying something under his loose denim jacket. I was willing to bet it wasn't a box of candy.

I gave them a few minutes to get clear. Then I ran back to Ackroyd's Morgan and drove it back to where the Caddy sat. There was a free parking space four cars down. I wheeled the Morgan in, parked it, and got out. I walked back to the Cadillac, wiping my sweaty hands on my trousers.

Then I let the air out of Lorenzo's tires.

I started with the rear ones. When both were fully deflated, I did the front. I was just finishing when I felt a tap on the shoulder. I whirled to see a ten-year-old standing behind me, clutching a huge skateboard. "Whatcha doin', mister?"

I looked him up and down. "Nothing," I said quietly. "A little trick on my friend."

"The big fat guy? I'm gonna tell."

I sighed and dug out my wallet. Pulling out a five, I passed it to the kid. "Take this," I said. "Go buy yourself a puff adder. And keep your mouth shut, okay?"

The kid nodded happily. I took off, heading in the direction of the Conservatory.

Lorenzo and Festus were standing outside, looking suspiciously at the crowd. I slipped up behind Lorenzo, tapped him on the outside shoulder, ducked back the other way, and gave Festus a wide smile. "What's happenin', fellas?"

Festus shifted his stance a little, showing me the sawed-off under his jacket. "Watch it, motherfucker," he hissed. His eyes were bright, the pupils cranked down to pinpoints. Whatever he was riding on right now, it hadn't improved his disposition.

Lorenzo looked down at my empty hands. "Thought you was ready to deal, Donovan."

"It's heavy, remember? A hundred pounds at least. I left it in the car." I pointed off toward the road. "Come on. It's in the trunk."

"Shit." He gathered his bulk together and we moved off back toward the car. "This better be on the level. Otherwise, Festus is gonna rip you asshole to appetite."

"Relax. I just want to get this over with." We reached the Morgan and I took the keys out of my pocket. "It's in the trunk here."

Lorenzo looked at the Morgan. "This your wheels? I don't believe it." He let out a low whistle.

"I did a little business out of town," I said, "and it paid off. It paid off well." I tapped the hood of the Morgan. "She'll do over a hundred on the freeway. I had her up there most of the way up from LA yesterday. Best ride of my life."

"That where you got the car? LA?"

I nodded. "Yeah. It was a nice deal, actually. It's not completely new, of course. The, ah, previous owner's whereabouts being more or less unknown, I managed to get the car at a substantial discount."

"It's hot, you mean."

I smiled. Now for the hook. This, I thought, will make it or break it. "No, it's not hot. That's the best part of it. It's had a paint job and new plates put on." I reached over and snapped open the glove compartment. "But best of all, it's got clean papers." I tapped an envelope inside the glove compartment. "Along with the car, I bought a clean transfer document. No name on it."

Lorenzo straightened up. "No name?"

"That's right. I just fill in whatever." I paused. "Course, I haven't got around to it yet. I guess I'll go on down to Motor Vehicles tomorrow morning sometime. I wanted to get rid of the weed first and get us square, y'know?"

He nodded. "Yeah. Good idea." He kept looking at the Morgan.

I opened the trunk. "Here."

They moved forward to inspect the sack. Lorenzo opened it, pulled out a clump of buds, broke some of them apart, and sniffed deeply. A wide smile spread like a rash across his face.

"All right." He stood up and hefted the bag, grunting with effort. "Okay, we got a deal, Donovan. Festus, grab this here bag."

I helped Festus put the heavy sack in the trunk of the Cadillac and waited while they climbed in.

Lorenzo looked at me from behind the wheel. "A piece of advice, Donovan. Keep out of my way from now on, you hear? I still ain't forgot about the Imperial you trashed. Far as I'm concerned, you still owe me for that little trick. I see you around in the neighborhood, I'll tell Festus to trash you. Got that?"

"Got it," I said. "You two have a nice day, now." I loped back to my car as Lorenzo ground the starter.

I fired up the Morgan and pulled out just in time to see Lorenzo and Festus erupt from the Caddy, swearing. I stopped alongside. "Anything wrong?" I said.

"Some fucker let the air out of our tires!" Lorenzo said.

Festus came around the side. "They all flat, man."

I shook my head. "Tough luck, guys. I'd give you a lift in my new car, but there's not enough room for both of you. Be glad to call a tow truck, though."

Lorenzo turned. "Nah, shit—" His eyes fastened on the Morgan. "Wait a minute." He looked at Festus, grinning. "How'd you like to ride home in something like that?"

Festus nodded. "Be smooth as a shaved pussy, I bet."

"Yeah." He held out a greasy paw. "Give me the keys, Donovan."

Be still, my heart, I told myself. "What keys?" I just had to say it.

"Your keys, dink! We're takin' your car." He turned. "Show him the gun, Festus, and then get that bag out of the trunk."

I opened the door and got out. "Hey, no need, man. I don't want trouble. Take the car, go on. I'll come by later on and collect it."

Lorenzo chuckled as he wedged himself in behind the wheel. "You do that, Donovan. You just do that."

Festus heaved the garbage bag into the trunk of the Morgan and hopped in, grinning like the proverbial possum.

I stepped back and watched them roar off, around the Circle and onto JFK, taking the turn hard out onto Oak Street, headed for the Bay Bridge and home. I turned, whistling, and almost bumped into the kid with the skateboard. His face was thickly covered with what looked like dried chocolate ice cream.

"They just took your car, mister. Aren't you gonna call the cops?"

I smiled. "Yeah, kid," I said. "As a matter of fact, that's exactly what I'm gonna do."

* * *

"San Francisco Police, Homicide." Luther Crake's throaty roar was music to my ears.

I spoke through my handkerchief. "Listen carefully," I said. "I'm only going to say this once. District Attorney Delbert Ackroyd is the head of a dope ring. Even as I speak two of his henchmen are in his car delivering a load of drugs for him. They're on Oak, headed toward the Bay Bridge. Check it out."

"This is Homicide, buddy. We don't deal with drug busts."

"Then pass it on to whoever does. But check it out all the same. Ackroyd's letting his car be used for drug deliveries, and one's in progress right now. It's a bright red Morgan two-seater, license number—"

"I know the district attorney's car, goddamnit. Now look, who is this?"

"The tooth fairy. You'd better hustle; they're getting away. Oh, and be careful of the black one. He's got a sawed-off twelve-gauge, and he'll use it."

"Listen, friend, just tell me—"

"Check it out," I repeated, and hung up. There was a grin from ear to ear on my face that just wouldn't go away. I stepped out of the booth and snagged a passing cab. I lay back in the seat, whistling softly with my eyes closed.

On the way back to the Eager mansion we had to wait in a line of traffic for more than ten minutes. "Must be a fire truck, ambulance, some kinda emergency," the cabbie said.

A cop finally waved us through. As we crept slowly by, I could see three police black-and-whites blocking Ackroyd's Morgan. Lorenzo and Festus were being led to the salad wagon by four cops with pump shotguns at the ready. The Morgan looked as if it had kissed a telephone pole pretty hard, and the windshield was blown mostly out.

"Look at that, will you?" I murmured as we slid past.

"Fuckin' cops," said the cabbie.

CHAPTER TWENTY-EIGHT

Bone looked up. "Where the hell have you been?"

"Out and about," I said. "What's happening?"

He waved the glass he was polishing toward the ballroom behind the French doors. There were two or three hundred people inside swilling down the food. Most looked as though they could do without the extra calories.

"They're just about finished with the main course. Creamed breast of chicken and artichoke hearts. The speeches will start after dessert. Mrs. Ackroyd'll do the national anthem to kick things off." He shook his head. "All this for only a thousand dollars a plate." He gave the glass another swipe with his towel. "We didn't find a damn thing upstairs, Max. Freddie and Sam finished looking on this floor and went down into the cellar about fifteen minutes ago."

"I'll go down and check on them, then. Back in ten minutes."

Just outside the door I collided with Costello, looking about as relaxed as a pregnant fox in a forest fire. "Christ, Maximilian, there you are!" he hissed. "Where on earth have you been? Things have been just frantic–"

"Sorry, Mr. Costello," I said. "They wanted someone to help unload and sort the, ah, tumbrils."

He cocked his head at me like a bantam rooster. "What? Oh, never mind. At least you're here now. We'll be serving the pineapple flambé in just a few minutes. Get some of the serving trays laid out on the long table, and check with the kitchen to see if they're ready. Hurry, now."

"Sure thing, Mr. Costello," I said as I headed for the kitchen and the door into the cellar.

* * *

It was cool and quiet in the cellar, and I moved through the rooms looking for Sam and Fat Freddie. Too quiet, I thought. Was something wrong or was I just jumpy?

The cellar rooms were ordinary – ordinary, that is, for someone very rich. There was an extensive wine cellar, which I glanced briefly through, and a huge pantry next to it with a dumbwaiter-type arrangement to send food up to the kitchen. In one corner, masts, folded sails, and other boating paraphernalia were stacked and hung neatly. In another room the gardener had stored his tractor-mower with its wide-blade attachments. There were shelves from floor to ceiling full of paint, varnish, tools, and odds and ends.

"Freddie?" My voice echoed oddly in the silence of the cool damp. No answer. I called again. I started wishing I'd brought a gun. I came through the toolroom, out toward the large double garage doors leading to the sloping hillside below the tennis courts, when I caught sight of the small wooden door set into the wall.

Just a closet, I thought. I grasped the handle and pulled, surprised at the weight of the door. Inside there was nothing but blackness; whatever it was, it was deeper and larger than a closet.

A bomb shelter? I listened carefully for a moment, hearing nothing, and then stepped inside, feeling along the wall to my right. My fingers closed around the light switch, and I snapped it on.

My eyes, adjusted to the dim cellar light, blinked twice in the brightness that flared suddenly. I caught a snapshot of Freddie and Sam seated on the floor in front of me, gagged and with their hands bound behind their backs.

Then something hard and cold crashed down against the back of my head. There was a terrible pain, the sensation of falling, and then blackness.

* * *

J. Whitney Eager's face looked like a distended clown's mask, a grotesque balloon as it hovered inches away from my own. "Waking up, Maximilian? Good. I thought for a minute there I'd hit you too hard."

I grunted and lifted my head experimentally. It hurt like hell. Warm sticky stuff was sliding down my neck into my shirt. I assumed it was blood. Because I could more or less see and hear, I also assumed that I was alive. Well, that was something. The fact that my hands were securely tied behind my back wasn't great news, however.

Eager moved around in front of me. In one hand he held the pipe that had recently made contact with my skull. In the other, an elegant little snub-nosed lady's gun. Made for a purse, it used .22 shorts and had hardly enough punch to break windows. Fired at close range, however, it could kill you just as dead as an MX missile.

Eager must have been a mind reader. "You're what they call dead meat, Maximilian," he said. "Your own fault, of course. I'd just finished tying up your two friends here" – he gestured negligently with the gun toward Sam and Freddie; I saw Freddie cringe, his eyes wide, as the gun moved in his direction – "when I caught sight of you entering the basement."

He pointed to a small bank of TV monitors hanging from the low ceiling. There were nine of them, little five-inch Sonys. They showed views of the approaches to the house and several interior hallways, including the cellar stairs. On one of them I could see the crowd eating in the ballroom, the waiters and waitresses bustling to and fro with food and drink. All of it silent and in miniature.

"One of you managed to short-circuit the burglar alarms," Eager was saying, "but you missed this. It works on an antenna system – no wires." He took a beeper from his pocket. "And I have this, which tells me if anyone tries the door here. That's how I knew your two friends had penetrated my little hideaway." He smiled, his fleshy lips parting to show big teeth, square and white as sugar cubes.

I looked around at the room. It was large, lit with indirect fluorescent lamps and, here and there, a spotlight on tracks. The walls were filled with display cases and cabinets, making it look like a museum. Most of what I could see seemed to be artifacts in metal, wood, and pottery. Eager must have spent a hell of a lot of money to make this room so private and secure, I thought. Which probably meant that the items in the cases were worth plenty.

"The room is totally soundproof and absolutely secure." He motioned with the gun toward the heavy bar bolts on the back of the door I had come through. He glanced up at the television monitors. "They're just starting dessert," he said. "I should be back upstairs in twenty minutes."

"You killed MacKenzie, didn't you?" I said. "The Australian in the motel room."

Eager nodded. "Of course I did. I crushed his skull — with that." He pointed to a stone ax hanging on display over the fireplace. "A poor specimen, really." He smiled. "The ax, I mean, not MacKenzie. I only kept it because it was the murder weapon, you see."

"Why?" I said. "Why kill him?"

He turned back from the fireplace. "He annoyed me, that's why. For that, he died. Perhaps you'll understand if I tell you about this room — why I built it and what it contains. Do you have a few moments?" He laughed, a harsh ugly sound in the silence. "Of course you do. You have all the time I choose to give you."

He bent over me. "It's a terrific feeling, you know — the power of life or death. I wish I'd discovered it earlier." He sighed. "But better late than never. Come on, I'll give you a little tour."

He turned away from me to look again at the TV monitors. As I struggled to my feet, I caught Freddie's urgent stare. He glanced at Eager to make sure his back was still turned, and then turned to show me his hands, bound behind his back with nylon rope. He had popped one of the strands somehow and was almost free. I nodded, and Freddie hid his hands behind him again.

"Down here," said Eager. "And move along, please — we don't have much time."

We began to walk slowly down the long room, past the display cases and shelves. "I had this room built years ago, when I bought the house. I'm a single man, and I work very hard for my money. There are stresses and strains which — well, which ordinary people like yourself couldn't begin to comprehend. I decided a long time ago that I needed ways to be private, to be myself."

He gestured to the objects on the walls. "So I became a collector. Of things which, for the most part, I cannot display publicly." He took a key from his pocket and opened one of the cases. "My special little hobby, you see. I collect artifacts. Unicums, to be precise."

"Unicums?"

"Unique pieces, one of a kind. I collect only the rarest and most valuable of whatever is available. Most of them, of course, have been acquired illegally." He reached into a display case. "Take a look at this, for example."

He brought out what appeared to be a small mask, of abstract design, hanging from a twisted length of string. As he brought it closer I saw that it was a human head – or rather the skin of a human head, shrunk and stretched over an interior frame of some kind.

Eager dangled the obscene object before me; I couldn't tear my eyes away. The skin was very brittle and had been distorted into a stylized form, with an elongated skull and high forehead. The nose was gone, and here and there pieces of skin were missing, chewed perhaps by insects. The eyeholes stared vacantly at me as I gazed upon the shriveled, reptilelike mouth.

"It's a headhunter's trophy, from West Irian." Eager's voice broke the spell. He spoke softly, as if to avoid waking the sleeping head. "Unique for several reasons. Excellent workmanship, for one thing – most of the skin's intact. That alone makes it a rarity. But not unique."

He held the head up for close inspection. "The people who made this head were a small, fierce tribe of headhunters, among the last of the groups discovered by the Dutch administration. Because they were so isolated, they had no immunity to our diseases. The Dutch patrol officer who made contact with them in 1961 also brought them influenza. Within two months the entire tribe was dead – wiped from the face of the earth. They burned their homes, their crops, and all their artifacts in a desperate attempt to appease their gods and stop the deaths."

He held up the head. "This is the last surviving piece, you see. It was sold to me by the Dutch official who made contact. The sale of such artifacts is highly illegal, of course. I paid a great deal of money for this."

I looked at the shrunken head, seeing in its empty eyes the dying villagers, the burning and abandoned bodies in the jungle clearings. The tiny face grinned mockingly at me, the last remaining remnant from a world gone forever, preserved now in a rich man's glass prison.

"MacKenzie," I said. "You still haven't said why you killed MacKenzie."

He replaced the head carefully and turned. "MacKenzie was a fool. Because I collect illegally, I'm known to people in the trade. He got my name from a dealer in Hong Kong and approached me several weeks ago with an interesting offer – a pair of live birds of paradise."

"The King of Saxony."

Eager looked at me. "You've done your homework, Maximilian. Who are you, the police?"

"No," I said, "but the woman in the other room is."

Eager smiled. "And I'm Alexander the Great." He shrugged. "Even if she is, no matter. You'll all be disposed of without a trace, I assure you. No one will ever find you. Where was I? Oh, yes, the King of Saxony. One of the rarest and most valuable of the species. I don't collect animals as a rule, but the idea grew on me. No private collector has these birds, you see. So I called him and agreed to meet."

"What went wrong?"

Eager frowned. "MacKenzie did a very stupid thing. We met in a sleazy motel, as he insisted. First he showed me some second-rate artifacts – nothing special, hardly above the category of airport art. I told him I was interested only in the birds. He opened his suitcase and produced the male. He claimed the female had died in transit. Then he had the nerve to ask ten thousand dollars for the male alone. It had been his original price for the pair."

"And?"

Eager's face darkened. "I thought he was trying to get more money out of me. He could see that I wanted the birds, badly. I told him to go to hell." His voice grew hoarse. "And when I did he lifted the bird up – that beautiful, beautiful bird – and he wrung its neck like a chicken. He... he threw it down in front of me and said, 'Up yours, mate.'" His voice dropped to a whisper. "And so I killed him."

His eyes glittered as he looked at me. There was spittle at the corners of his mouth now and a strange note in his voice. "It was easy, actually. I hit him with the stone ax he'd just tried to sell me. I hit him once and he fell to his knees in front of me. I hit him again. I kept hitting him until I knew he was dead. Then I took the ax and the dead bird and left." He paused. "I called the district attorney when I got home."

"And Ackroyd protected you," I said.

"I'm paying to get him elected," Eager said simply. He looked at his watch. "I have to get back. The speeches will start soon."

Freddie and Sam were still in the same positions. "Sit down across from them on the floor," said Eager.

I slid down the wall until I was seated, my feet out in front of me. I watched Freddie's face carefully. I raised my eyebrows in a question and saw him nod. He was untied.

"You'll never get away with this," I said. It was all I could think of. Highly original.

Eager laughed. "Of course I will." He raised the pistol to Sam's head. "The power of life and death is incredible, you know. Just incredible. I think I could really get to like this." His finger tightened on the trigger.

I swung my feet out in a wide arc, moving them as fast as I could. They caught Eager's ankles and swept him sideways, knocking him to the cement floor with a thud and a sharp whoosh of air. The pistol flew out of his hand and clattered to the floor six feet away.

He crabbed sideways on the floor and I managed to get in a glancing blow to his head with my feet. Then he was out of range, dragging himself up the wall, his eyes wild as he searched frantically for the pistol.

Freddie's arms came out from behind his back and he stood up. Eager hissed with surprise and drew back. "Oh, no," he whimpered. "Don't hurt me, please."

Freddie stood still, looking at him.

"The gun," I said quietly. "Get the gun, Freddie."

He turned tortured eyes to me. "I can't, Max. I– I'm afraid to touch it." He looked over at the gun in the corner, and then away.

"Do it, Freddie," Sam whispered. "Now. Get the gun." Freddie took a step over to the corner, and then stopped, trembling. "I can't, Max. I just can't."

Eager had straightened up while we were talking. Now he began to move slowly along the wall toward the corner where the gun lay.

"Get the fucking gun, Freddie," I said between clenched teeth. "Bend down and pick it up. For God's sake."

Freddie bent and touched the gun, withdrew, and touched it again. His trembling hand closed around it.

"Good," I said. "Now pick it up." My voice sounded very small in the room.

Shaking, Freddie raised the gun, keeping it well away from him.

Eager inched slowly toward Freddie, his eyes glued on the gun. Blood trickled slowly down his forehead from where he had hit the floor, and his face was beaded with sweat. His eyes glittered behind his glasses.

"Give me the gun, my boy." His voice was paper rustling in the wind. "Give it to me, now."

"Don't do it, Freddie." My voice was a harsh croak. "He's going to kill all of us! You've got to stop him!"

Tears ran down Freddie's cheeks, and his big shoulders heaved in pain. He squeezed his eyes shut and shook his head from side to side. "I can't, Max! I can't, I can't!"

"Yes, you can," I said quietly. "I know you can."

His eyes opened and locked on mine. I nodded. "I *know* it," I said.

Freddie brought the gun up, and Eager stopped.

"Don't be silly," Eager whispered. "Give me the gun. Do it now. I won't hurt you. I promise." He moved toward Freddie, his hand outstretched.

Freddie kept the gun high, backing up slowly until he bumped into the wall. He shook his head. "Stay away."

Eager's outstretched hand was inches away from the gun now. A small smile of triumph appeared on his face. "The gun," he snapped. "Give it to me now, before I get angry." He took a last step forward.

The shot boomed out in the small room. Eager stood stock-still, his taut smile frozen on his face. The smell of cordite filled the air as the pistol dropped from Freddie's trembling fingers.

Then Eager folded quietly and decorously to the floor and lay there in a tidy heap, unmoving.

CHAPTER TWENTY-NINE

We stood in the hallway and watched the assembled crowd as they settled back in their chairs, getting ready for the speeches. Behind us, in the kitchen, the staff was putting away the dessert dishes and getting the cigars and brandy snifters ready. Up on the speaker's platform, Eager's place was conspicuously vacant. Ackroyd peered this way and that, searching the crowd for him.

Beside me Freddie spoke softly. "I really shot him, didn't I, Max? It seems like a bad dream."

I put my arm around him and gave him a hug. "You really shot him, Freddie. And you did good. You didn't even hurt him very much. The bullet went clean through his shoulder. I think he was more surprised than anything else."

"Think we oughta tell Ackroyd that Eager isn't gonna make it?"

I shook my head. "Let's not spoil the party. The doctor'll be here in a few minutes. Let him break the news."

Sam was grinning from ear to ear. "Boy, is Ackroyd in trouble. This is going to make a lot of people in the office very, very happy."

"Uh-oh," said Freddie. He pointed to the speaker's platform. "They're gonna start."

The applause was building as Mrs. Ackroyd moved to the microphone, her huge bosom thrust in front of her.

"Good God," muttered Bone. "She's going to sing."

Freddie was staring at Ackroyd, who beamed as he applauded his wife. "Know what I wish, Max?"

"What's that?" I said.

"I wish I had a way with words, that's what. If I could just find the words, I'd like to walk up to Ackroyd, y'know? Right here in front of all his friends. I'd walk up to him and I'd look him in the eye, and then – and then I'd say something really sly and snide, y'know?"

"Something sly and snide? Like what?"

Freddie thought for a moment. "Like 'fuck you.'"

Just then there was a commotion in the hallway behind us, and I turned to see a phalanx of San Francisco Police crowding through the door. Luther Crake was in the lead, his face as grim as a cast-iron doorknob. In his hand he clutched the registration papers for Ackroyd's car. Behind him two cops dragged a heavy garbage bag across the marble floor.

I looked at Crake, a slow smile spreading across my face. I put my arm back around Freddie's shoulders. "I think, buddy, that's all being taken care of."

In the ballroom, Mrs. Ackroyd burst into song.

CHAPTER THIRTY

The fire had burned down to coals. We lay snuggled together on the blanket on top of the warm sand; sipping the last of the wine, looking at the nighttime stars and each other. Across the fire I could see Freddie and Kathy at the water's edge, holding hands, engaged in quiet conversation.

"He's going to make it, isn't he?" Sam's voice was soft in my ear.

I nodded. "Yeah, I think so. I've never seen him looking better. He weighed himself again this morning, and guess what? Fifteen pounds down so far, and still dropping. It's not just the way he looks, though – it's the way he is."

Sam smiled. "The power of love."

I looked at her. "And shooting J. Whitney Eager. Freddie's good deed."

Sam giggled. "'A good deed.' Is that what you call it?"

"You bet. Freddie needed to break out of the circle – to confront an enemy, a person who was so obviously wrong and evil that he could overcome his block. If he could do that – and win – he'd be free." I stroked her cheek. "Of course it helped a lot that he didn't actually kill Eager."

"Guess what?" said Sam. "Kathy told me this morning that Freddie asked her to marry him."

I raised up on one elbow. "Maybe we'd better take him in to see the doctor again. Is she going to accept?"

Sam smiled. "She said she'd see. She wants to make sure we all make it through the season."

I nodded. We'd been running fishing charters for just over three months now and business was booming. Our first big outing had been a success and word had quickly spread. I flew down from San Diego twice a week, and the Cessna was full every time. We had bookings into September, the boat was almost paid off, and the bank account was slowly growing.

We were going to finish the season in the black, and then some. We made little jokes with each other about it – whether it was Kathy's food, Sam's drinks, Freddie's expert navigation, or my bad jokes that kept 'em coming – but we were careful not to talk about it too much, lest the luck disappear. It was still a little too fragile to talk about directly.

"We're going to make it," I said. "It'll all work out, you'll see."

"It already has worked out, Max," said Sam. "Eager's in jail, Pastor Fairley's being extradited, and Lorenzo and Festus are going to trial next week. And Mohinder Das's money went to repair Randolph Armlin's campaign chest, with no one the wiser."

"Don't forget Ackroyd," I said.

"That's the best one of all. Not only did he lose the election to Kathy's dad, but now he's being prosecuted for election fraud, extortion, and concealing evidence. Eager told the jury all about it."

She came close and kissed me softly. "And you and I are here in Mexico together. What's left to want?"

We lay back, feeling each other's warmth. It was a blissful feeling, and I gave myself fully to the moment, knowing that it wouldn't last forever. Lorenzo and Festus would eventually get out of jail, but in the meantime there were other fish in the sea to watch out for. I thought about them, the sharks waiting out there, out beyond the safety of our pitifully small jerry-built reefs, the big heavy predators who knifed silently through the deeps searching for prey.

Sam nudged me with her finger, hard. "Ouch."

"You were thinking," she said in an accusing voice. "And not about me."

I poured the last of the wine. "I was thinking," I admitted. "About the next time." She looked questioningly at me, her almond eyes somber. "There are too many things with sharp teeth out there. I'm a finder, Sam. And sometimes when I go looking for something, turning over the rocks and poking my head into the holes and cave mouths, things jump out that I don't expect."

She shivered. "Like this time."

"Like this time."

* * *

We packed up the things silently and put them in the jeep. We put out the fire and buried it, leaving no trace that we had been there. Tomorrow the early morning wind off the Gulf of California would fill our footsteps, and the gulls would find and devour whatever tiny scraps of food we might have left behind.

The moon was full, hanging just above the horizon. I started the jeep and maneuvered it through the soft sand down to the water's edge. The tide had gone out, leaving a wide avenue of packed wet sand to drive on. The sea was alive with phosphorescent plankton, glowing brightly with tiny Christmas-tree colors as the water lapped against the shore.

I flicked on the headlamps and started down the beach to the tiny fishing village, ten kilometers away. The salt air felt good in my lungs, the wine was singing softly in my head, and Sam's hair was soft against my cheek.

Our headlamps illuminated thousands of tiny crabs feeding along the sand. They parted before us, as if to royalty, as we drove through the warm night under the full moon.

THE END

If you enjoyed this book, please let others know by leaving a quick review on Amazon. Also, if you spot anything untoward in the paperback, get in touch. We strive for the best quality and appreciate reader feedback.

editor@thebookfolks.com

www.thebookfolks.com

Also in this series

WITH TOOTH AND NAIL (Book 2)

When a hitman kills a policeman and makes his getaway by stealing Max Donovan's car, the army veteran makes chase. His quarry is a cunning and violent man heading for another kill and won't welcome Donovan's efforts to stop him. A thrilling game of cat and mouse in the jungle and savannah of Senegal ensues. Only one man will come out on top.

THE SERPENT'S LAIR (Book 3)

Max Donovan has survived a bomb explosion in Colombo, Sri Lanka, but is handed a powder keg in the form of a mission to protect the author of a manuscript exposing insurrectionist plans. He's up against powerful forces, not least the ocean and jungle, that he'll have to strike at the heart to subdue.

All FREE with Kindle Unlimited and available in paperback!

More fiction by the author

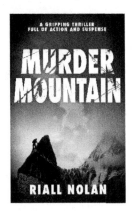

MURDER MOUNTAIN

A standalone action thriller

Wanted by the FBI and hiding out on a remote island in the Pacific, Peter Blake has an unwelcome visit. He's been rumbled by a man who "trades in information" and the price for not being handed over to the authorities is to use his mountaineering experience to lead a team on a dangerous mission to recover a fallen satellite. If he fails, it will cost him his life.

FREE with Kindle Unlimited and available in paperback!

Other titles of interest

THE PIPER'S CHILDREN
by Iain Henn

The first standalone book in a new series of mysteries set in the US

A boy is found wandering in the woods, dressed in medieval clothes and speaking a strange language. When another child turns up, it doesn't shed any more light on the mystery for FBI agent Ilona Farris. Only by digging into her own past will she begin to work out what is going on, and who these children are, seemingly lost in time.

FREE with Kindle Unlimited and available in paperback!

YOUR COLD EYES
by Denver Murphy

A serial killer is targeting women. He is dressing them up
and discarding their bodies. Detectives become convinced
that it is something about the way the victims look that is
making them be selected. They need to find out just what
that is, and why, to hunt down the killer.

FREE with Kindle Unlimited and available in paperback!

Sign up to our mailing list to find out about new releases and special offers!

www.thebookfolks.com

Printed in Great Britain
by Amazon